Wrekin
Rebels and Romans

Allan Frost

WREKINbooks

For C.A.T.S.
— *Caroline, Anthony, Tim and Sarah.*

Text, maps, illustrations and cover design © Allan Frost 2006.
All rights reserved.

ISBN-10: 1-872989-07-1
ISBN-13: 978-1-872989-07-5

First Edition

British Library Cataloguing in Publication Data:
A CIP catalogue record for this title
is available from the British Library.

Published by Wrekin Books
1 Buttermere Drive, Priorslee, Telford,
Shropshire, TF2 9RE, England.

Printed and bound in Great Britain by
Cox & Wyman, Reading, Berkshire.

Contents

Next page, top: Tim's map of the district around Caer Gwirocon.
Bottom: Caroline's plan of Caer Gwirocon.

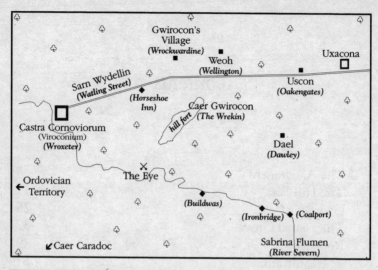

Gwirocon's Village
(Wrockwardine)

Weoh
(Wellington)

Uxacona

Sarn Wydellin
(Watling Street)

Uscon
(Oakengates)

(Horseshoe Inn)

Caer Gwirocon
(The Wrekin)

hill fort

Castra Cornoviorum
(Viroconium)
(Wroxeter)

Dael
(Dawley)

Ordovician Territory

The Eye

(Buildwas)

(Ironbridge)   *(Coalport)*

Caer Caradoc

Sabrina Flumen
(River Severn)

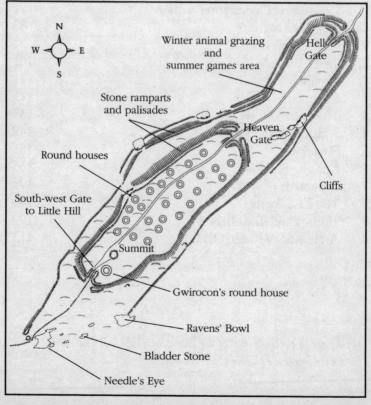

N
W — E
S

Winter animal grazing
and
summer games area

Hell Gate

Stone ramparts
and palisades

Heaven Gate

Round houses

Cliffs

South-west Gate
to Little Hill

Summit

Gwirocon's round house

Ravens' Bowl

Bladder Stone

Needle's Eye

CHAPTER 1

The Assignment

Both Tim and his twin sister Caroline were feeling decidedly fed up with History. They had it thrown at them at home as well as at school. And now they were being set a history assignment to do in the school holidays. It really was too much!

Mr Hart, the history teacher ('Brave' to his pupils, but not within earshot) was droning on about how history is not just full of events. They were events caused by people. People made history because of their choices and decisions.

Tim's mind wandered. He was fascinated by Brave's appearance. Long, unruly hair tumbling from a shiny bald circle. Moustaches swinging from side to side, with a piece of breakfast fried egg clinging on for dear life to one of them. It begged the question: what lurked inside the overgrown pointed beard which looked more false than the Headmaster's wig? Probably a sausage or two and a chunk of fried bread, for mid-morning break.

Caroline gave Tim a sharp nudge with her elbow. He jerked out of his reverie. Brave noticed. His eyebrows rose above the top of his glasses.

'Ah! Tim Dale! Welcome back to the present! What were you thinking, my boy?'

Tim looked back at him, uncertain what to say.

Caroline put a hand to cover her mouth as discreetly as she could. 'You were wondering who to write about,' she whispered.

'I was just wondering who I should write to,' said Tim.

Brave's eyes lit up. Tim couldn't tell whether they were friendly or full of malice.

'Why, you can write to me! No less than a thousand words. About an event, or anyone who lived or worked, in the Telford area during the last two thousand years. That should give you plenty of scope! And that goes for the rest of you!'

A hand shot up at the front of the class, a finger stabbing sharply at the ceiling. It was Susan the Swot.

'Please, sir! Telford hasn't existed for two thousand years,' she said, smugly.

'You are quite right, Susan. Perhaps I should have said in the area now known as Telford. Well spotted!'

'Do we have to confine our essays to Telford, sir? I'd like to write about Charles Darwin. He was born at Shrewsbury in February 1809.'

Susan seemed unaffected by the thirty or so daggers embedded firmly between her shoulder blades.

Brave thought for a moment. Her father was a school governor. Better not upset her.

'Good idea, Susan. Yes, Shropshire, then. Not just Telford.'

Another hand shot up.

'Sir, I'd like to write about Jack the Ripper!' exclaimed Ralph the Rebellious.

It was interesting to see how consistent Brave was in treating his pupils.

'Ralph, were you born stupid or have you worked hard to attain such a high level of sub-intelligence?'

'It comes naturally, sir. My dad says I should have been born two thousand years ago when Herod was around.'

'I can see his point.'

The bell rang. Group lethargy miraculously changed to a concerted effort to escape, matched only by fire evacuation practices.

'Don't forget your assignments! Two thousand words about something that happened or someone who lived in Shropshire during the last one thousand years,' Brave's voice struggled to be heard above the turmoil of the scrum at the doorway.

'Please, sir, you got that the wrong way round! It's one thousand words and two thousand years!'

'Susan, stuff it!' Someone shouted from within the stampede. She found herself swept away with the outgoing tide.

The classroom was deserted except for Brave. He sighed, relieved.

'Yes, Susan. Stuff it. I really don't know why I bother.'

Tim and Caroline arrived home earlier than usual. Now that school had broken up for the holidays, there was no need to do their homework straight away. There would be plenty of time to write the essay during the next couple of weeks.

Their father greeted them with a smile.

'Well, how was the last day?' he asked.

'Brave's given us an assignment,' Caroline said, glumly.

'What about?'

'Anything that happened or anyone who lived in Shropshire since the year dot,' Tim replied.

'Any ideas, dad?' said Caroline.

'How about Thomas Telford? The town's named after him and you'll find plenty of stuff in the Library.'

'Telford's boring.'

'OK. How about Charles I? He declared war on Cromwell's Parliamentarians a few miles away. Or Abraham Darby and Ironbridge.'

He could see they weren't impressed. If anything, there was too much choice. It was all right for dad to come up with suggestions; he had written several books on local history. More to the point, he was interested. Tim and Caroline weren't. Definitely.

Ever since they were small, they'd been dragged, whining, around almost every castle in Shropshire, Wales, Yorkshire and anywhere else they'd been on holiday. It was difficult to relate to piles of weathered ruins, however much remained above the surface. It was the ultimate turn-off. But they hadn't the heart to tell him.

'Forget all about the assignment for today. Something'll turn up. But don't leave it too long. It's easier to do homework early on in the holidays rather than leave it to the end.'

For once they took their father's advice. Tim retired to his bedroom to play on the computer. Caroline switched on the television and flicked through the channels until something caught her eye. Things to do in the school holidays. Some juvenile presenter was prattling on about displays at English Heritage sites.

Really! Some of these television people seemed to think they were so wonderful. Talk about ego trips! They might be able to talk and smile at the same time, but they didn't have two IQs to rub together! And they were more interested in hearing their own voices than listening to what their guests had to say.

The programme showed scenes of Roman soldiers and Celtic warriors re-enacting battles at nearby Wroxeter, the fourth largest city in Roman Britain. Scattered around the ruins were several tents featuring aspects of life before and during the Roman Invasion. Caroline found it all quite interesting.

'Tim!' she shouted up the stairs. 'Come here! Quick!'

'What is it?'

'Something on the telly.'

A few moments later, Tim came in and sat down on the settee.

'Wroxeter? Boring!'

'Oh! Look! There's The Wrekin Hill in the background.'

'So?'

Caroline sat back in a huff.

'I thought you'd find the weapons and the fighting interesting.'

They watched in silence. It wasn't long before Tim was as fascinated as Caroline.

Their father entered, wondering why they were both so quiet and not arguing as they usually did.

'What're you watching?'

'Hush!'

He sat and watched with them until the feature finished.

'Dad, what do you know about the Romans?' asked Tim.

'I thought you weren't interested in history.'

'This isn't history. It's about people.' He couldn't believe he'd repeated Brave's own words, let alone agreed with them.

'And the way they lived,' added Caroline.

'Mum will be back soon. Let's have something to eat and I'll tell you what I know this evening. Unless you'd rather do something else.'

Tim and Caroline gave each other a quick glance. Caroline acted as spokesperson.

'No, that's OK, as long as you make it interesting.'

As soon as they had finished their meal, Mr Dale ferreted about in his study and returned to the lounge clutching a few books. Tim was relieved to notice that they were all modern paperbacks, not his father's dusty old dog-eared tomes.

Mrs Dale sat sketching in her usual armchair while Tim and Caroline sat on either side of their father on the settee.

'OK, dad. Why did the Romans invade England?' asked Tim, eagerly.

'And what was life like for the people already here?' said Caroline.

Mrs Dale looked up momentarily. She knew her children were bright but found it amusing that, suddenly, they wanted to hear what her husband had to relate about The Past. Until now they'd shown little or no interest in their father's occupation, even if it did put food on the table. She turned back to her sketch.

'Steady on!' said Mr Dale, smiling at their newly-discovered enthusiasm and relishing the thought that they were desperate to hear what he had to say. 'The Romans didn't invade England, they invaded Britain. England didn't exist then.

'We're not too sure of the precise reasons why the Roman emperor decided his legions should be sent to these shores,' he continued. 'Historians have different opinions on the subject and there is very little written evidence.'

'Dad, don't get boring! You promised to make it interesting,' complained Caroline.

Mrs Dale smiled to herself. Her husband was not known for keeping things simple. History, especially ancient history, was full of ifs, buts and grey areas. She sighed and wondered who would lose patience first; them or him.

Mr Dale pondered for a few moments before continuing.

'OK, then. We'll start again.'

Caroline gave Tim one of those eyes-raised-to-the-ceiling looks.

'Apart from a special alphabet used only by druids, and then very rarely, the ancient Britons didn't know how to read or write. Their history was recorded in spoken stories, memorised by bards. The Romans, on the other hand, were able to write things down in their own language.'

'Latin,' said Caroline.

'That's right. Latin. And because they had libraries in Rome, much of what we know about their culture comes directly from their writing. The problem is that they only give one side of the story.'

'And because the Britons weren't able to write, we don't know what happened from their point of view,' said Tim, feeling quite proud of himself.

'That's exactly right. We know a lot about the early years of the invasion; when the legions first arrived, a few of the major battles and the directions in which they advanced.'

'How?' asked Caroline.

'By the letters and books written by some of the generals as well as politicians in Rome.'

'Since when has anyone believed what politicians say?' said Tim. 'You're always moaning that they can't answer yes or no even to simple questions.'

'True, but a lot of what they said has been confirmed by archeological finds, like at Uiroconium. Archaeology has also revealed a lot about the Britons; how and where they lived, for example.'

'Like on top of The Wrekin, you mean.' Caroline could remember seeing her dad's aerial photographs showing the outline of huts within the embankments of the British fort on top of the hill.

'Yes.'

'What about people?' asked Tim. 'Our assignment is to write about a person.'

'Or an event,' added Caroline.

'Hm,' Mr Dale considered for a few seconds. 'We know there was an early Roman fort a short distance away from where the town of Uiroconium was later built. The governor at that time would probably have been Plautius. It was his job to invade Britain. Or perhaps it was his successor, Scapula,' he pondered. 'I'm not too sure ...'

'What were the names of the Britons then?' asked Caroline.

Their father pulled a face. It usually meant he'd been caught out. Eventually he spoke. 'I think the main one in this area would have been Caradoc, or Caratacus as the Romans called him. He was one of the sons of King Cunobelin who ruled the lands just north of where London is now. Do you remember seeing Shakespeare's play *Cymbeline* on television a few weeks ago? Well, Cymbeline and Cunobelin were the same person, although there's no historical proof that what happened in the play actually happened in real life.'

'Could the bards have passed the story on from one generation to the next?' asked Caroline.

'Possibly, but the bards had long gone by Shakespeare's time. The stories could well have become folklore by then.'

'This guy Caradoc,' said Tim. 'How did he get to be in Shropshire?'

'Shropshire as a county didn't exist until much later. The lands around here belonged to a tribe called the Cornovians. Caradoc's army was defeated by the Romans in two major battles soon after the legions arrived in the year 43. Caradoc realised that the invading army was too strong to defeat in open battle, so he resorted to guerrilla warfare – hit and run attacks – and was very successful. Bit by bit, however, the legions advanced until Caradoc was pushed back into this part of the country. Not long afterwards he sought refuge in the Welsh hills.'

'When the Romans won, was Caradoc killed?' asked Tim.

'No. His last battle may have been in Shropshire or somewhere nearby in Wales.'

'I thought you said after losing the first battles, Caradoc only used guerrilla tactics,' said Tim, accusingly.

'He did. We don't know why he chose to fight another pitched battle.'

'What happened to him?'

'You'll have to find out for yourselves. Read the books.'

'Oh, that's not fair!' protested Caroline.

She looked at Tim; both were a little surprised how interesting this all was and how much their father knew. Even their mum had put her sketch pad down to listen.

Tim frowned.

'How is all this going to help with our essay?' he demanded. 'There can't be enough to write a thousand words.'

Mr Dale smiled.

'Read the books,' he insisted in an annoyingly tantalising way. 'It shouldn't take you long. And we'll go to see the display at Uiroconium on Sunday afternoon. I'm sure you'll find out a lot more from the people there. And I think you may find a thousand words won't be enough.'

'Yeah, right!' Tim was unconvinced.

Caroline picked up a book on Early Celts and flicked through the pages.

Tim selected one on the Roman Invasion of Britain.

They'd have to start their essays sometime. Hopefully, the books would be easy to read and tell them something useful.

They must have done, because their parents had to prise them from their fingers when it was bedtime!

Mrs Dale couldn't believe her luck on Saturday, the first day of the school holiday. The children were normally a pain, not knowing what to do with themselves. They didn't want to go shopping at the supermarket, there was nothing on the telly and they couldn't be bothered to do anything other than mooch around the house with miserable faces dragging along the floor.

But this Saturday was different. Tim didn't go to his Judo club and Caroline didn't go riding at the stables. They had been as quiet as mice ever since their noses first dipped into the books their father had lent them. All day long, Tim and Caroline sat or lay on the floor, reading constantly, only pausing for lunch and a couple of drinks during the whole day.

They complained about the noise caused by their mother when she returned home with the shopping and by their father when he decided this would be a good time to mow the lawn with the ancient mower which sounded more like a pneumatic drill. The only time the house had been so quiet was when Mr Dale had a migraine or when they were all asleep in bed.

The books, of course, couldn't explain everything, and Tim and Caroline found themselves jotting down questions to ask their father or some of the people at Uiroconium.

At the end of a very long day, during which even the television hadn't made a sound, the young historians retired to bed without a murmur.

They did, however, smuggle a couple of books upstairs to learn just a little bit more before going to sleep. In fact, they fell asleep with the books still open on their beds.

It was late morning on Sunday when the family set off in the car to visit Uiroconium at Wroxeter, the name of the nearby village. It was only a short journey, no more than seven miles.

They passed The Horseshoe Inn on the way; it was somewhere the twins had always wanted to go for lunch and their father promised to take them there as a special treat sometime during the holidays 'but only if you complete your assignments'.

Uiroconium was mobbed when they arrived, so much so that nearby fields had to be used as overspill car parks. They joined other visitors and ambled back along the lane to the entrance of the Roman site. The Wrekin Hill, Shropshire's most famous landmark, rose above the ground in the east, keeping silent vigil over the ruins.

Mr Dale presented his English Heritage membership card to the curator and the family went through the souvenir shop into the small museum beyond. They spent a few minutes looking at items found during the many excavations at the site before leaving the building.

They walked past an impressive wall which once served as the entrance to the Roman baths and soon arrived at the exhibition field. Mr and Mrs Dale exchanged smiles when Tim and Caroline ran off to explore the display tents.

Caroline found herself unbelievably interested in the displays of what living conditions were like for the ancient Britons and asked the attendants countless questions. Tim, on the other hand, was fascinated by the explanations of fighting tactics illustrated by people dressed up as Roman soldiers and Celtic warriors. The aspect of the event which thrilled him most was being chosen to operate the ballista and catapult, Roman war machines.

All things considered, history wasn't such a boring subject after all. The visit to Uiroconium had been an outstanding success.

As their father said, 'You can't beat seeing the real thing.'

Little did he know how true his words would be.

Tim and Caroline enter the Needle's Eye on The Wrekin Hill.

CHAPTER 2

The Hill Fort

The following day was a Bank Holiday and, although Tim and Caroline wanted to carry on reading, their parents decided they should go somewhere for a picnic rather than stay indoors. The weather looked promising so the idea was adopted with enthusiasm.

But where should they go? As this was to be an outing for all the family, Mr Dale decided not to mention his desire to visit picturesque Stokesay Castle in South Shropshire. Similarly, Mrs Dale kept silent about wanting to see the inside of Sunnycroft, one of the newly-acquired National Trust properties in Wellington-under-The-Wrekin.

It was Caroline who came up with a suggestion which pleased everyone.

'Why don't we go up The Wrekin?' she asked. 'It's not too far and I'd like to see the view from the top. I've never been to the actual summit.'

'Brill!' agreed Tim. 'And we'll be able to see what's left of the old hill fort.'

'Go and get ready, then,' smiled their mum.

'What do we need to take?' said Caroline.

'Suitable clothes, for a start,' said their father. 'And walking boots. It's dry now but it'll still be muddy from last week's rain. You could take a map and compass if you want to identify the landmarks visible from the summit. And any other odds and ends you can think of. But you'll have to carry them yourselves!'

'Just like when we go camping!' groaned Tim.

He and Caroline ran upstairs to get their things.

'I'll make up some food and drinks,' called Mrs Dale after them. 'Make sure you leave room in your backpacks and remember to take a sweater! It may be cold on top of the hill.'

Both children stuffed a variety of things inside their backpacks; if nothing else, their parents had taught them well over the years. Better to be prepared. However, Caroline wasn't the only one with a bemused expression when Tim appeared with his father's extremely long climbing rope slung over his shoulder.

'What do you need that for?' asked Caroline.

'Just in case.'

'Isn't it a bit too long?'

'I daren't cut it; Dad would go ballistic!'

'Well, I think it's a waste of time taking it.'

They set off on foot. After fifteen minutes or so they reached the road which ran along the base of The Ercall, the low hill east of The Wrekin. It was quite quiet, apart from occasional chirping from birds and a gentle breeze rustling in the trees. It didn't take them long to arrive at the foot of The Wrekin.

Caroline's heart sank a little. She'd forgotten how steep the path up the hill was. It was at times like this she appreciated horse riding. Tim, on the other hand, found hill walking with his father something of a challenge. Although quite tall for his age, he struggled to keep up with his father's long strides. Mr Dale liked to walk on ahead, his logic being that it gave him a longer break when they all stopped to catch their breath or take in the view.

Today was no exception, except that Tim found it more difficult than usual because he wanted to ask questions about the hill and its history. Mr Dale could talk for hours without it affecting his pace but Tim found himself almost running to keep up at times. And there was no way he was going to ask his father to slow down; that would be an admission of defeat.

Caroline and her mum refused to succumb to pointless exhibitions of masculinity; they were quite happy to stroll up the path through the woods, admiring the rural tranquillity. Caroline loved being out in the countryside and especially enjoyed its simple natural pleasures, such as sunlight streaming down in shafts through the treetops and lighting up the undergrowth with its myriad shades of green and brown.

It wasn't long before they arrived at the Halfway House, a cottage in a clearing which, according to Mr Dale, had been a very popular venue when he was a child. There were once swing boats to play on, but they'd disappeared years ago, and refreshments (including ice cream). Tom, the present owner, had tidied the area up considerably and now sold drinks and snacks to hill walkers. He gave them a cheerful wave as they passed by.

A few metres after the Halfway House (which was, in fact, nowhere near halfway to the summit of the hill), the well-trodden path veered sharply to the left. The family paused to look down on Wellington-under-The-Wrekin and other townships in the Telford conurbation, and heard the muted droning sound of traffic drifting up from the M54.

They continued on their way, up the slope they used for sledging during the winter. It all looked so green in spring, unlike the grey-and-white landscape which sped past as they hurtled down on their toboggans, taking as much care as possible not to crash into the large tree by the bend in the path.

After a few strenuous minutes, the party reached a flat piece of ground and paused again to look at the view. They gazed at the Shropshire Plain stretching northward as far as the eye could see. Not far away, a long plume of white steam drifted from the tall towers of the sugar beet factory which was soon to close down.

They then climbed up a short passage between the high bank called Hell Gate; it had once been the lower eastern entrance to the Iron Age hill fort. Beyond it a stretch of gently rising ground led to Heaven Gate, the upper eastern entrance to the fort. The television station and mast, 'a veritable blot on the landscape' according to Mr Dale, lay in a cutting to the right.

The top of the hill was also quite flat apart from a few natural mounds and innumerable circular hummocks which presented some evidence of the roundhouses lived in by the ancient Britons. The only large trees near the summit were those on the northern face of The Wrekin, planted by the Forestry Commission many years earlier.

The family strode to the white concrete pillar which marked the highest point of the hill. They each touched it in turn, as local custom demanded. They looked around to admire the scenery. Today was one of those days everyone who climbed the hill hoped to experience after the tiring walk. You could see for miles in every direction; the urban sprawl of Telford beyond the Ercall Hill in the east, the steam-belching cooling towers of Buildwas Power Station to the south and the South Shropshire Hills between there and the west and finally the patchwork-quilt of fields and hedgerows to the north.

'That's Caer Caradoc with The Lawley hill in front,' said Mr Dale, pointing to distant hills in the south-west. 'And those are the Breidden Hills,' he added, moving his hand more than ninety degrees to the right. 'Both also have Iron Age forts.'

'Did Caradoc live on the hill named after him?' asked Tim.

'Quite possibly,' nodded his father. 'Although there's another hill of the same name just beyond the south-western border of Shropshire.'

'So he might have lived on both of them?'

'That's something we'll never know.'

'Come over here,' called Mrs Dale, who stood a few metres behind them. She was pointing at a small stone cairn with a large stainless steel plate on its top. Engraved on the shiny surface was a toposcope showing the shape of the horizon all around The Wrekin, the names of the hills and their distances measured from where they stood.

Tim took off his backpack and rummaged in it until he found his orienteering compass. He also took out an Ordnance Survey map from the flap pocket, opened it out and laid it on the top of the cairn. He then explained to Caroline how the engraving compared to the map, pointing out prominent features, including where Uiroconium was, a few miles west, although they had some difficulty seeing the ruins until Tim dug out his pair of trusty binoculars.

Mr and Mrs Dale smiled at each other with a touch of pride. Every parent likes to think their children are clever and takes great pleasure in seeing the proof.

'Just a couple of more things to see before we have lunch,' said Mrs Dale.

She led them to the southern edge of the hill not far from the concrete pillar.

'That outcrop of rock is called the Raven's Bowl. Near the top is a small cup-shaped hole filled with water which is supposed never to dry up. And down there,' she turned towards another, much bigger, outcrop of rock, 'is the Needle's Eye. Tradition says that you can't be regarded as a true Shropshire person until you've been through the Eye. Be careful if you want to give it a try. It's very narrow and there's a steep drop on the other side.'

Mr Dale smiled to himself.

'Aren't you forgetting the other tradition,' he said, with a twinkle in his eye.

Mrs Dale blushed. Caroline noticed.

'Tell us, mum.'

'I'm not sure I should,' she said, giving her husband one of those you-wait-until-we're-alone looks. 'Folklore says that if a woman wants to have a baby, she must climb through the Eye from the other side without help.'

'Really?' said Caroline, her eyes wide open. 'Does it work?'

Mrs Dale blushed again, this time giving Mr Dale a look withering enough to curdle milk.

'OK, I went through and you two were born nine months later.'

Caroline jaw dropped so much it almost touched the ground. Tim and his father burst out laughing. Mrs Dale turned sharply on her heel and marched off towards the shelter of the trees.

'I think it's about time we had something to eat!'

Tim and Caroline weren't feeling particularly hungry but their parents tucked into sandwiches and soft drinks before lying down on a car blanket 'just for forty winks'.

'Let's go through the Needle's Eye,' said Caroline.

'Which way?' said Tim, mischievously.

'Don't be stupid,' responded Caroline. 'It's just an old wives' tale. Unless dad made it up to embarrass mum.'

She reached the southern edge of the hill and gingerly made her way down the steep slope towards the bottom of the outcrop. Tim followed her. Suddenly, a piece of turf gave way under his foot and dislodged the soil beneath. He slid downwards, unceremoniously on his backside, until he crashed to a halt when his feet caught Caroline's shins. She fell over.

'Are you all right?' he asked, his voice full of concern.

Caroline rubbed herself. 'I think so. How about you?'

'My bum's sore!' he smiled.

'What happened?'

'Some soil fell away. Up there.' He pointed.

Caroline looked up the slope. Her eye saw something glinting in the sunlight.

'What's that?' she said, scrambling upwards. Her hand brushed the dirt away until she was able to tease out a small, almost circular piece of heavily tarnished metal. Gripping it tightly, she eased her way back down the slope to Tim.

Her brother took out a hanky, spat on it and gently rubbed the metal until he had cleared away most of the dirt.

'It's a pendant!' exclaimed Caroline. 'Let me see!'

She snatched it back and examined it closely.

The silver pendant was seven or eight centimetres in diameter and engraved with an assortment of symbols, including a sun, moon, star and a tree with wavy lines beneath, perhaps a river. In the centre was what seemed to be the shape of a hill.

'Let's take it to dad,' suggested Tim.

'Not yet,' said Caroline adamantly. 'Let's go through the Eye first. We should be able to get back to the top by climbing round the other side of the rock.'

'Hang on,' said Tim. 'I've got some string in my backpack.'

He took out a small ball of string and a penknife, cut a short length and threaded it through the top of the pendant. He tied the ends together and placed the loop over Caroline's head.

'What else have you got in that bag?' said Caroline, laughing. 'The kitchen sink?'

'Dad says you should always be prepared. Anyway, I bet you've packed some strange stuff in your bag. Women always do.'

'Don't push it! You may be an hour older than me but it doesn't mean you're cleverer!'

'More clever. There's no such word as cleverer.'

He began to climb up into the Needle's Eye before she could have the last word. Caroline followed close on his heels. He could be a right pain sometimes but he'd do anything for her.

It only took a minute to squeeze through the Eye itself and neither seemed to notice the strange shimmering of the rocks on either side of them. They gazed in horror at the gully on the far side of the Eye.

'Do we have to climb down there?' asked Caroline, her voice trembling.

Tim looked into the gully and at the rock walls on either side.

'It's only about three metres deep and about a metre wide,' he said confidently. 'There are loads of footholds. Tie the rope around your waist and go down first.'

Caroline did as she was told and, with more than a little apprehension, slowly eased her way into the gully. Tim directed her while keeping a tight grip on the rope.

'Be careful!'

Caroline held her breath and wedged both feet on either side of the chasm. She released one foot and, taking the pressure on her hands, eased her body down slightly until the boot found another foothold. She continued in this way until, after a couple of minutes' hard effort and butterflies in her stomach, she stood safely at the bottom. She untied the rope.

'Your turn,' she called up.

Tim recoiled the rope and slung it back over his shoulder.

A few moments later he was standing, slightly breathless, next to Caroline.

'Women must be desperate to have a child if they attempt to climb up that way,' she observed, wryly.

Tim looked around, slightly puzzled.

'What's up?' said Caroline.

'Dad once said there was a massive boulder blocking the exit from the gully,' answered Tim. 'Someone must have cleared it away. Oh, well,' he shrugged his shoulders. 'Ready to carry on?'

She nodded.

The side of the hill fell away sharply to their left. Tim sensed something else had changed but couldn't think what it was. He looked up at the rocks on the right.

'The outcrop doesn't look too steep on this side,' he said. 'Plenty of hand and foot holds. Do you want to go first? I'll catch you if you slip.'

Caroline led the way. The climb wasn't too arduous or very long, but they were both aware that something wasn't quite right when they reached the top. Caroline was first to realise.

'Tim,' she said, her voice faltering.

Tim's eyebrows furrowed.

'What's the matter?'

'I don't know. I've got the strangest feeling.'

Tim watched her closely while she looked around the hill top. He saw her eyes widen in disbelief and her jaw drop. She was trying to tell him something but words just wouldn't come out. He put his arms around her. She was shaking like a leaf. Several leaves.

'Calm down,' he said softly. 'If you can't speak, point.'

Caroline's hand rose.

Tim looked towards where she was pointing. He couldn't see at first, it was all too obvious. The concrete pillar and the toposcopic cairn had disappeared! So had the television mast! All the trees had gone! And there were countless thatched round houses scattered all over the summit!

They looked at each other. One pair of fearful eyes met another.

'Where's mum and dad?' Caroline almost screamed. She looked around desperately. They were nowhere to be seen.

Tim held her hand tightly and led her towards the spot where the cairn should have been.

'Caroline,' he said, his voice barely audible. 'What can you see?'

'Huts,' came the faint reply.

'What else? Look around.'

They turned slowly, trying to see what else was different since they had stood on the same ground with their parents.

The Buildwas Power Station and the sugar beet factory had vanished. So had the M54. And Telford! Large fields had been replaced by light woodland in all directions as far as the eye could see!

The sudden appearance of huts on top of the hill was not the only thing which caught their attention. The grassy slopes of the hill had been replaced by stone walls surmounted by a wooden palisade.

'I'm scared,' Caroline murmured, still gripping Tim's hand. 'What's happened?'

'It's almost as if English Heritage have done a reconstruction of what The Wrekin was like when the Romans came.'

'But they can't have done it all in less than half an hour,' exclaimed Caroline. 'And what's happened to all the buildings and towns?'

Tim couldn't answer her. There were no answers. What would dad do in a crisis? Keep his head. Think. Weigh everything up before doing anything.

'Let's sit down and have something to drink. We mustn't panic!'

Caroline nodded and sat down while Tim opened his backpack.

After they had taken a few sips of warm lemonade and rested, they plucked up courage to explore the hill top village. Caroline stood aside as Tim tentatively pushed open the door to one of the huts.

He peered inside.

'It's OK. No one here,' he whispered.

'Then why are you whispering?'

'In case there's anyone nearby. C'mon.'

She held on to his backpack for comfort and followed close on his heels.

The hut was very gloomy, lit only by the shafts of sunlight streaming through cracks in the wattle walls and thatched roof. There were several earthenware bowls, rags and rough twine scattered around the floor. The floor itself was covered with straw, turned grey with age. A circle of ash lay in the centre.

Caroline lifted a long piece of timber partly covered by the straw, some of which fell into a hole beneath. Tim knelt down to have a closer look with his torch. He reached inside the hole and pulled out a handful of grain. He sniffed it. 'Smells like wheat. Mouldy wheat.'

'It must be a pit beneath the hut. The Celts stored supplies in pits for use during the winter months,' said Caroline, knowledgably.

Tim threw the grains onto the floor.

'Let's check out the other huts.'

They spent a short while peering into a few more houses, all apparently deserted, working their way towards Heaven Gate. They were amazed when they saw the gate itself. It had been restored to its former glory.

There were two small rooms, probably used as sentry chambers, built into the dry-stone masonry on each side. Wooden gates hung open on primitive hinges across the entrance. The stockade above the walls crossed over the gateway.

They almost ran up the wooden ladder onto the walkway behind the stockade. For a moment all their fears were dispelled by this remarkable discovery.

Until they looked towards Hell Gate.

A procession of more than a hundred people, all strangely dressed, was walking slowly away from them down the hill.

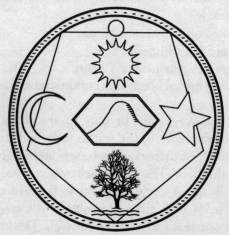

The pendant found by Caroline near the Needle's Eye.

CHAPTER 3

Gwirocon

Tim and Caroline ducked down out of sight. 'Did they see us?'

'I hope not,' whispered Tim. 'Let's follow them!'

The procession reached the foot of the hill. It was led by a tall man wearing a black robe and carrying a long staff.

The spies took great care to keep out of sight and noted that, although the Halfway House and public conveniences were no longer there, the pathway followed the same route as they had taken earlier. They also noticed the modern road in the valley between the foot of The Wrekin and The Ercall had been replaced by a narrow track, hardly a path, which meandered between trees and dense undergrowth, following the course of a small stream.

The man dressed in the black robe was about forty years old with a mass of grey hair tumbling around his shoulders from a bald circle on top of his head. His weatherbeaten and heavily lined face was partly hidden behind a long white beard. Around his neck hung a silver pendant. His staff was highly polished and, judging from the way he held it, quite heavy.

He waited a few moments for stragglers to catch up, then continued southward. After about half a mile, the ground became increasingly marshy underfoot. Large willow trees, their drooping branches wafting lazily in the breeze, towered sturdily above countless grassy mounds surrounded by small, shallow pools of green, stagnant water. Apart from the grassy mounds, the whole area was quite flat.

Tim tripped on an exposed root and slipped down the muddy bank into a pool. He quickly scrambled out. Caroline saw someone turn and look at the ripples in the water, frown, then turn away again.

'That was close,' she hissed. 'Watch your step or we'll be discovered!'

The man in black halted near a shallow hole around which several men were leaning on rustic shovels and sweating profusely. Four more men were standing next to a roughly-made stretcher upon which lay the badly charred body of a man. The people gathered around the shallow grave. No one uttered a word. Tim and Caroline crept a little closer and hid behind the fronds of a willow tree.

The man in black turned around to address the throng and, while he raised his outstretched arms to the skies and chanted, the four men carried the stretcher to the front and gently lifted the corpse into the hole. Some of the women stepped forwards and laid small bunches of wild flowers on and around the body. Two men, obviously warriors judging from the long swords hanging from their waists and the strangely ornate tattoos on their faces and arms, carefully placed a battered shield, a dagger, long sword and bent spear beside the body. They resumed their places in the crowd.

Tim and Caroline felt as though they were intruding on something private and very special and were more than a little scared in case they were discovered. Tim did his best to be brave and squeezed Caroline's hand occasionally to give her the reassurance he certainly didn't feel.

The dead man must have been someone very important. The respect felt by the throng for him was evident by the looks on their weathered and careworn faces.

Tim and Caroline crawled a little nearer through the undergrowth so that they could hear and see more clearly. They were surprised beyond belief when they heard the man in black speak; even though his words were of a language they had never heard before, it was as though they were wearing headphones and someone was translating for them a split second after the original words had been spoken. At first it was quite unnerving but they soon became accustomed to the experience.

'Men and women of the Cornovian tribe, hear my words!'

The man in black spoke with the authority of one who does not need to shout to gain attention.

'Here lies Madoc, your king, my brother, cruelly slain by the hand of Rome! He was too great a man to be cremated! Let us consign his body to the earth so that his spirit may join our ancestors!'

The grave diggers began to fill in the hole. The people watched in silence for almost an hour by which time the diggers had built a mound some two metres high on top of the grave. Caroline noticed that the mound was about the same size and height as the others in the vicinity. Perhaps they were all burial tumuli.

The man in black raised his arms again.

'It is done! Return to your homes and reflect on King Madoc's life! I shall consider who should be our new king and what action should be taken against his killers!'

'We want you for our king,' said one of the warriors.

'That's right,' agreed another. 'There is no one else.'

The crowd murmured its support.

The man in black looked at them for a few moments as if examining their innermost thoughts. Kingship was not something to be taken lightly and could conflict with his own beliefs.

'I shall give the matter a great deal of thought and decide what is best. You!' he beckoned to one of the warriors. 'Do you have the bronze sword of our forefathers?'

The warrior nodded and lifted a battered and bent old sword in his right hand.

'Take it to where King Madoc's body was recovered and cast it into the river. It will be our offering to the spirit of the water. Take two men as witnesses.'

'It shall be done.'

The warrior bowed briefly. He motioned to two men in the crowd to follow him and silently led the way further southward along the track.

As soon as they had disappeared from view, the man in black spoke again to the people.

'Return to your homes. I shall send word when I have made my decision.'

He sat down on a rock and watched as the crowd dispersed. He fingered the pendant around his neck and observed the small flash of sunlight it reflected onto the ground. He smiled when he directed the reflection onto the warm ground of Madoc's grave.

'Goodbye, my brother. Your memory will live on forever. I shall name one of these hills after you. But who can we find to succeed you as our king?'

He closed his eyes and sat in silence.

Tim and Caroline lay in the undergrowth for what seemed ages. Even though she hated creepy crawlies, Caroline watched them going about their business with a courage she didn't feel. She was more scared of what the man might do if he discovered them.

It was a great relief when he stood up and ambled slowly back along the track. Tim and Caroline realised they had no option but to follow him at a discreet distance. They were not really surprised when he began the arduous ascent to the hill fort. Climbing the rugged path a second time on the same day was not something they particularly wanted to do but there was an air about the man which gave them a little comfort in this alien world.

It was not long before the man reached the summit and sat on a rock, staring at the ground in deep contemplation. Tim and Caroline took refuge behind one of the huts and watched.

The man in black sat in silence for the best part of an hour. It was almost as if he was in a trance. The sun was now very low in the sky and the man's shadow stretched a long way across the ground in front of him.

At last Caroline spoke. 'Is he asleep?' she whispered.

'He could be, but I can't be sure.'

'We can't stay here for ever.'

'Could you understand what he was saying?'

'Yes. Strange, wasn't it? I didn't recognise any of the words he spoke but I knew what they meant.'

'Same here. Were you upset?' asked Tim with some reluctance. He'd found the burial ceremony deeply moving.

'I don't want to witness another, if that's what you mean. It was a bit like watching it on telly. You know, you see it but seem a bit removed from it, as if it's not real.'

'It was real all right!'

'Who are these people?' asked Caroline after a short pause. She thought she knew but the implications, if she was right, were incredible.

'You heard what he said. He called them Cornovians and said the Romans had killed King Madoc.'

'But how ...?' Caroline didn't want to say what she was thinking. It was too scary.

'Somehow we've gone back in time. That's why the fort is complete again. That's why everything – Telford, the power station, you name it – has disappeared. None of it existed then.'

They sat in silence again, considering what all this meant.

'We'll never see mum and dad again!' said Caroline. She felt an overwhelming feeling of sadness well up inside her. A tear trickled down one side of her face.

Tim noticed. He put his arm around her and gave her a gentle hug.

'I told you: everything'll be OK,' he said. But he wasn't convinced. 'I wonder who that man is. He must be important.'

'A druid?' speculated Caroline. 'But I thought druids were supposed to dress in white robes.'

Tim shrugged his shoulders.

'Dad says you can't believe everything you read in books. You have to witness things for yourself.'

'We're certainly doing that!'

Tim smiled.

'It'll help with our assignments. Brave will be impressed!'

Caroline let out an involuntary laugh. She and Tim exchanged anxious glances and simultaneously looked to see if the man had heard them.

The man's head rose. For a moment, he seemed to look straight through them. He closed his eyes and dipped his head again.

'Phew! That was close!' said Tim, relieved.

'Sorry, I couldn't help it. It was just the thought of Brave seeing us now.'

'He'd be green with envy!'

'So would dad! He'd give anything to be in our shoes!'

'I wish he were here. He'd know what to do.'

'The first thing he'd do is take photographs as proof.'

'Camera!' exclaimed Tim.

'Hush!'

Tim was already rummaging in his backpack. He took out his camera.

'I completely forgot I'd brought it,' he said with more than a hint of pride.

He pointed the camera directly at the man in black. He pressed the trigger. The shutter clicked loudly and seemed to echo in the stillness. The flash went off.

The man in black opened his eyes and looked in their direction. He smiled warily at them.

'You can come out now! I thought my eyes were deceiving me!' His voice seemed amused and friendly.

Tim and Caroline exchanged nervous glances before rising very slowly to thsaideir feet.

The man beckoned them to sit beside him. He eyed them up and down for several, very long, minutes. He seemed both fascinated and confused by their appearance. He was particularly interested in the pendant hanging around Caroline's neck.

Tim noticed and compared it to the pendant around the man's neck. It was exactly the same as Caroline's except that his was newer and not tarnished!

'The pendant we found is exactly the same as his!' Tim exclaimed before he could stop himself.

'So, you can speak!' the man in black said with a broad grin.

'You can understand us?' said Caroline.

'I hear strange words but understand what they mean.' He pondered for a few moments before continuing. 'You are not of this time, that is evident from your attire. The talisman has a magic of its own which even I have been unable to fathom.'

'We don't know how we got here, either,' explained Tim apologetically. 'We found the pendant a few minutes before we went through the Needle's Eye!'

'The what?'

'The Needle's Eye. The cleft in the rock.'

The man was genuinely surprised. And very concerned.

'You passed through the cleft?' he said, incredulously.

'Yes,' replied Caroline. 'What's wrong with that? Thousands of people do it every year.'

'The cleft is a sacred opening. Between this and another world. We are not permitted to go anywhere near it!'

'Our mum and dad have been through it loads of times,' said Tim. 'And nothing ever happened to them.'

'Except we were born after mum went through once,' said Caroline.

'Mum came through from the other side,' said Tim. 'Not the way we went.'

'Then it must be the talisman,' said the man in black. 'But why are you here? That is what we must consider.'

He was obviously troubled by their presence.

'Perhaps it would help if you told us who you are and what's been happening,' said Caroline. 'I'm Caroline Dale and this is my brother Tim.'

The man took a deep breath. It's not every day you see ghosts, let alone ones that can hold a conversation.

'My name is Gwirocon, chief druid of the Cornovians. My brother Madoc was king of our people as was my father Bravix before him. Our country is being invaded by men called Romans who come from a land very far away and who seek to dominate the world!'

He paused, as if uncertain whether to continue.

'Are you wraiths here to help us?'

Tim's jaw dropped.

'Wraiths? Did you call us wraiths?'

Gwirocon nodded. 'I did, for that is what you are, are you not?'

Tim and Caroline shook their heads.

'We're not wraiths, we're people like you!'

'I think not!' said Gwirocon, emphatically. 'People I can see clearly. You are but transparent shadows. Look!'

He pointed to the ground. Caroline gasped with disbelief. Gwirocon's shadow lay quite black along the ground. Her shadow was very faint, barely visible. Tim's was the same.

'Well, I don't feel dead,' said Tim with some relief. He touched Gwirocon on his sleeve. 'Did you feel that?'

The druid nodded, then frowned. He lifted his staff off the ground and offered it to Tim.

'Can you hold this?'

Tim held the staff. It was very heavy. He handed it back to Gwirocon, who still frowned.

'I need to witness more. What do you have in your bags?'

'All sorts,' said Caroline. 'Food, clothes, odds and ends.'

'And what is that?' he said to Tim, indicating the camera still in Tim's hand.

'It's a camera. It takes pictures.'

A puzzled expression crossed Gwirocon's brow.

'Let me see.'

Tim handed him the camera but Gwirocon was unable to hold it. His fingers passed through both Tim's hand and the camera as if they were made of air.

'Put it on the ground.'

Tim did so. Again, the druid was unable to pick it up.

'This is very interesting, but weird. I cannot touch you, but you can touch me. You can hold my staff but I cannot grasp your ... camera, or even see it when it is in the shadows.'

No one said a word for several moments. It was really quite spooky.

'But how did you get here?' asked Gwirocon. Nervously, he continued. 'Are you ... gods?'

It was all very confusing.

'No, we're not gods. Perhaps there's magic in the pend– ... talisman.' Tim changed the subject. 'Tell us about yourself. Please. We know a bit about what happened when the Romans invaded Britain but we'd like to learn more.'

'Very well,' said Gwirocon. He was more relaxed now that the 'wraiths' seemed friendly. 'I'll be brief as it will soon be dark. The Cornovians are a poor tribe, mainly farming folk. Apart from our cattle, we produce salt in our northern lands and sell to neighbouring tribes. We are not strong enough to resist the advances of Rome.'

'How did Madoc die?' asked Caroline.

'A scouting party of Roman soldiers came into our territory from the south, along the banks of the Sabrina.'

'The river Severn,' Tim explained to Caroline. She threw him a foul look to remind him she wasn't totally ignorant.

'Madoc led a small party of warriors downriver last night in their coracles. All they intended to do was find out how far the enemy had advanced. Unfortunately, they came upon the Roman camp not far from the Pitch Pool. Madoc was killed by an arrow and his torch fell into the coracle. It burst into flames and drifted until it sank. We recovered his body this morning and carried it to the sacred ground for burial.'

'Where's the Pitch Pool?' asked Caroline.

'Not far from the Tar Tunnel near Coalport, I should think. They probably use the pitch to make the coracles waterproof,' said Tim.

Gwirocon nodded. He was impressed with Tim's knowledge despite the boy's apparent youth.

'Madoc has ... had a farm not far from here, an hour's walk to the north,' the druid continued. 'This hill fortress is named after the king of the time, Caer Madoc. If I decide to accept the vacant kingship the fortress will be known as Caer Gwirocon.'

'Don't you want to be king?' asked Caroline.

Gwirocon shook his head.

'No, but there is little choice. I became a druid because Madoc was the eldest son and we do not like a king's brothers to serve under him as warriors. It can lead to conflict. Disputes of power. Druids have a special place in our society, even above kings.'

'Then wouldn't it be better for you to be both king and druid?' said Tim. 'Your people obviously have a lot of respect for you as a druid. Won't they have even greater respect for you if you were their king as well?' It made sense to him. Caroline nodded in agreement.

Gwirocon thought long and hard. Eventually he spoke.

'Perhaps you are right, although I do not relish the prospect. Now that the Romans are approaching, it will be a very difficult time for us, especially as we have so few warriors.'

'Can't you join up with another tribe?' said Caroline.

Gwirocon sighed.

'We do not get on well with our neighbours. It is the same all over Britain. There is so much mistrust, not just between tribes but also between the under-kings within each tribe. Unity is almost unheard of. Only King Caradoc has been able to offer any real resistance to the Roman legions.'

'Then why not join him?' said Tim.

'If only it were that simple,' said the druid. 'Caradoc ruled in the east and fought two great battles to forestall the Romans when they began this invasion some years ago. Unfortunately, his army lost and his so-called allies made treaties with the invader. Caradoc has been fighting a hit-and-run war ever since.'

'Then he has no lands of his own,' said Caroline.

'Not any more,' said Gwirocon, shaking his head. 'Despite his successes, all he has managed to do is hinder the Roman advance. He has no fortress to call his own and has to rely on the generosity of other kings. And they only offer help when they themselves are threatened. In fact, he and his followers have just moved into the fort on that hill, over there.'

He pointed towards the hill Mr Dale had earlier identified as Caer Caradoc.

'It belongs to me. But now that the Romans have advanced to Cornovian territory, it won't be long before Caradoc is forced to retreat into the mountains and hills in the west.'

Both Tim and Caroline felt sorry for the druid and his people. It must be awful to be so defenceless against such a powerful enemy.

'What will you do?' asked Tim. 'Surrender?'

Gwirocon gritted his teeth.

'Never!' he said with determination. 'You have helped me make up my mind. I shall become king! And I'll play the Romans along.'

'What do you mean?' Tim didn't understand.

'I and my people will welcome their legions here with open arms. We aren't strong enough to do otherwise. But we shall also give Caradoc all the help and support we can!'

'How?' asked Caroline, mystified.

'We can give his warriors food. We can make weapons for them.

We can tell him what the Romans are doing, their movements and strength. Good information is worth a thousand warriors!'

He stood up decisively. 'It has been useful talking to you both. Now I know what I must do!'

Tim stood up. Gwirocon looked at him very closely, as if reading Tim's innermost thoughts. He smiled.

'Thank you, Tim. And you, too, Caroline. There is hope if future generations are like you!'

'Where are you going?' enquired Tim.

'To Madoc's village.'

'May we join you?' asked Caroline. 'We've nowhere else to go.'

'Of course you can. But keep out of sight as much as possible. I don't want my people scared by ghosts!'

'Gwirocon ... do you mind if I ask you why you came all the way back to the top of the hill after Madoc's burial? Wouldn't it have been easier to go home rather than climb the hill again?'

'Ah, Tim! Life is not always about taking easy options. If only it were! I often come here when I need solitude to deliberate on important matters, particularly when the weather is fine. No one lives on top of the hill except during the winter months, and it is such a beautiful place with wonderful views in all directions. Peace and tranquillity help clear the mind. There are no distractions here, apart from my friends the ravens; they come and play with me occasionally. Very clever birds, ravens.' He smiled, nodding towards the Ravens Bowl where more than a dozen of these stockily-built, black-feathered creatures stood watching him closely. Caroline shuddered, partly because of the chill in the air and partly because these enormous birds seemed so threatening.

'You saw how restless my people were after we laid my brother to rest,' Gwirocon continued. 'I needed to get away from them, otherwise I, or they, might have said or done something which would be difficult to undo later. Decisions are best reached after careful, uninterrupted, thought. Come, it's getting late.'

He stood, stretched and led the way towards Heaven Gate. An owl hooted. It was now quite dark. Tim and Caroline followed him with a mixture of excitement and apprehension.

Tim glanced at his watch, pressing the button to light up the face. It still showed the time when they had climbed through the Needle's Eye.

What would happen next?

And would they get back to their own time?

Or were they destined to spend the rest of their lives lost in this period of Time?

The Ravens Bowl outcrop on The Wrekin Hill.

CHAPTER 4

The Sacred Grove

They didn't get to sleep until well after midnight. Gwirocon was as much fascinated by Tim's powerful Maglite torch as they had been by the druid recounting the story of his life.

It had taken almost an hour to accompany Gwirocon down The Wrekin and along a woodland track northward for a few miles until they reached a small village. Both Caroline and Tim thought it was roughly where the village of Wrockwardine is today.

Half way along the track they crossed over a wide lane which the druid said was Sarn Wydellin, the major route from north of London to a large island which Tim understood to be Anglesey. Apparently there was a large centre on Anglesey to which druids from all over Europe as well as Britain travelled to study their arts and beliefs. Unlike kings and tribes, druids were so highly regarded that they could travel anywhere in the Celtic world without fear of attack or imprisonment. They could even walk within a heated battle knowing that no warrior would dare injure them; such was their power.

Interesting as all this was, Tim and Caroline were so tired that they fell asleep almost immediately when Gwirocon took them into his large yet almost unfurnished hut. They snuggled down on a pile of straw in one corner of the circular room, surrounded by pots and leather bags full of aromatic liquids, herbs and potions.

Gwirocon woke them shortly after dawn the next morning. He warned them to stay out of direct sunlight so no one would be alarmed by their faint shadows and to keep themselves hidden and quiet until he was able to assess precisely how visible or audible, if at all, they were to his people.

The druid opened the door to let in light and fresh air to dispel the gloom and stuffiness inside. Tim and Caroline politely refused his offer of a chunk of bread and a slice of rancid chicken for breakfast. They still had their lemonade and sandwiches and were, for once, grateful that their mother had given them far too much for just one picnic. Even after they had eaten there was still enough for another couple of days if they ate only what they needed.

Caroline sat to one side of the doorway and spent a few minutes jotting down some notes and drawings on what had transpired the day before; she'd kept a diary for years so Tim wasn't unduly surprised. He wished he'd brought a notebook as well; even though they'd experienced the same events, they each saw things in a different way and Caroline didn't take too kindly to Tim's suggestions on what to write. It was her book, after all.

When Caroline had finished writing, she and Tim peered through the open doorway and welcomed the gentle breeze as it wafted across their faces. It really was very warm inside. The room was surprisingly tidy; everything had its place, including the rustic cot-like bed covered with sacking and straw on the side opposite the door and the small stone-bounded hearth in the centre. One side of the room was filled with bundles and sacks of herbs awaiting preparation while another contained pots and bags of ointments and other medicines. Several low stools surrounded a roughly made wobbly old table.

They peered outside and saw there were quite a few more huts of varying sizes inside a grassy compound surrounded by a metre high wattle fence. The houses were, without exception, round like the ones on The Wrekin. None of them had windows.

All had a single doorway set in a wattle and daub wall upon which rafters rested to support a thatched roof. The roof, shaped like a conical lampshade, extended below the top of the low wall to prevent wind, rain and snow entering the main living area below and was further supported by four timber posts inside. It was impossible to pass through the doorway without bending low.

There seemed no definite pattern to the layout of the village. Houses had been erected in a rather haphazard manner on either side of a central track whose well-trodden curve wound its way from the entrance to a very large house at the centre. Gwirocon's hut lay nearest to it.

Outside the compound fence, Caroline noticed that several small cultivated fields had been cleared from the surrounding woodland. Sparsely-sown wheat and barley grew rather weakly in some of them while cattle and sheep nibbled the grass in others. A stream burbled along its narrow course down one side of the compound.

Within the village, chickens, dogs, oxen and horses roamed around at will. Very few of the animals seemed particularly well grown or healthy. Women sat chattering away in small groups preparing food, skinning hares and baking bread while their children ran around playing or helping their mothers. Elsewhere, men were busy making pottery, leather goods and metal implements.

Gwirocon was standing in the middle of a group of warriors and older men. They were obviously having a heated discussion. Caroline put a finger to her lips and jerked her head at Tim. He understood and followed her across the open ground into the shadow of the largest hut outside which the discussion was taking place.

'I shall willingly be your chosen king but our people are simply not strong enough to withstand the might of Rome,' they heard Gwirocon say. His tone was both reasonable and authoritative. 'We have to face facts.'

'I think we should make a stand,' said one of the warriors. 'There is no shame in dying with honour!'

'I agree there is no shame but glorious deaths will not help our people to survive!' insisted Gwirocon. 'You know as well as I that our neighbours will not ally with us. And there is no point in all our warriors being wiped out by the Romans in a pitched battle. It would achieve nothing!'

'The druid is right,' said an old man. 'I have witnessed too many battles where the deaths of too many warriors have caused much hardship to their families. There comes a time when another course of action must be found for the good of the majority.'

But not everyone was convinced.

'What other possible course of action is there?' demanded another warrior. 'Warriors are meant to fight!'

'There are other ways to oppose Rome,' said Gwirocon quietly. 'Consider this: our main aims must be to preserve our people, territory and livelihoods. It is inevitable that the enemy will enter our lands; even Caradoc cannot stop them, only hinder.'

A warrior opened his mouth to speak; Gwirocon raised a hand and the man backed down.

'We have several choices. One is to fight and suffer the consequences. The second is to capitulate and do whatever the Romans dictate. The third is to welcome the Romans with open arms, appear to be their friends but,' he added, with a twinkle in his eye, 'give whatever support we can to Caradoc and his freedom fighters!'

'What sort of support?'

'Food; we are a farming people. Weapons; we are metalworkers. Information; if we are friendly, the enemy is bound to tell us things which will be of interest to Caradoc, apart from which we have eyes and can see how soldiers are disposed. We know this land; they do not.'

'This plan depends on the people doing as they are told,' said the old man. 'What if someone tells the Romans?'

'Anyone found guilty of treason, for that is the crime at issue here, shall be executed ... along with all immediate relatives and co-conspirators. These are desperate times!'

The group fell silent. The idea had a certain appeal. The warriors would not lose face; everyone could do something, however small, to support Caradoc in his struggle.

'This will not be an easy course,' continued Gwirocon. 'The Romans will demand a proportion of all our produce to feed their own men. It will mean our farmers will have to work that much harder to increase the harvest to support themselves as well as Caradoc's men.'

'The people will not like that.'

'What are the options? Slavery or death at Roman hands. Or survival.'

'I still maintain we warriors should fight. We are not peasants!

We do not dirty our hands with soil!'

'If a warrior wishes to fight, he may join Caradoc's forces,' said Gwirocon. 'If we are seen to have few warriors, it will add credibility to our cause. The enemy is unlikely to attack when he sees we are defenceless and can feed his army.'

The group nodded their agreement to Gwirocon's plan. Most of them seemed convinced. A few had severe doubts.

'I think the ceremony to appoint the druid as our king should take place without delay,' said the old man. 'The Romans are already in our territory and, now Madoc is dead, all Cornovians need to know who gives the orders. They trust the druid but he is not their king and, as Madoc left no heir, it is only right that we choose his brother.'

Again, the group nodded assent.

'I promise I shall act in the best interests of all my people,' said Gwirocon with deep sincerity. 'Instruct the under-kings and their druids to meet in the sacred grove at Weoh in seven days' time! They can listen to what I have to say and, if they agree, elect me as their king.'

Soon afterwards, the group dispersed and before Tim and Caroline could speak to him, Gwirocon was assailed by another warrior who rode into the compound in a great hurry. He hastily jumped down from his horse and, after the briefest of bows, spoke urgently to the druid.

'Gwirocon, Caradoc has sent me to warn you that he intends to attack a Roman camp at The Eye during the hours of darkness! To avenge Madoc's death. He wishes you to ensure none of your own people are in the area before the attack begins in case the enemy is alerted.'

Gwirocon thought for a moment before replying.

'I shall do my best. What is his battle plan? The Eye gives a clear view of both sides of the river and the enemy is bound to hear approaching horses even if they cannot see them.'

'We shall drift silently in coracles downstream to the camp under cover of darkness,' replied the messenger. 'Other warriors will be hiding in the surrounding woods. After the sentries have been despatched we will attack from all sides at the same time.'

'Tell Caradoc we shall not disrupt his plans. And wish him a successful outcome.'

The messenger bowed and remounted his horse.

'I need to speak to Caradoc urgently. Ask him to come here as soon as he is able.'

The man nodded and rode off as quickly as he had arrived.

While Caroline had been listening to the conversation, Tim looked at his map to see where The Eye could be. Only Eye Farm, on the northern bank of the River Severn and some two miles south of The Wrekin, seemed to fit the brief description given by the messenger.

Nothing much happened during the next few days. Tim and Caroline, interested as they were by the domestic activities in Gwirocon's village, were becoming a little restless. Although they knew they were no longer able to enjoy the modern benefits of central heating, flushing toilets and electric lights, living in such harsh, primitive conditions made them tetchy at times.

They loathed not having a television to watch, a computer to play on, having to go to bed at dusk and getting up at dawn. All that was bad enough, but they sorely missed not being able to speak with their parents, visit their friends or just trot down to the shops. Gwirocon was, whether they liked it or not, their whole life. And it was annoying not being able to keep track of the time during the day now that Tim's watch had stopped.

They also found the basic diet of the ancient Britons somewhat uninspiring. Warm milk, boiled eggs, barely cooked hare or chicken and hard, crusted bread with stodgy dough in the middle seemed to be the mainstay, and occasional fish, boar, deer or wild birds depending on what had recently been caught.

The visitors from the future were more than grateful that their own food supplies lasted so well, although they soon became rather partial to raw honeycombs and even weak ale and imported wine, both of which were fortunately sweet and not very strong.

Neither of their parents would have condoned the ale or wine, but it was safer to drink them than cloudy, unpurified stream water.

Gwirocon helped to relieve some of the boredom by getting them to strip leaves from sprigs of herbs and grind all sorts of seeds into powders and oils. He seemed to enjoy their companionship and did not resent answering their countless questions.

They had more fun when he asked them to perform simple experiments. It seemed that no one except the druid had seen them; their semi-transparent shadows were just visible, but only if the twins stood in bright light. On the other hand, their voices could be heard so they had to take care not to speak when in close proximity to anyone else.

Some of the things Gwirocon asked them to do caused mirth to all three, particularly when Tim flicked some dough along the ground as a woman was about to pick it up, and Caroline made it disappear in one hand before rolling an egg back from the other.

Gwirocon, on the other hand, was always busy. Messengers came from other Cornovian settlements as well as neighbouring tribes, all bearing news which obviously troubled him. Many druids and Madoc's former under-kings arrived and were accommodated at other farmsteads in the area.

The highlight of the week came when King Caradoc, tall and dignified, arrived in a small chariot accompanied by a few of his warriors, including a Gaul named Cunorix who appeared to be Caradoc's trusted friend and adviser.

Such was the excitement that everyone in the compound crowded around their illustrious visitor. Many of them touched him and shook his hand, believing that physical contact would, in some way, make them stronger or give them good fortune.

Gwirocon, Caradoc and Cunorix spent several hours together in close conversation. Cunorix had a different way of speaking than the others but, as they had come to expect, Tim and Caroline understood every word.

During the meeting, Caradoc told Gwirocon that the attack at The Eye had gone according to plan; the camp had been destroyed and the enemy massacred.

The freedom fighter spoke with authority and took no pleasure in describing the harshness of the attack or its outcome; they were victims of an invasion and had to do what was necessary, in their eyes, to preserve the British way of life.

Gwirocon then spoke of what he intended to do if elected his brother Madoc's successor. Caradoc and Cunorix listened intently and approved his ideas. Plans were agreed on how the Cornovians could best help Caradoc and a system of communication set up for when the next wave of Romans arrived, as they must surely do.

Gwirocon's guests agreed to remain at the compound until after the day of King Choosing. They occupied Madoc's large house; no one, not even Gwirocon, was permitted to claim it until a new king had been elected but, in keeping with Celtic tradition, guests were permitted to enjoy the best comforts available in any village.

The evening of the ceremony at Weoh arrived. Gwirocon, wearing a voluminous white robe tied with a cord around his waist, led the way eastwards through the woods for some two miles. A great many people of all ranks of society joined the human train.

Tim and Caroline were amazed to see the size of the crowd assembled in the sacred grove which was lit by countless burning torches. Tim estimated that the grove was situated in what would become the parish churchyard in Wellington-under-The-Wrekin, their home town in north Telford.

The grove itself was a small clearing in the woods. Several springs bubbled out of the ground near an enormous oak tree covered by a throttling mass of mistletoe and ivy. Several large and ancient yew trees provided an air of gloomy sanctity to the scene.

In front of the oak was a flat topped boulder upon which already lay a sword in a scabbard and a round, highly ornate shield, all illuminated by a row of tallow candles. Gwirocon laid his own staff and a short golden ceremonial sickle on top of the boulder.

Tim and Caroline stood behind the oak tree. They guessed that about two hundred fully armed under-kings and warriors mingled behind the fourteen druids who stood waiting in a semicircle in front of the boulder. Hundreds of other people crowded beneath the trees at the sides of the grove, straining to get a better view.

King Choosing ceremonies were very rare occasions and no one wanted to miss the spectacle.

Gwirocon raised his arms and called for silence.

'Brother Druids! You have heard why I wish to stand as candidate for the kingship of Cornovia! Have you deliberated?'

One of the druids stepped forward. Nervously.

'Chief Druid Gwirocon, we are divided. There is no precedent for a man becoming both druid and king.'

The crowd murmured.

'I am well aware of that but it does not mean it is not lawful. What are the options?'

'Again, we are divided. Some of us wish to elect one of the under-kings so that the appointments remain separate.'

'And the others?'

'Agree with what you propose.'

'Have you cast your votes?'

'We have. Seven for your election. Seven against.'

'Then I have the deciding vote?'

'You are not permitted to vote. You have an interest.'

'Then how shall we decide?'

There was no answer. The crowd murmured again.

Caradoc stepped forward.

'There is no time for prolonging this affair! Cornovia needs a king! Gwirocon is right and should be elected!'

The spokesman for the druids gave him a withering stare.

'It is not your place to advise on such matters! That is the sole privilege of druids, not mere kings! And you are not even of our tribe!'

Caradoc was livid. He drew his sword and held the point at the druid's throat.

'If you and your kind are so clever, why have you not thought about the consequences of indecision? These are troublesome times and the Romans are a powerful enemy! If you elect the wrong king, you will be spiritual leaders for a tribe of dead men and slaves!'

'Lower your sword, King Caradoc. It has no place here,' said Gwirocon calmly.

Caradoc did so and, with a face like thunder, bowed to him before returning to his place among the warriors.

'There is only one course of action left,' continued Gwirocon, looking directly at the druids. 'We must ask the spirits of the Grove for guidance.'

He turned around and was relieved to see Tim and Caroline crouching in the darkness beneath the low branches of the great oak, their faces just discernable in the weak candlelight.

'I need your help,' he whispered urgently. 'Listen to my words; you will know what to do!' He turned to face the druids again.

'Let the spirits of our forefathers decide!' he proclaimed. 'Should I continue as a druid, armed only with my staff and sickle? Or should I be king, armed with the sword and shield? Or should I be both druid and king, armed with all four symbols of office?'

He paused. He could see the druids were still divided. Half were smiling. They were the ones who opposed his appointment to kingship.

He raised his arms to the dark heavens.

'Join me!' he commanded the druids. 'We must all have a hand in this appeal!'

The druids, in a display of solidarity, also reached to the sky and accompanied Gwirocon as he chanted to the spirits.

Tim and Caroline were mystified.

'What are we supposed to do now?' whispered Tim.

'You heard what he said! C'mon, stupid! You go that side, I'll go this!' said Caroline. She stooped down and waddled to the sickle side of the boulder.

'Hang on!' said Tim, reaching for his camera. 'Smile!'

Caroline stood and turned to face Tim.

A bright flash almost blinded the onlookers. A united gasp of awe and fear pierced the air. The druids stopped chanting.

'A s-spirit!' A druid stuttered.

He can't have been the only one to catch a fleeting glimpse of Caroline when the flash went off. Gwirocon tried not to smile.

'Silence!' he ordered.

Druids, under-kings, warriors and the assembled crowd could

not believe what happened next. Eyes and mouths opened in astonishment. Only Gwirocon's voice could be heard, his powerful chant reaching all corners of the grove.

The sickle was the first thing to catch their eye. It rose from the top of the boulder and drifted magically through the air until it slid behind the cord tied around Gwirocon's robe.

The sword was next. The belt of its scabbard fastened itself around the druid's waist.

Finally, both shield and staff drifted into the air and hovered in front of Gwirocon. He reached out and grasped them, one in each hand.

The druid spokesman was first to regain his composure. He joined Gwirocon behind the boulder.

'We have all witnessed this amazing visitation from the spirits of our ancestors! Let there be no more differences! Gwirocon is our chief druid and our new king! Follow his leadership and advice, on pain of death!'

Caradoc raised his sword.

'Long live King Gwirocon! Death to the Romans!'

Everyone cheered.

Gwirocon tried not to grin; it wouldn't do to seem too pleased with himself. Struggling to maintain an air of dignity, he raised his arms again and called the crowd to be silent.

'Fellow druids, kings and Cornovians! I know how much you're looking forward to having a celebratory drink or two, so I'll be brief! I thank you sincerely for the trust you have placed in me. I promise to do all within my power — with or without supernatural help — to protect you from the evils Rome will undoubtedly bestow upon us. In the meantime, enjoy yourselves! Tomorrow's perils will arrive soon enough!'

Gwirocon glanced down at the boulder.

'Thank you, my friends. You have helped change the course of history!'

'Who are you speaking to?' asked the druid spokesman, perplexed. He couldn't see anyone in the shadows.

'Just the spirits,' answered Gwirocon with a knowing smile.

'Can you see them?'

'No, but I know they're close by. Do you not feel their presence?'

The spokesman shrugged his shoulders and glanced around nervously. He didn't feel confident enough to question Gwirocon's word and had no wish to seem lacking in druidic faith. But he certainly didn't feel comfortable with unexplained magic.

He gave Gwirocon the briefest of nods and turned away.

Perhaps, just perhaps, Gwirocon was destined to be a great king after all.

Map showing the principal tribes of southern Britain together with the locations of some Roman towns and forts.

CHAPTER 5

Romans!

Gwirocon was an extremely busy man during the next few weeks. It was remarkable how energetic he could be when occasion demanded. One moment he was deeply involved in matters regarding his kingship, the next he acted out his duties as chief druid of the tribe.

He moved a few of his meagre belongings into the king's house next door but left his druidic accoutrements in his old home. It was there that his wraith-like guests would live. They were less likely to be disturbed or discovered there since it was strictly out of bounds to everyone unless they had the druid's express permission to enter. It was a place of mystery and reverence.

Tim and Caroline gradually became reconciled to the fact that it was most unlikely they would ever see their parents again, let alone return to their own time. Even so, every now and then they were overcome by a strong sense of loss and on the verge of tears. At least they found consolation in each other's company, united, as they were, in adversity.

It was a relief to them both as well as to Gwirocon that they adapted so quickly to the ancient British way of life. They became accustomed to the meagre and uninspiring variety of food and the constant lack of proper washing facilities for themselves and their clothing.

The most important thing they had to be wary of was carelessness in case someone discovered them. Gwirocon did his best to make life as interesting and bearable for them as he possibly could. Now that he was king he was able to involve himself in kingly pursuits, diversions which had previously been denied him because of his religious and social position.

He was impressed by Caroline's horse riding and Tim's persistence in trying to match her abilities despite his constant com-

plaining of having a permanently sore backside. He was convinced
his sister had more padding in her bum than he did.

All three enjoyed riding in Gwirocon's wicker chariot; not only
were Tim and Caroline able to stand on either side of the druid on
the narrow platform of the vehicle but it saved a lot of time when
Gwirocon had to visit other parts of his kingdom 'unaccompa-
nied', such as when he went to the sacred groves at Weoh, Uxcon
and Dael. (Tim thought the latter two were near modern-day
Oakengates and Dawley but he couldn't be sure. The countryside
covered by his map of modern Telford's roads and buildings was
hopelessly up to date.) The druid king visited all three groves once
every four weeks during the summer to officiate at judicial hear-
ings.

No one suspected their presence. Why should they? The
thought that visitors from another time would come among them
never crossed their minds and, even though almost everyone
believed in spirits and ghosts, no one had actually seen one apart
from the one they thought they saw during the King Choosing ceremony at Weoh. But it was enough to strengthen their belief in
the supernatural.

Gwirocon's authority had never been so highly regarded. The
'visitation' at the grove had strengthened his position and elevat-
ed it to new heights. Druids from other tribes sought his advice
and territorial disputes with neighbouring kings dwindled almost
completely away, at least for the time being.

Immediately following the Weoh incident, Gwirocon began the
unpleasant task of advising his under-kings and warriors that they
must give up the sword or leave their lands to join Caradoc's wandering rebels.

Many found it a difficult decision to make. Some of the older
warriors decided to stay but most of the younger men with fire still
coursing through their veins chose to leave, taking their wives and
children with them amid heart-rending scenes of torn loyalties to
their tribe and defence of their country. It made Tim and Caroline
realise just how traumatic invasion and war could be and how
many sacrifices had to be made.

Their lives adapted to meet the needs of changing times.

Cornovians worked harder to produce more food and ate less to prepare themselves to support both Caradoc's army as well as the expected demands of future Roman occupation.

Fear and uncertainty increased when a larger force of Roman auxiliaries advanced northward along the banks of the River Severn which, at that time, marked the western boundary of enemy occupation. They passed the carnage caused by Caradoc's army at The Eye and continued a few miles further until they reached the river crossing near what would later become the city of Uiroconium.

The invaders erected a small but strong wooden fortress there and, as it was now late in the campaigning season, prepared themselves to survive yet another harsh winter in this bleak and forsaken land.

Most of these auxiliaries came from or had served for many years in much warmer climes: Spain, Italy, Greece and other countries around the Mediterranean Sea. They loathed the dismal, cold and wet British weather. They hated having to carry their own supplies as well as heavy weaponry, but knew it was necessary if they were to survive in this inhospitable land. They were only men doing their duty and couldn't understand why so many Britons looked on them with such contempt and suspicion.

The first thing they did after building the fort was to cut down all the trees within a hundred metres or so to reduce the likelihood of a surprise attack by the natives. They then sent out heavily armed groups to forage for additional food in the immediate neighbourhood. At first, Caradoc's men were able to attack these parties with some success but the soldiers learned from their mistakes and took measures to protect themselves more effectively.

The fact that Roman auxiliaries now controlled the main river crossing made it more difficult for Britons to carry out their normal trading activities without having their goods searched and animals confiscated. Alternative crossings were found both up and down river but faster currents in those stretches led to inevitable drownings and goods being swept downstream by the force of the turbulent water.

The Cornovians were beginning to experience the hardships suffered by those tribes already under Roman rule. Gwirocon did much to encourage his people and, taking advantage of the fact that the soldiers were unlikely to venture too far away from their fort until reinforcements arrived the following spring, instigated a system of 'hidden' fields and pits for the production and storage of surplus food.

Every daylight hour was filled with an activity intended to sustain the lives of both ordinary people and Caradoc's men.

Swords, daggers, shields, bows, arrows, slings and pebbles were made or collected and transferred in coracles across the quieter reaches of the river to waiting carts and chariots on the other, unconquered, side.

Blocks of salt from the northern territory, earthenware pottery, honey and a wide variety of other products were stockpiled in readiness to meet the anticipated demands of their own people as well as the Romans in the not too distant future.

Gwirocon was adamant that his tribe should be seen as friendly and willing to support the occupying forces when they arrived in much larger numbers. And if his people could take money from the enemy, so much the better.

The Cornovians were, as a tribe, unfamiliar with the concept of money and much preferred the traditional system of barter, but that would have to change. Convincing them not to fight to defend their land was one thing; getting them to trade with the enemy was something which needed nurturing to avoid any chance of open conflict.

Tim and Caroline were impressed by Gwirocon's initiatives and understood what he hoped to achieve, but they didn't have the heart to tell him that Rome would eventually be victorious and change the British way of life forever.

Inspired hope is infectious: an acceptance of what is inevitable leads to despair. The poor Cornovians needed all the encouragement they could get. Unless Tim and Caroline could change the course of history in a dramatic way.

Autumn witnessed the customary migration of both animals and people from their widespread farms within the woodlands to the restricted confines of the hill fort. Animals were free to roam within the larger Hell Gate compound while the Cornovians occupied hastily repaired roundhouses behind Heaven Gate, with several families to a hut. They were ready to spend the winter months huddled together in what was, in effect, voluntary imprisonment. There was safety in numbers here.

Gwirocon had the largest hut all to himself, which made it safe for Tim and Caroline. But they found it very frustrating and cramped, especially when the weather worsened and howling blizzards swept across the hill top. Again, the druid king came up with inventive ways to ensure they were not confined to spending the whole winter period inside his quarters. After heavy falls of snow, he asked individuals to visit him on one pretext or another so that Tim and Caroline could walk in their footprints to avoid detection. That way they could benefit from exercise and fresh air.

They thought living conditions were pretty bad from the very beginning and couldn't possibly get much worse. But they could, and did. Gwirocon relied on them to mix herbal potions while he tended the sick. Food supplies were meagre but after four months of confinement even maggots in the salted meat were desperate to escape!

Eventually spring arrived, heralded by a shaft of sunlight resting on a rock called the Bladder Stone at midday on the Vernal Equinox. The effect on the hill top population was remarkable. Gwirocon was put under great pressure to initiate the Animal Cleansing ritual so that everyone could vacate the huts and return to the comfort of their own farmsteads.

Tim and Caroline smiled at the druid's deliberate denial that spring had come. The people implored him to act. He asked if they were sure spring had come. They insisted it had, they had seen the sunlight on the stone. At length, Gwirocon agreed to begin the ceremony. The crowd cheered and heaped piles of timber on either side of Hell Gate.

Gwirocon then lit both fires and waited until they were fully ablaze before allowing those cattle and sheep that had survived the winter to be driven between them, through the open gateway and down the hill. The whole fort was deserted in less than an hour.

The druid king smiled as the last of his people passed through the gateway.

'It's the same every year,' he explained to the spirits from the future. 'They say it's spring, I say it's not. Eventually I agree and send them on their way in a joyful mood.' He paused for a moment or two. 'I wonder if they'll be as happy this time next year ...'

His ominous words filled them with foreboding.

Barely two weeks passed before the terrible news arrived. A travelling merchant called at Gwirocon's homestead to pay his respects. He presented him with an amphora of Italian wine as payment for permission to peddle his wares in Cornovia.

'Governor Scapula is now approaching Letocetum,' he said grimly. 'He's keen to reach the new fortress on the Sabrina during the next week or so.'

'How many men does he have?' asked Gwirocon, anxiously. Letocetum, now called Wall, was only some twenty miles away to the east.

'A whole legion,' the man replied. 'Plus auxiliaries and the usual hangers on.'

Gwirocon thanked the merchant for the information and wine and retired to his hut.

'We heard,' said Caroline. Her voice trembled.

'Our troubles will begin in earnest now that a whole legion is about to enter Cornovian territory,' said Gwirocon.

'Is there anything we can do?' asked Tim.

The druid shook his head.

'Nothing that we haven't done already.'

'So we just sit and wait,' said Caroline.

'Yes. Be patient and keep our heads. I hope my people do the same. If not ...'

'Things will be fine,' said Tim with a conviction he didn't really feel. 'You'll see.'

'I pray you are right.'

It wasn't long before a scouting party of Roman auxiliaries from Letocetum reached Red Hill and quickly erected a transit camp for their protection. Shortly afterwards came the cavalry and infantry and, a few days later, a vast number of roadbuilders and engineers whose job it was to widen the ancient trackway and improve its surface to make it easier and faster to move troops and supplies.

Gwirocon was uncharacteristically indecisive about whether or not he should make contact with the oncoming forces immediately or wait a little longer. He decided to wait a while longer but rode off in his chariot with Tim and Caroline to assess the situation for himself rather than rely on the often exaggerated accounts of well-meaning messengers.

By now, Gwirocon had become accustomed to his guests taking their backpacks with them wherever they went but understood it was just a precaution; they could be transported back to their own time at a moment's notice.

Their brief journey took them through Weoh and along Sarn Wydellin to Uxcon and up a steep hill beyond. Ahead of them they could see the dark sandy soil of Red Hill excavated around the Roman camp to make a ditch and bank within which lay countless rows of leather tents.

Gwirocon let Tim take the reins and pointed along a narrow trackway which ran slightly away from the Sarn. Eventually they reached a small field surrounded by a low embankment. The charred remains of a hut stood in one corner of the enclosure.

The druid gritted his teeth and jumped down from the back of the chariot.

'Stay here!' he ordered, entering the ruins. They saw him look around and stoop down for a few moments. He returned grim-faced.

'What's happened?' asked Caroline.

Gwirocon took the reins and whipped the horses along another track leading northward through the trees.

'Was there someone in the hut?' said Tim.

'Not alive,' he replied ominously. 'And all his cattle have gone.'

'Romans?'

'Who else? No Celt would have done such a deed!'

They rode in silence until they could hear the sounds of intense activity coming from inside the Roman fort. An earthwork gateway came into view. Gwirocon stopped the chariot behind a large holly tree.

They could tell Gwirocon was extremely unhappy at this turn of events. It was obvious that the invading army would take what they wanted, kill whomever they wanted and do whatever they wanted in their efforts to subdue Britain and its disunited people.

Tim and Caroline felt rather proud that Gwirocon treated them seriously and listened to what they had to say concerning the present position. Even though the druid knew what had happened since the Romans first set their unwelcome feet on British soil, his 'spirits' seemed to understand the overall picture of events and their implications to his tribe far more comprehensively than his own advisors.

Mr Dale would have been equally proud to know how his children had behaved in this unique crisis. But that was impossible; how could they tell him? Tim and Caroline had to make the most of their current situation, if only for their own survival.

They noticed that on the eastern side of the main fort was another area of neatly pitched goatskin tents also surrounded by a dirt bank and shallow ditch; presumably this was the temporary camp for the auxiliaries who would soon march on to the next suitable spot for another camp. If, as they had read, there were about fifteen miles between forts, this section of the Roman army was on its way to meet up with those already occupying the temporary fort at Uiroconium.

Gwirocon put a finger to his lips and jumped down from the back of the chariot. Tim and Caroline followed close on his heels as he stealthily darted from behind one tree to another until he was as close to the main camp as it was safe to be. Tim used his binoculars to get a closer view. Gwirocon watched him with frustrated interest; he would have given anything to be able to hold and look through them.

Soldiers were everywhere. Everyone had a specific task. Several groups of men were erecting a sturdy fence to prevent mules, horses and stolen cattle from wandering, others strengthened the walls of the fort and dug the ditches deeper. Nearby trees were being felled to provide a clear view on all sides.

Caroline couldn't help but notice the uniforms worn by the legionary soldiers; although almost identical to those she had seen at the Uiroconium re-enactment, they were filthy, torn and faded. The auxiliaries, on the other hand, had quite a wide variety of clothing and weaponry.

Within the fort, more men were erecting wooden huts (presumably to make a permanent fortress here), cleaning equipment and performing all manner of domestic chores. Tim and Caroline were astounded by the efficiency and discipline, a marked contrast to the Cornovians. The entrance to the main camp was guarded by only one sentry, who seemed more intent on picking his nose than keeping watch.

'I'm going inside,' announced Tim.

After some deliberation, Gwirocon nodded.

'Don't do anything stupid.'

'I won't!'

Tim strode boldly through the entrance knowing that the overcast sky would not give him away. He stood to one side of the gateway in case someone walked into him. He surveyed the scene.

He couldn't believe how small and cramped the inside of the fort was but realised that only a small contingent would remain when the rest of the army moved on. Those left behind would patrol the road between here and Letocetum, the nearest camp to the east, and Uiroconium in the west, making sure lines of communication and supply were kept open.

Tim spotted two men in highly decorated uniforms entering the general's very large tent in the centre of the camp. He dodged between soldiers and tents until he stood to one side of the entrance flaps. He was relieved to discover he understood everything being said inside.

'The scouts advise us to continue to the river crossing as soon as possible,' said one man. 'This fort will be finished in a day or two. Order the auxiliaries to move on tomorrow.'

'Yes, governor Scapula.'

Tim's heart pumped like a galloping horse. So this was the famous Scapula!

'What is the name of this place?'

'It is near a hamlet the natives call Uxcon,' replied the officer.

'Uxacon?' said Scapula, not hearing the officer's reply quite correctly. 'Then we shall name the fort Uxacona. Any signs of unrest from the locals?'

'Not yet, governor. It's abnormally quiet.'

'Calm before the storm, General Quintus, you mark my words.'

Quintus still didn't know just how far he could go with the new governor even though he had served under him for almost two years. Still, five years under the authority of the previous governor Plautius had almost been more than even the most hardened legionary could bear. He still remembered a conversation he had had with Scapula when the new governor first arrived in this god-forsaken land.

'The Second Legion has its hands full in the south-west,' Quintus had said. 'The Ninth protects the border with Brigantia in the north. And we of the Fourteenth are too spread out to hold Caratacus back.'

'Can we not make use of the Twentieth at Camulodunum? Governor Plautius did well to conquer so much ground, but our supply lines are far too long.'

'Governor Scapula, how can we? They are needed to maintain order in the east.'

'How many of our men are coming up for retirement? In all four legions?' asked Scapula, after some thought.

'Not more than two or three hundred.'

'Emperor Claudius has suggested we turn Camulodunum into a colony for retired veterans. If we do, that would release the Twentieth Legion to come here and campaign against Caratacus.'

'But we don't know where the rebel is exactly! We believe his base is to the west, but he attacks us even behind our own frontier!'

'Then we disarm all natives behind the frontier!'

'Even those allied to Rome?'

'Even those.'

'But how? There are so many settlements over such a wide area!'

'By force. If any object, kill them and burn their homes! Whole settlements if need be! It is the only lesson they will understand!'

'The men will enjoy that!' Quintus grinned maliciously.

'See to it. I want the Twentieth stationed at Glevum by next spring. We have to gain full control over the territory we've already taken, however long it takes. We'll campaign against Caratacus as soon as we have our rearguard safe.'

The invasion of this miserable country was only supposed to take a few months. Unfortunately, countless Britons living in Camulodunum had been massacred when the Romans took possession, a fact which caused understandable resentment and would, ten years later, result in a revenge rebellion led by Queen Boudicca. Camulodunum was not a good example of Romano-British co-operation.

Furthermore, the new offensive to track down Caradoc who had, by this time, joined forces with the Silurians under their king Ruticon, was not going well. The Twentieth Legion had spent over a year relentlessly chasing the rebel king all over the mountains of South Wales, without success.

The Silurians knew their land so well that the Twentieth Legion had suffered countless attacks and ambushes and had little to show for their efforts apart from a very gradual occupation of the valleys. Scapula's almost fanatical determination to capture or kill Caradoc was no longer simply an order from the emperor; it was a personal vendetta, an obsession.

'Any news of the Twentieth, sir, if you don't mind me asking?' said Quintus.

'They're still chasing Caratacus around Silurian territory.'

'But I thought Caratacus was responsible for the attack near here.'

'He was. He's obviously moved northward. Assuming he hasn't retreated into the hills to the west, he'll still be somewhere near here. With a bit of luck, the Twentieth will be able to create a new frontier between Glevum and our next fort and cut him off. He'll be trapped between the river Sabrina and the new frontier, unable to get help from the Silurians or the Ordovicians! Then we've got him!'

Quintus nodded, although he found it difficult to believe Caradoc would be so stupid as to get himself caught so easily. Still, Scapula was in charge. Orders had to be followed, even if they didn't always make sense.

Tim had heard enough and wanted to report to Gwirocon as quickly as possible. Before he made his way back, he couldn't resist releasing several guy ropes from the restraining pegs of the general's tent, causing it to collapse on top of its occupants. He burst out laughing when he heard Scapula's muffled voice bellowing in anger.

'Which idiots put this blasted tent up? Get us out of here! Now!'

Present day ruins of Uriconium city with The Wrekin Hill in the distance.

CHAPTER 6

The Infiltrators

A gloomy atmosphere hovered over Cornovians living around The Wrekin during the following weeks. Now that the enemy had entered their territory, the war and its implications began to sink in. Although life was never easy, every year had followed a regular pattern, where everyone knew the familiar cycle of events. That had all changed. No one knew how they would be affected by the presence of the Roman army.

Gwirocon also suffered under a cloud of foreboding. Had he done the right thing persuading his people not to take up arms against the invaders? Only time would tell. In the meantime, he kept a close watch on developments.

It did not take long for the assembled army at Uxacona to complete the last stage of their journey to the fort at Uiroconium. With such a large presence there it was essential that the fort, now far too small for their needs, should be greatly enlarged. Work began straight away and it was not until the job was finished that Scapula felt he was in a strong enough position to turn his attention back to the Caratacus problem.

Tim, Caroline and Gwirocon observed the initial stages of occupation with great interest. The surface of the ancient Sarn was vastly improved and the road witnessed an incredible increase in traffic both to and from Uiroconium.

The amount of timber, livestock, produce, weaponry and people now travelling along the road was substantial; it had to be, considering it was impossible for the invaders to rely on regular and freely-provided supplies from the aggrieved British people.

The fact that the enemy was so engrossed in establishing a major centre of operations at Uiroconium meant that, for the time being, little heed was paid to Gwirocon or the Cornovians. Life continued as it had done for generations with the added advantage that the Sarn was now much easier to travel; however, care had to be taken to avoid army patrols or attract unwanted attention.

The Romans had all but abandoned the difficult and narrow route along the upper Severn valley by which they had originally entered Cornovia, concentrating instead on the ancient Sarn which provided a faster and safer line of communication.

Furthermore, it became obvious to Gwirocon that the army was under strict instructions not to advance any further into hostile territory or antagonise the natives any more than was absolutely necessary until Scapula was ready.

This current state of affairs was more than welcomed by one man: Caradoc. The rebel leader took advantage of the situation realising, as Gwirocon had, that he was, for the moment, safe from patrols specifically intended to hunt him down.

His long-established policy of guerrilla attacks again proved a sharp thorn in the side of his enemies. Several successful ambushes were launched on supply trains in the Worcester area, where Caradoc's men could quickly retreat to the west bank of the Severn and disappear into the hills, making it impossible or unwise for Romans to pursue him.

Scapula called the enlarged camp Castra Cornoviorium, 'the fort of the Cornovians', a name the site was to keep for almost thirty years before being changed to Uiroconium Cornoviorum.

Many important visitors came to see him during the next few weeks. Every legionary commander and a few British kings, who had proved their allegiance to Rome's authority and were considered trustworthy, were summoned to tell him what the current situation was in their parts of the country.

Governor Scapula was well aware that his emperor was not at all happy with the mounting cost of the campaign. Both Emperor Claudius and the Senate were astonished that Britain remained unconquered after some seven years. Claudius needed more signs of success so that he could counter criticism from his political enemies in Rome. It didn't take much to be deposed (emperors had a bad track record when it came to assassination) and conspiracies were rife. Scapula's own fate was very much tied to his emperor's. And he knew it.

Gwirocon was both pleased and anxious that the new governor had not yet made direct contact with him. This was, from what he could tell, extremely unusual. Ever since the Romans embarked on their campaign after Caradoc's earlier defeats, their generals had, almost without exception, sought out the kings of newly-invaded lands to impose their laws and tax demands.

So far, this had not happened in Cornovia. And Gwirocon was worried in case Caradoc's recent successes were seen as being due, if only in part, to his support for the legendary rebel. If Scapula suspected Gwirocon's motives, all the plans made for his people's survival would be in vain.

Gwirocon needed to know what was going on inside Castra Cornoviorum but he did not wish to approach Scapula voluntarily, nor were any of the visiting kings trustworthy. They would be only too willing to spread rumours against him if it meant they could gain political advantages or tax concessions for their own benefit. There was only one course of action possible.

'Do you understand the Roman tongue?' he asked.

Tim nodded.

'I could at Uxacona,' he said. 'And if I can, so can Caroline,' he added.

'Can you read their words?'

They shrugged their shoulders. Their father had often shown them Latin inscriptions in his history books and on monuments but they had never actually tried to translate anything.

'I suppose we might be able to read their words; they use the same letters as we do,' said Caroline after a moment's thought. 'But so far we've only understood speech.'

'Why do you want to know if we can read Latin?' asked Tim.

'In case you see anything written down,' replied the druid. 'I have a basic knowledge, learned as part of my druid training, but am not completely confident.'

'Well, it's a pity you don't practice more,' observed Caroline.

'Everything we know about this period in British history was written from the Roman point of view. Being here now has taught us that we can't rely on what they wrote.'

'Why don't you write something yourself?' said Tim. 'In Latin. It's the language of the future. And keep it somewhere safe, to be found years from now. That way historians would know what really happened and what life was like before and during the Roman invasion.'

'But you know what things are like,' said Gwirocon.

'Yes, but how can we prove it?' said Caroline. 'Even if we do return to our own time, no one's going to believe us unless there's proof.'

Gwirocon considered what they had said.

'If I survive the next few years, I'll give it some thought. But you've made me forget what I was talking about.'

'About understanding the Roman language, Latin,' prompted Caroline.

'Oh, yes,' nodded Gwirocon. He looked earnestly at them. 'You have both been a great comfort and help to me since you arrived. You understand what I hope to achieve and I know I can trust you above all others. I should like you to do something important for me and my people. It will be dangerous.'

Caroline felt rather nervous. He hadn't spoken like this before.

'What is it?' asked Tim.

'I want you to enter Castra Cornoviorum.'

'Why?' said Caroline, her voice faltering slightly.

'I need to know what Scapula's plans are. Not just as far as the Cornovians are concerned, but also what his intentions are towards Caradoc.'

Caroline looked anxiously at Tim.

'I could go on my own,' said Tim, bravely.

'If you're going, so'm I,' said Caroline adamantly.

'You don't have to do anything you don't want,' said Gwirocon. 'I have no right to ask but I cannot think of any other way.'

'We'll go first thing tomorrow,' said Tim decisively.

Shortly after they had finished their usual uninspiring breakfast of brittle bread and fresh milk, Gwirocon took them in his chariot westward along the Sarn. After a couple of miles he turned onto a narrow track through the woodland. Eventually he pulled the horses to a halt. They were only a few metres from the edge of the trees. The Roman fort stood some two hundred metres further on.

Gwirocon looked skyward. He frowned.

'It won't be long before the sun burns away the morning mist,' he said. 'You'd better hurry. Are you sure you want to do this?'

'Yes,' said Caroline emphatically.

Tim nodded. 'It's the only way we'll find out what Scapula's plans are.'

'Take care. I'll wait here until nightfall. And remember, keep away from sunlight in case you're seen.'

Caroline led the way along another narrow track until they emerged from the trees. The mist was already dispersing; she could feel the first rays of the sun's warmth on her back.

They hurried between the stumps of felled trees and bushy undergrowth surrounding the fort. Soldiers were busily going about their daily duties tending their mules and horses, fetching water from the river and finishing off the construction of the wooden ramparts.

'The gate's open!' exclaimed Tim. 'Run!'

They rushed across the open ground in front of the gateway. Suddenly, as they approached the gate, a shaft of sunlight burst through the clouds. At the same time, a soldier, whistling to himself and carrying two leather buckets hanging from a yoke around his shoulders, came out of the gate. Tim swerved sharply and managed to avoid crashing into him. Caroline was not so lucky.

She ran straight into one side of the yoke, spinning it and the Roman round in a complete circle. Breathless and alarmed, Caroline rapidly recovered her wits and ran through the gate into the shadow beyond.

'You OK?' whispered Tim.

Caroline nodded. 'Did he see us?'

Tim peered around the corner of the gateway. The soldier had recovered his balance but his face was an absolute picture! He was completely confused. He turned and looked into the gateway, then all around where he stood. He scratched his head, then shook it in disbelief.

Another soldier carrying water approached him.

'What's wrong with you, Marcus? Seen a ghost?'

'I could have sworn someone shoved me,' Marcus replied. 'Did you see anything?'

'No. But then, I didn't have a skin full last night!' He laughed and continued walking into the fort.

Marcus set off towards the river bank, muttering to himself.

'That was close,' said Caroline. 'Where do we go now?'

'Let's get our bearings first,' said Tim. He pulled her away from the gateway and further into the shadows.

They spent a few minutes looking around. Like at Uxacona, everyone had a job to do to ensure the smooth running of the fort and make sure no one had too much time to spend being idle. Idleness leads to mischief and lack of discipline, neither of which were tolerated in the Roman army. Especially in a hostile land.

The inside of the fortress was filled with wooden barrack buildings and workshops separated by straight streets. Nearest to them were stables. Beyond the stables were rows of soldiers' barracks. Tim could just see another wooden building further down the main street. It seemed to be right in the centre of the fort. He pointed.

'That must be the commander's quarters,' he said. 'I've got to get inside.'

'*We've* got to get inside, you mean,' Caroline corrected him. She didn't want to be left out of the action.

Tim sighed. 'Look, if anything goes wrong, one of us has to get back to Gwirocon. Someone has to stay outside.'

'Why should it be me?'

Tim was about to say something about her being a girl but thought better of it. Caroline had strong views on equal rights for women.

'Because it was my idea,' he said.

He could see she was annoyed; she was pouting and had her arms folded.

'Are you just going to stand there? We'd better make a move; the sun's getting stronger. Remember what Gwirocon said: stay in the shadows.'

'I know! I'm not stupid!'

They walked stealthily along the foot of the fortress wall until they found themselves at another gateway. This one was closed but had sentries standing above the gate.

'Why've they got another gate?' asked Caroline.

'The fort's roughly square-shaped. They always have a gate in the middle of each side. Opposite gates are joined by main streets so that they meet smack in the middle. That's where Scapula's quarters are. See?'

He turned and pointed. Caroline saw an important-looking soldier dressed in a shining and colourful uniform exit the doorway of a building near the crossroads. He walked purposefully along the road and turned a corner.

'You'd better get by the door ready for when it opens again,' said Caroline. 'You can't very well open it yourself in case anyone sees you.'

Tim nodded.

'You stay here.'

'Tim,' Caroline's voice faltered.

'What?'

She gently touched his arm.

'Take care!' she said quietly and sincerely. 'I don't know what I'll do if ... you know.'

Tim squeezed her hand reassuringly.

'Don't worry, I'll be OK.'

He ran along the side of the road and crouched down in the shade near the door. He was just in time. The important Romans, whom Tim now recognised as Scapula and Quintus, were walking straight towards him. They were in the middle of a conversation.

Tim was relieved to see they left the door open. He followed them inside.

'What about the local king? Shouldn't we make contact with him?'

'What's his name again?'

'Uirocon of the Cornovians. He has a settlement a few miles east of here and a fort on top of the hill.'

Tim wondered why he had called Gwirocon 'Uirocon'.

'What do you know about the fort? Is it strong?

'You saw it on the way here. The defences are the usual stone wall and wooden palisade. There are two ways to approach. The ground is very steep on the south-western side; it could present problems. There's a much easier path from the north-east, but there are double defence gates on that side. Even so, they shouldn't give us too much trouble if you think an attack's worthwhile.'

'Is it well defended?'

'As far as I can tell, it's not even occupied, except over winter and on odd occasions during the year.'

'Is there any point attacking it?'

'Only from the point of showing our power.'

'I'll take that as a no, then. They're already aware of our strength. No point in risking any more casualties, at least for the moment.'

'No, sir.'

'What do we know about this King Uirocon?'

'Nothing much. I gather he was a druid before we killed his brother King Madoc. He may still be a druid for all I know. Rumour has it that he doesn't want to fight; certainly, we've only had that one lot of trouble, when our first scouting party arrived. If you recall, they killed Madoc while he was spying on them from a coracle on the river.'

'And all the scouts were massacred afterwards,' said Scapula, with more than a hint of regret in his voice.

'But that could have been Caratacus. It must have been. The Cornovians are mainly farmers and there aren't that many of them, so I shouldn't think they were responsible, however angry they were at losing their king.'

'So who has been ambushing us along the Sabrina valley?'

Quintus shrugged his shoulders. 'Again, it has to be Caratacus.'

'If it is, why doesn't King Uirocon do anything to prevent Caratacus wandering all over his territory and occupying one hill fort after another?'

'What can a weak tribe do to stop a strong opponent? Nothing.'

'So they shouldn't cause us any trouble?'

'No.'

'If that's the case, I'll be able to concentrate on pursuing Caratacus?'

'If the gods permit, yes.'

'What have these Cornovians got to offer us?'

'No resistance for a start; that's worth a lot. And they produce salt. And corn and a lot of cattle. My spies tell me there's iron and lead in the area as well. Uirocon could be a useful ally.'

Scapula fell silent, thinking.

'Has he tried to make contact with us yet?'

'No.'

'In that case, we'll pay King Uirocon a visit in a few days' time.'

'If the Cornovians are like every other tribe we've encountered so far, most of them will be assembled in the king's hill fort on Midsummer's Day. That's in three days' time.'

'Then our presence will give them something extra to celebrate!'

'How many men should we take?'

'Leave the auxiliaries behind on this occasion,' Scapula smiled. 'We'll just take a cohort from the Fourteenth. With the Legion's eagle standard. Make sure they're turned out smartly.'

'Take the eagle? Regulations say it should remain in the camp.'

'Sod the regulations. We want to make a good impression!'

'Do you expect trouble?'

'I shouldn't think so. He hasn't done anything yet and he's had plenty of time and opportunity to hinder the enlargement of this fort. But would you welcome a bitter enemy with open arms? Of course not! No, we'll show King Uirocon how strong the might of Rome really is! And if he plays fair, he'll see how good we can be to our friends.'

'He won't like it when we demand food supplies.'

'Don't mention it to him. We can, well, bring that subject up later, after he's committed himself to supporting us. We'll give him a few amphorae of wine beforehand, just to butter him up. Word will soon reach the Silurians and Ordovicians; that'll make them see him as an enemy and he'll be all the more willing to help us in every way he can. He won't want them on his back as well as us!'

General Quintus grinned. He was beginning to understand Scapula's way of thinking.

'Have you ever thought about going into politics?'

'Me? Do you think I'm mad? Have you any idea what politics is like in Rome? No thanks, I'd rather take my chances here, on the field of battle, than risk assassination by my friends!'

They laughed.

Tim had heard enough. He had to get back to Gwirocon as soon as he could.

Druid king Gwirocon's roundhouse on The Wrekin Hill.

CHAPTER 7

Omens and Divine Intervention

Tim told Gwirocon and Caroline everything he'd heard while they made their way back to the farmstead at Wrockwardine. The druid king was worried, of that there was no doubt, but at least he was able to explain why Scapula had referred to him as 'Uirocon'.

Apparently the Romans were unable to pronounce the 'gw' sound; 'w' or 'u' was the closest they could manage. They also often Latinised the names of people and places, so Caratacus was the name they gave Caradoc. Both Caroline and Tim were pleased to discover this because it proved that several of the local place-names, especially The Wrekin, Wrockwardine and even Uiroconium, must have been named after Gwirocon.

By the time they returned home, Gwirocon knew what he had to do. He immediately despatched messengers to his under-kings, telling them to hide their good weapons away from their homes so that the Romans would not discover them, and to yield all rusty swords and useless spears when required to do so. On no account was anyone to offer resistance; the Cornovians had to be seen as friends of Rome.

Advising his neighbour, the Ordovician king Madrun, was a different matter entirely. Whether or not Madrun acted on Gwirocon's advice was up to him; he had no power in his territory and could do no more than warn him that the Romans were likely to invade Ordovicia in the near future.

Midsummer's Day was the most eagerly anticipated day of the year. No one wanted to miss out on the fun and excitement of the occasion. Many tribesfolk travelled for several days to be there and everyone living close to the hill was expected to open their doors to accommodate visitors.

The event began at the onset of dusk the day before. It was traditional for members of every household to gather together and eat a small meal before setting off to the fortress on the hill. As soon as darkness came, Gwirocon let Tim and Caroline light an enormous bonfire on the summit.

Some families travelled on foot, others in whatever transport they had, including horses, mules and ox-drawn wagons. Everyone held a torch or mutton-fat candle to light their way through the gathering gloom in the forest and struggled to carry sacks containing enough food and drink to sustain them throughout the coming event.

The sight from the top of the hill was enthralling. Spasmodic flickers of light appeared and disappeared all over the surrounding countryside, indicating where a group of people had passed through a woodland clearing.

The hours wore on, the torchlights became more concentrated as one group joined another, then another, until they formed a continuous dancing, winding line of flame from the foot of the hill to the bonfire at the top.

Once everyone had gathered, huddled together within the restricted space of the inner fortress, the druid called for silence. With arms raised high, Gwirocon gave praise and thanks to god and the spirits for their bounty and support and beseeched them to yield a good harvest and protection from the Romans. His voice was unshaking, powerful, commanding; his exhortations skilfully timed to end when the first shaft of summer sun exploded in a blood-red lake beneath the greenish blue of the heavens.

A loud cheer erupted. Everyone took turns to cast the remnants of their candles and torches into the bonfire as votive gifts to the spirit of fire.

Gwirocon again called for quiet. Children who had been born since the previous Midsummer's Day were brought to him. One by one he held them gingerly over the smouldering embers of the bonfire. This was to purify their souls and make the parents aware that, from that point on, any misfortunes affecting their offspring were solely due to the influence of Man and not god or the spirits.

Then, all who wished to marry on this special day were invited to come forward. Smiling brides, hair adorned with wild flowers and wearing clothes freshly cleaned, stepped forward, affectionately clutching the hands of their intended husbands, some of whom seemed less enthusiastic than others.

The druid conducted a collective wedding ceremony; individual oaths of mutual love and support were exchanged. Gwirocon then awarded grants of land to the newly-weds and exhorted their families and friends to help prepare their allotments for early habitation and cultivation.

The druid king spoke a few more solemn words concerning the sanctity of marriage, reminding everyone that they all had a responsibility to treat the newly-weds with respect and not be tempted to do anything, anything at all, to jeopardise the success of their union.

Formalities over, the entertainment began. By this time the sun had risen enough to dispel the half-light of dawn. Several new fires were lit and the carcasses of pigs, cattle and sheep hoisted over them on spits to provide fresh hot food. Containers of ale, mead, milk and water were also on hand. Enjoyment is thirsty work!

Whereas the older generations were content to sit in groups, chatting and nibbling, the women organised games and races for the younger children. Young boys and warriors took part in archery and slingshot competitions and travelling jugglers, acrobats and bards performed throughout the day.

Tim and Caroline found the whole event not only fascinating but also totally unexpected. None of the books their father had lent them gave any idea that this sort of thing had ever taken place in ancient Britain. They had always thought that the Celts were backward, uncouth and barbaric. The more they saw for themselves, the more they realised that pre-Roman Britain was a highly civilised and well ordered society. Life was, without a doubt, very hard but the people certainly knew how to enjoy themselves!

The wraiths from the future found it very difficult to remember to keep in the shade whenever the sun shone, especially when they wanted to get a better view of one of the performances. They prayed for the sun to hide behind one of the scudding clouds so that they could emerge from the shadows and walk around unseen and unnoticed for a few minutes.

Gwirocon, of course, kept as close an eye on them as he possibly could. As usual, he'd warned them against exposure, even though he knew he could trust them. Nevertheless, it didn't stop them from grabbing portions of food and drink, much to the confusion of individuals who could have sworn there had been one more piece of bread or another mug of milk on the ground beside them.

The Cornovians were in an exuberant mood, although they knew Scapula and his cohort of soldiers would arrive at any minute. In the meantime, they intended to follow tradition for as long as possible. Midsummer's Day only came once a year and had to be enjoyed to the full!

It was approaching noon when one of the lookouts standing on the walkway above Hell Gate ran up the hill into the inner fort to tell Gwirocon that a large group of Romans was approaching. They would reach the foot of the hill very shortly. Gwirocon spread the word and warned everyone to be on their very best behaviour. Under no circumstances must anyone annoy or anger the enemy. All items used in the weapon competitions were hastily hidden in empty storage pits inside a few of the huts.

Tim and Caroline managed to get close to the druid king.

'It's just a thought,' said Caroline, 'but the Romans are supposed to be terribly superstitious.'

'And it's a certain fact they could wipe everyone out if they wanted. Let us know if you need us to do anything,' Tim added.

Gwirocon nodded. He'd already had one or two ideas, but much depended on what Scapula did. And the weather. Dark, storm-laden clouds were rapidly approaching from the west.

'I'm sure you'll know what to do if I need your help,' he said, mysteriously.

Gwirocon grabbed his staff and strode purposefully through

Heaven Gate and across the outer fortress compound. He stopped and stood resolutely in the entrance to Hell Gate. A small crowd of people assembled behind him, anxiously watching and waiting. They were very aware that they were totally defenceless and completely at the mercy of the approaching enemy. All their unspoken, respectful trust rested in the druid king.

They did not have long to wait. Scapula and Quintus, both on horseback, were first to appear. Behind them walked the signifer, the legion's standard bearer, carrying a long pole with a highly polished steel eagle at its top. A long train of fully equipped legionaries marched smartly at the rear.

Scapula pulled his horse to a halt halfway along the level ground in front of Hell Gate and raised his hand. His army came to an immediate and silent halt. Gwirocon was understandably impressed by their discipline and uniforms.

Highly polished breastplates and helmets glistened in the sunlight; bright red tunics and cloaks and large ornate shields added brilliant colour to the scene. Long spears stood rigidly to attention, nervous hands twitching as they gripped the staves. Gwirocon could not see their deadly short swords but knew they could appear from behind the shields at a moment's notice. He waited to see what Scapula did next.

'Bring King Uirocon of the Cornovians to me!' commanded Scapula.

Gwirocon struggled for a few seconds, trying to remember his Latin. It had been a long time since he had needed to use it. His delay frustrated the Roman governor.

'I said, bring King Uirocon of the Cornovians to me!' he shouted testily, much louder than before.

Gwirocon wondered why people always thought shouting at foreigners would help them to understand better.

'There's no need to shout. I heard you twice the first time,' he called back as amiably as he could. 'I am Gwirocon. Please do not take offence if I am slow to understand your words.'

Scapula was bemused by Gwirocon's attempt at humour. Or was it an insult? He couldn't be sure.

'Come here!'

'I would rather offer you the hospitality of my fortress.'

Gwirocon stood his ground. He didn't want to risk capture, nor did he wish to offend Scapula. But he wanted the Roman to know that he was not afraid. And a king.

Scapula's eyes flashed with annoyance. Gwirocon noticed. Perhaps humour was inappropriate, for the present at least.

'Please enter,' he continued, standing to one side and showing the way with an outstretched arm. 'Have no fear, my people are not armed.'

Scapula was deeply suspicious and somewhat taken aback by Gwirocon's attitude. The last thing he expected was an invitation. He could handle conflict, but not kindness.

He flicked the reins and his horse moved slowly forwards. Quintus did likewise and motioned his men to follow. The soldiers closed ranks, their shields forming a barrier on both sides as they entered Hell Gate.

By this time, the Cornovians had abandoned their celebrations and were standing on either side of the main path all the way from Hell Gate, through Heaven Gate and onwards to the summit. Gwirocon walked a few paces ahead of Scapula and stopped when he reached the top.

'Will you join me in some refreshment?' he asked Scapula. 'We are simple folk but our food is good.'

Scapula hesitated before dismounting. Neither he nor his men liked being surrounded by the enemy, but he had not been pro-voked into taking drastic action. Yet.

Gwirocon motioned a woman to give Scapula food and a mug of good wine. Seeing that the Roman was reluctant to partake, Gwirocon ate a morsel and sipped from the mug to satisfy Scapula that neither was poisoned.

The governor understood Gwirocon's actions and nodded his approval before helping himself.

'Why did you welcome me into your fortress?' he demanded, chewing a chunk of meat.

'Why shouldn't I?' asked Gwirocon. 'Your soldiers have done nothing to harm me or my people. Besides which, we are not war-riors, merely farmers and craftsmen.'

Scapula surveyed the silent Cornovians. They seemed normal and the younger men did not appear warrior-like. And no one carried a sword, just small daggers and knives used for cutting meat. He nodded.

'Am I to understand you bow willingly to Roman rule?'

Gwirocon smiled.

'I had hoped to reach an agreement with you,' he said. 'Neither of us has anything to gain by conflict.'

'Then who killed the scouting party by the river?'

'We believe it was Carad– ... Caratacus. It was certainly none of my people,' replied Gwirocon, truthfully. 'We do not make war.'

Scapula didn't know whether to believe him or not.

'I know you British,' said the Roman scornfully. 'Always fighting and grabbing each others' territory! What makes you so different? If you don't fight, why have you not been taken by neighbouring tribes?'

Gwirocon fingered the silver pendant around his neck. It caught the sun and cast its small but bright reflection on the ground. The druid tried hard to stop himself grinning when the reflection flashed in the direction of the Raven's Bowl and a raven jerked its head in his direction.

'Because we are protected by unseen powers,' he said in a matter of fact way.

Scapula frowned. Was this a threat?

'Explain!'

'Do you believe in omens?' he asked, again fingering the pendant. The raven watched the reflection dance across the rock and pounced, trying to catch it.

'All Romans believe in the supernatural.'

'Is any bird more powerful than the eagle?' asked Gwirocon.

'No. The eagle is Rome. Rome is stronger than any other city or country. Why do you ask?'

'Watch.'

The druid king pointed towards the signifer's standard. Everyone turned to look at it. While they were distracted, Gwirocon manipulated the pendant so that the reflection enticed the raven from its rock and into the air. The ominous black bird emitted a chilling caw, alerting the other ravens in the murder. They launched themselves into the sky and swooped down in a unified attack on the shining eagle.

The signifer had no option but to do the unforgivable; let go of the pole while he tried to fend off the unrelenting onslaught. The standard fell to the ground, its silver eagle mauled by the ravens' strong, clawed feet and sharp beaks. None of the soldiers dared intervene; ravens were the ultimate in bad omens.

A dark cloud moved across the sun. Gwirocon released the pendant and clapped his hands. The ravens, no longer able to see the reflection and alarmed by the clap, cawed again and flew back to their rock.

'So you see,' said Gwirocon casually. 'We would rather grow food for ourselves than fight others. As far as I'm concerned, you and your people are our neighbours and we'll do what we can to provide food and other supplies.'

The way he spoke and what he said so soon after this supernatural demonstration had the effect he was hoping for. He had shown both hospitality and apparently divine power. The Roman governor would be stupid to act against him. But still Scapula was not completely convinced.

'How do I know this display was not contrived?' he asked. His tone was different now; almost respectful and not so imperious. 'If someone did attack you, how would you defend yourself?'

Gwirocon frowned. He hadn't anticipated this.

'Tell him your enemy's own weapons would protect you!' said invisible Caroline in a loud whisper.

'What are you playing at?' said Tim. 'Are you trying to get us all killed?'

'I know what I'm doing!' she retorted. 'Gwirocon! Do as I say! Please!'

Gwirocon frowned again. Scapula took the delay as a sign of weakness.

'Well?' he demanded with a slight sneer.

'My enemy's own weapons would protect me,' Gwirocon replied with some uncertainty.

Scapula smiled. There was an evil look in his eyes.

'How do you mean? Like this?'

He drew his sword and pointed it at Gwirocon. Quintus moved closer, expecting trouble. He signalled his men to be at the ready.

The smile in Scapula's eyes turned to fear when an unseen force slowly and firmly turned the blade away from Gwirocon and sideways towards his own throat. He let it go and stepped back in alarm.

He bumped into Quintus, lost his balance and fell over. Quintus leapt backwards and inadvertently knocked over the spit upon which the remains of a small pig were roasting.

The pig fell onto the flickering flames beneath, sending sparks and embers flying wildly into the air. The breeze carried them towards the huts; the thatch on the nearest one caught fire. The flame began to spread. Someone raised the alarm and pushed others away from the blaze.

Before anyone could do anything, one of the Roman soldiers felt his cloak being ripped away from his neck. He turned around, ready to face his assailant. There was nobody there except another soldier whose eyes and mouth were wide open in astonishment.

The cloak drifted up and began to beat the flames on the roof. Shreds of burning thatch exploded into the air and settled on the next roof. It, too, caught alight. As did the next.

Women grabbed their screaming children and crashed into one another, desperate to escape the blaze; they gathered in small groups in the safety of open spaces away from the huts. Fire, especially during a dry spell, was something that terrified them. They could lose their possessions ... and lives.

Spurred on by the cloak mysteriously acting on its own, Britons and Romans sprang into action. Fire was something they all dreaded. Flames were thrashed relentlessly with cloaks, sacks and hastily-hacked branches. Meagre supplies of water in buckets and ale and wine in earthenware containers of all shapes and sizes were poured over the flames without a second thought.

Desperation in the face of a common adversary can have the remarkable effect of uniting sworn enemies. It took a while for the wind-fanned flames to be brought under control. Three huts were beyond salvation, their thatched roofs riddled with smoking holes.

Cornovian men, seeing the hitherto immaculate Romans with smutty faces, singed hair and dirty armour, couldn't stop themselves laughing now that the danger had been overcome. At first, the soldiers didn't understand why. But realisation dawned and they, too, saw the funny side of things. A few drinks, just to ease dry throats, of course, soon brought both sides together in a rare show of friendship.

Quintus looked around in panic. He grabbed a spear from one of his men and waved it about threateningly.

'Where's Governor Scapula?' he yelled. 'What have you done with him?'

A muffled groan came from inside the pile of shields and spears, dumped by soldiers when they tackled the blaze. Scapula's feet were sticking out from underneath. Gwirocon saw them and unceremoniously dragged the dishevelled governor out.

Quintus thrust the spear at Gwirocon.

'Let him go,' he growled. 'I've seen enough of your tricks!'

His voice trailed away when he, too, felt an unseen power pull the spear away from Gwirocon, who smiled and knelt down to help Scapula back to his feet.

Quintus tried his utmost to resist the invisible force. After a few moments he gave up. He let go of the spear and stood back in amazement when it turned in the air and embedded itself firmly in the ground.

Marcus, the bucket-carrying soldier whom Caroline had crashed into at Castra Cornoviorum a few days earlier, couldn't contain himself any longer and snorted involuntarily as he struggled not to laugh. Quintus was incensed at this affront to his authority.

'You!' he shouted. 'Retrieve the spear! The rest of you get back in line!'

The soldier edged his way uncertainly towards the spear while his comrades fell back into lines. He slowly extended his arm. Suddenly, the spear uprooted itself, turned and slid into his open palm. Puzzled, he snatched it and retreated rapidly to take his place in the ranks.

Quintus glowered at him.

Marcus kept his face straight and stood rigidly to attention.

Meanwhile, Scapula dusted himself down, his eyes fixed on this unassuming British king who stood respectfully waiting for him to regain his composure and dignity. He just couldn't make up his mind.

Was everything he had witnessed some kind of clever illusion or was Gwirocon indeed blessed with divine protection? Did it really matter? The king had extended the hand of friendship and didn't appear to pose a threat as long as good relations were maintained.

The sky was getting darker by the minute and a strong wind began to whistle across the hill top. A flash of lightning and a growling roar of thunder heralded a sudden outburst of torrential rain. Gwirocon put his mouth close to Scapula's ear.

'Tell your men to shelter with my people in the huts!' he yelled. 'Let them help themselves to food! Come with me!'

Tim and Caroline had retreated into Gwirocon's hut as soon as the storm began and were already curled up behind a pile of sacking at the far side of the building. It seemed odd that they got wet only when they made a move towards the hut, but they didn't give it any more thought.

Caroline popped her head up momentarily when Gwirocon entered to let him know they were there: light cast through the open door lit her face briefly. She ducked down again when Scapula and Quintus followed him in, brushing raindrops off their uniforms.

Gwirocon gave them beakers of wine, mulled over the small indoor fire. The three sipped in uncertain silence, reflecting on the recent events. After some consideration, Scapula spoke.

'King Uirocon, I'm not sure what I have witnessed today, but I do know I've never seen anything like it. If what you have said is true, then I am willing to accept you as a friend of Rome. But I must warn you ... if there is any trouble, any trouble at all from you or your people, I shall have no alternative but to treat you as I would treat any other tribe. One more thing,' he said, lowering his voice significantly. 'I think it would be a good idea if we, er, managed to forget what, er, happened here today.'

'I am pleased to hear this,' said Gwirocon with genuine relief. 'I can promise you that, if you treat us well, fairly and without oppression, both you and your soldiers will find us a worthy ally.'

He extended his right hand to Scapula. The governor gripped it firmly.

'If that is what the gods decree, so be it!'

Gwirocon hid a smile and glanced vaguely in Tim and Caroline's direction.

'I am sure that's what the gods intend!'

Caroline gives the spear to puzzled Marcus.

CHAPTER 8

Angels of Mercy

News of yet more strife in all corners of occupied Britain were reported to Gwirocon during the following months. Every legion continued to carry out its orders, disarming each and every Briton whenever they discovered another settlement. Carrying arms had always been an accepted right for Celts throughout the ages and the execution of Scapula's edict was met with incredulity. But the people had to face the harsh reality of their situation; they were completely and utterly oppressed, powerless in their own land.

Scapula's orders gave his soldiers a wonderful opportunity to vent five years' worth of frustration and anger against an inhospitable country and devastating guerrilla attacks by their sworn enemy, Caratacus. The druids, with the power and authority to influence many British kings, gained considerable support and took every opportunity to encourage dissension against the invaders.

Scapula believed that an unarmed enemy would be so much easier to control. In some ways he was right, but the destruction of whole villages and the inhumane cruelty exercised by troops over-enthusiastic to fulfil their duties resulted in deepening hostility towards his rule. Many who were captured while defending their property were taken into slavery and shipped away to public auctions in Rome. Countless others, ordinary people, women and children, were massacred.

More and more disenchanted warriors fled to join Caradoc's army whose attacks became bolder and more frequent, yet Scapula continued to increase his brutal control over lowland Britain. He knew where his priorities lay.

Even those kings and queens who had sworn allegiance to Rome, like Queen Cartimandua of the Brigantians, and had remained neutral when the invasion began, discovered they were

not exempt from his tyranny. Kingship was no longer an heredi-
tary right passing from one generation to the next; Rome decided
when a ruler needed to be replaced, and who the new king would
be. This was the price Britons paid for centuries of internal strife
and mistrust, culminating in such weakening disunity.

Only Caradoc had the charisma to bring a few of the diverse
tribes together with the common aim of pushing back the Roman
advance, but had the Britons come to their senses too late?

As far as Gwirocon was concerned, his decision not to resist the
Roman army had been a wise one. His own people followed orders,
even if they didn't always agree with them, but were relieved to
find that handing over their useless weapons seemed to satisfy the
enemy. Perhaps the druid king was right, after all.

Gwirocon's main problem was with the kings of other tribes in
whom he confided; they found it difficult to believe his motives or
that he was helping to feed, clothe and arm Caradoc's men.
Gwirocon dreaded the prospect of what might happen to his
defenceless people if Scapula ever discovered the truth.

He and the Roman governor were on reasonably good terms.
Gwirocon ensured regular supplies of grain, livestock and other
provisions were delivered to Castra Cornoviorum and Scapula
kept his soldiers in check, rigorously enforcing a no-victimisation
policy in favour of the Cornovians. Regular patrols of small groups
of soldiers in the woodland around the Roman fort had little effect
on the lives of the natives.

Knowing that enemy troops were unlikely to explore much of
the area, the druid king was able to keep his 'hidden' fields and the
metal working activities in the heavily wooded Severn Gorge a
closely-guarded secret. Consequently his people enjoyed virtually
no persecution and maintained their humble standard of living
while the rest of occupied Britain suffered.

Life in the confines of Caer Gwirocon was about to resume its
usual, monotonous course over the winter period. The last few
families had just left their farmsteads in the forest to join the rest
of the Cornovians in the area. Everyone pulled together to ensure

they, their livestock, food and meagre possessions were safe within the confines of the hill fort.

There was still much work to be done. Cattle, pigs and sheep were slaughtered, salted and stored on hooks suspended from the roof supports inside the huts and grain was poured into the pits beneath the floor. Leather and wooden buckets were filled with water from one of the springs bubbling up from the north facing slopes of the hill. Groups of teenage girls ventured into the surrounding woodland to forage for nuts, edible roots, herbs and plants to supplement their diet.

For their own mutual protection against possible attack by wolves, boar or bears, the girls were instructed to stay within earshot of each other and to rally round, shouting and screaming loudly, if anyone got into difficulty to frighten wild animals away.

That was the theory and, in practice, it usually worked. However, it was easy to get separated from the crowd when engrossed in foraging. It was also almost impossible to hear cries for help from any great distance; sounds are soon absorbed by trees and hollows in the ground.

While Gwirocon was engaged in overseeing preparations on top of the hill, Tim and Caroline decided they would take the opportunity to get some exercise. They followed one group of girls through the south-western gate and down the steep path which led to the tree-covered Little Hill (or Primrose Hill as it is sometimes called).

The girls spread out, wending their separate ways in search of nature's produce. Some stopped to pick hazel nuts, others grubbed away at the undergrowth with their bare hands to pull out tuber-like edible roots. Whatever was reaped was put into one of the small sacks hanging from plaited ropes slung over their shoulders. Every now and then, someone called out and the others shouted back. It was a simple but effective way to ensure everyone in the group was safe.

As the morning passed, the girls spread out more and more. At times it was possible to judge where someone was by the sudden noise of wings flapping or a startled animal rustling through the leaf-strewn undergrowth.

Both Tim and Caroline realised many months before that, even though they could not be seen by humans, animals and birds were far more sensitive to their presence. Consequently, they made sure the way in front had been cleared by one of the girls so that they didn't startle the wildlife themselves.

After several hours of leisurely strolling around, numerous rests and occasional nut-nibbling, they found they had followed one of the girls some distance away from the Little Hill. Without realising it, she had all strayed a long way from the others. It was now late afternoon and beginning to get dark.

While the teenager was busily scratching out a shallow hole beneath a plant, Caroline saw two Roman soldiers walking slowly in their direction. She nudged Tim and pointed.

'Over there!' she whispered urgently. 'What shall we do?'

Tim ran between the trees until he was within earshot of the soldiers. He recognised one of them as Marcus.

'Are you sure this is the way?' said the other man. He seemed angry.

'No, I'm not sure, Ludo,' replied Marcus. 'If you hadn't gone after that deer, we'd still be with the rest of the patrol.'

'Well, I don't like it.' Ludo fingered his sword. 'It's too quiet.'

At that moment, the girl stood up. She saw the soldiers, screamed and began to run away.

Ludo ran after her. It didn't take him long to catch her. He threw her to the ground.

'Well, look what we have here,' he said with an evil smile on his pock-marked face. 'My, you're a pretty one!'

The girl struggled and screamed again. Ludo slapped her hard across the face.

Marcus caught up with him.

'What the hell are you doing?' he shouted. 'You know what Scapula ordered. Don't harm the natives unless they harm you first!'

'Her beauty struck me,' smiled Ludo. 'That's reason enough!'

He struggled with his clothing. Marcus realised what his intentions were.

'You can't do that! Let her go! She's only a girl!'

Marcus tried to pull him away. Ludo was incensed. The girl took advantage of the distraction and ran away into the gathering gloom. Ludo turned and began to run after her. Marcus ran after him. Ludo tripped on something and fell crashing to the ground.

'I said, let her go!' yelled Marcus.

Ludo stood up and rounded on Marcus. Their noses almost touched. Ludo's nostrils flared.

'Call yourself a Roman? Taking sides with a Brit? Traitor!'

Suddenly, Marcus's legs gave way. He fell down, clutching his side. Caroline gasped when she saw the dagger in Ludo's hand.

Marcus writhed on the ground and tried to pull himself up by grabbing hold of a low branch.

Ludo replaced his dagger, helped Marcus to his feet, then gave him such a punch on the jaw that Marcus almost flew backwards into a bush. He lay motionless, the wound in his side pumping blood at an alarming rate.

'Goodbye, Marcus. You'll be dead soon enough. Serves you right for interfering! When I tell Scapula the natives did this, it won't be long before he lets us do what we like with them!'

He strode back along the way he had come.

Caroline ran to Marcus's side and pressed hard on the oozing wound to stem the flow of blood. She couldn't tell whether he was dead or concussed.

Tim felt he had to do something. Quickly. If Ludo reported Marcus had been killed by the Cornovians, all hell would break loose. Gwirocon's plans and efforts would be a complete waste of time and his people would suffer terribly.

He ran after Ludo, rummaging in his bag on the way, until he was close enough to flick his foot and trip Ludo up. The Roman fell and hit his head sharply against a tree.

While Ludo lay there dazed, Tim took out the offending dagger from its scabbard and used it to remove the brooch holding the villain's cloak around his neck. He put the brooch in his pocket and held his torch under his chin and waited.

After a few moments, Ludo came out of his daze. He groaned and rubbed the top of his head. A lump was beginning to take shape under his scalp. He opened his eyes.

Tim saw his chance. Pulling the most gruesome face he could, he switched on the torch. Fortunately for him, the failing light of dusk was just dark enough for the beam emanating from somewhere under his chin to have the desired effect.

Ludo's terrified expression was a picture! He uprooted himself and tore off as fast as his shaky legs could carry him.

Tim couldn't stop himself laughing out loud. But he had more important things to attend to. He picked up Ludo's cloak and ran back to join Caroline. She looked anxiously up at him.

'Oh, Tim! He's still breathing! What can we do?'

'You're the one who did First Aid.'

'I can't stop the bleeding.'

'I've got an idea.'

He tore Ludo's cloak into narrow strips and handed them to his sister. Caroline tied the ends together until they made a long bandage. Tim then folded the remnants into a wad and held it firmly against the gaping hole in Marcus's side. Caroline helped him lift Marcus into a sitting position and carefully wrapped the bandage very tightly around his body. Marcus was alive ... just.

'What now?' asked Caroline. 'Do we go to get help?'

Tim shook his head.

'We can't leave him here. We won't be able to find him in the dark. Besides, he won't be able to ward off wolves or boar.'

'Then we'll have to carry him.'

'He's much too heavy!'

Caroline's eyes fell on the sack bags left behind by the girl during her flight from Ludo.

'Give me a hand.'

It took them almost two hours to reach the foot of the Little Hill. Using the girl's sacks and a couple of branches, they'd managed to make a rough stretcher. Marcus was bound to it with Tim's coil of climbing rope. For once it had come in useful.

By now it was pitch black. The air was damp and cold, as it often is in early November. Tim's compass and the full moon, hidden at times by drifting mist, helped them find their way.

Caroline stopped, gasping for breath. She laid her end of the stretcher on the damp ground. An owl hooted. She looked up. She could just see a faint orange glow above the treetops.

'Look! Light from the bonfires!' she exclaimed.

Tim lowered his end of the stretcher and shone his torch at Marcus.

'He looks terrible!' said Caroline.

'There's no way we can carry him to the top of the hill. Go and fetch Gwirocon; the path's straight up from here. I'll stay with him.'

While Caroline went for help, Tim unwrapped the rope from around the stretcher and gently rolled Marcus onto the ground. Then he tossed the branches to one side and hid the sacking in the undergrowth. It might raise awkward questions if the Roman was discovered tied to a rudimentary stretcher and bound with invisible rope!

Caroline was gone for what seemed ages. Marcus was getting weaker by the minute. Tim was worried. He'd caught a glimpse of several pairs of yellow eyes and heard furtive rustling in the undergrowth. He was more than a little relieved when he saw the welcome sight of burning torches descending in the darkness. He flashed his torch on and off briefly. The dancing flames held aloft by the search party headed in his direction. Caroline was first to reach him. Gwirocon was not far behind. He ordered men to carry the body carefully and led the way back up the hill.

Everyone in the fort lined both sides of the path between the south-western gateway and the druid's hut. They watched silently with worried, weary eyes. How could they explain away a mortally wounded enemy found in their woods? They dispersed when the door of the hut closed behind the Roman and the druid. Everything now depended on Gwirocon's skill in the arts of medicine. They had every faith in their king, who seemed to possess powers not given to other men. How else was it that he knew the Roman was in trouble and exactly where he lay in the woods?

Tim and Caroline spent most of the night helping Gwirocon tend the injured man and explaining what had occurred.

After administering one of his many potions and cleaning the deep wound, the druid king sewed the skin together with coarse horsehair thread and a fine bone darning needle. All three took it in turns to keep the fire burning and wiping Marcus's fevered brow. Eventually the Roman's breathing became stronger and more regular, at which point they took the opportunity to get a few hours sleep.

At daybreak, they were woken up by loud thumping on the door.

'King Gwirocon! Wake up! The Romans are here!'

Gwirocon roused Caroline and Tim and briefly felt Marcus's brow before opening the door. A contingent of grim-faced legionaries had already marched through Heaven Gate and was rapidly approaching his hut. He drowsily pulled the door closed behind him and prepared for the conflict which was about to be unleashed.

'Good morning, Scapula! I've been expecting you!'

Scapula was somewhat taken aback by this friendly greeting. It was the last thing he expected. He ignored Gwirocon's outstretched hand.

'I thought I could trust you, King Gwirocon,' he said. There was genuine disappointment in his tone. 'I am here on serious business. Some of your people have murdered one of my best soldiers.'

'I cannot believe that is true. Who has been murdered and who witnessed the incident?'

Scapula beckoned one of his soldiers forward. It was Ludo.

'Tell him what you told me,' he ordered.

'We were on patrol duty yesterday afternoon. My friend Marcus and I got separated from the rest and came across a girl; I saw her here, in this camp, a few moments ago. She waved us to approach – as you know, we're under strict instructions not to speak to your people unless invited – and we were ambushed by many warriors. Marcus fell. I was lucky to escape with my life. I lost my dagger and cloak in the fray. That's all.'

'Where did this take place?' asked Gwirocon.

'About three miles away, between here and Castra Cornoviorum.'

'Do these belong to you?' Gwirocon showed him the dagger and cloak brooch Tim had given him.

Ludo examined them. How had they come into the druid's possession so soon? He kept his nerve.

'They do,' he nodded.

'Thank you, Ludo. Governor Scapula, this is a most serious accusation.'

'How do you know this man is called Ludo?'

'I think we should discuss the matter in private. Please come with me.'

He led the governor into his hut and shut the door behind them. It was very gloomy inside but not so dark that Scapula could not see the body covered in blankets near the flickering flames of the fire.

'Is that man sick?' asked Scapula. 'Not one of the men who killed Marcus, I hope.'

'It was certainly someone who witnessed the attack,' said Gwirocon. He picked up the stub of a candle, lit it with a spill from the fire and held it near Marcus's face.

'Marcus!' Scapula exclaimed in astonishment. 'He's alive!'

'Fortunately, yes.'

At that point, Marcus stirred. He groaned.

'Marcus! Wake up!' ordered Scapula.

'Don't shout so loudly!' urged Gwirocon. 'He has been unconscious since I found him.'

He went over to a wooden box, picked out a small clay bottle and sniffed the contents. Then, while Scapula propped Marcus up, the druid poured a thick green liquid between the patient's lips. Marcus coughed and spluttered.

'Where am I?' he croaked. His voice was hoarse.

'At Caer Uirocon,' said Scapula. Gwirocon was surprised by the governor's gentleness and concern. It seemed curiously out of character. 'Can you remember what happened?'

Marcus nodded. He felt very groggy but managed to speak.

'Ludo tried to ... attack a young girl. I went to stop him. He stabbed me ... knocked me out ... left me for dead. I don't know what happened next. I think the spirits of the forest carried me here.'

'Spirits?!' exclaimed Scapula.

'He must be confused. Oh, by the way, here are the remnants of Ludo's cloak. I used it to stem the flow of blood from the wound so that he could be carried here.'

Scapula stood up resolutely.

'That's all the evidence I need! I've seen enough! King Gwirocon, I am sorry to have doubted you. I bitterly regret this incident. Will you look after Marcus until he's well enough to return to my fort?'

Gwirocon nodded. 'Of course. And Ludo?' he asked. He knew what the answer would be.

'An unprovoked attack on an innocent girl is unforgivable. To attack a comrade and leave him for dead is ... well, let us say you will not be troubled by Ludo again.'

South-west view from The Wrekin Hill over the meandering River Severn with Caer Caradoc in the centre distance.

CHAPTER 9

Caer Caradoc

Spring came. The long winter had passed by without further incident but Gwirocon was concerned that Scapula's tactic of consol-
idation was proving too successful. Rome's stranglehold over lowland Britain was, to all intents and purposes, complete.

It couldn't be long before Caradoc would be hunted down in
earnest. The time had come for the British rebel to reassess his
position: he called a meeting of all free kings and their druids.
Now that the campaign season was about to begin, it would be
more difficult to travel as there was more likelihood of attack from
or arrest by Roman scouting parties and patrols.

Caradoc continued to occupy the majestic hill fort on the border between Cornovia and Ordovicia, even though it was only
about ten miles south of Castra Cornoviorum. Despite Romans
having control of the main crossing, Cornovians were still able to
cross the River Severn in several other places using their coracles
where the water was too deep for wading. So far, regular supplies
from Gwirocon continued to reach Caer Caradoc without difficulty but the situation was about to change.

Gwirocon prepared to visit Caradoc. The gathering would be
the most important one since the invasion. There would be continuous discussions and differences of opinion; this was to be
expected when so many representatives from such diverse back-
grounds got together. The future of Britain was at stake.

Of course, Tim and Caroline would accompany Gwirocon; they
had proved their reliability and usefulness on so many occasions.
Following Gwirocon's advice, Caroline filled lemonade bottles
with boiled and cooled fresh water and placed them in her backpack with a supply of fresh food. Gwirocon gave them each an
identical dagger 'just in case' and warned them not to take any
unnecessary risks.

Because they had to cross the river above the Severn Gorge, where the river coursed through wide meanders in marshy ground, they were obliged to travel on horses rather than in Gwirocon's chariot. They made use of a communal coracle, left upside down on the river bank for casual use by anyone with a need.

The river was abnormally high for that time of the year and the current fast-flowing, so much so that Gwirocon found it difficult to manoeuvre the large coracle without it spinning around out of control.

With Tim and Caroline safely transferred to the opposite bank, Gwirocon made three more journeys to lead the horses across one after the other. Once clear of the marsh they were able to mount the animals and continue their journey.

The going was slow but not too difficult. Caroline was surprised to find there were countless tracks leading over the hills and through the woodland, yet there were almost no lanes wide enough to take a mule and cart. They were constantly having to duck beneath low branches and skirt around boggy ground.

Eventually they arrived at the northern foot of Caer Caradoc. Caroline couldn't believe how many hours it had taken to travel such a short distance; it would have taken less than an hour in her dad's car. It didn't seem much different from how Tim and Caroline remembered it from visits to Church Stretton and the Long Mynd with their parents, unlike The Wrekin where the change had been so dramatic. The slopes of Caer Caradoc were still treeless and covered in grass, although outer earthworks at the summit were now surrounded by a low drystone wall surmounted by the customary wooden stockade. Tim could just make out the roofs of huts inside the fortress compound.

Gwirocon made them dismount and tethered their horses to his own horse's harness. The climb was very steep; they were forced to pause frequently to regain their breath. By the time they reached the narrow gateway they were sweating profusely, despite the strong breeze.

Word of their impending arrival had been conveyed to Caradoc; he was already waiting and greeted Gwirocon warmly. After the horses had been untethered from each other and left to graze freely within the compound, Caradoc led Gwirocon to the small hut set aside for his sole use during his stay.

Tim and Caroline followed a short distance behind and slid into the hut when Caradoc left to attend his other guests. A small fire in the centre helped counter the damp atmosphere.

After a few minutes, Cunorix the Gaul entered, holding a short piece of roughly cut timber upon which sat a bowl of ale, some bread and freshly cooked wood pigeon. When he had gone, Gwirocon shared the food with his 'spirits' and suggested they get a few hours rest before joining Caradoc and the others in the main hut. Discussions were bound to continue until well after midnight and they'd need to stay alert.

They were disturbed several times during their slumbers by noises made by the arrival of other important guests. Cunorix returned at dusk to take them to Caradoc's hut where a crowd of over twenty kings and druids from other parts of unoccupied Britain were already waiting.

They sat on straw-covered ground in a circle around the central fire. Smoke coiled lazily upwards and hovered like a thick cloud trapped by the exposed timbers of the roof. Women entered and offered food and drink to the hungry visitors.

Tim and Caroline sat immediately behind Gwirocon and made sure they did not get in the way of passing servants. They ate their own provisions; it would have been difficult for Gwirocon to pass food to them without anyone noticing.

At length, Caradoc cleared his throat and called, respectfully, for their attention.

'My friends, thank you for travelling so far for this gathering. I have called you here to discuss how we may continue the struggle against our enemies.' His voice was quiet but full of authority.

'The Romans have strengthened their hold over the lands to the east and south and are now encamped at Castra Cornoviorum. Gwirocon tells me it is Scapula's intention to bring the Twentieth Legion up from the south with the sole intention of dealing with me and my supporters. The hunt will begin in earnest very soon.'

'Can Gwirocon's word be trusted?' asked Madrun, king of the Ordovicians.

The hut fell ominously silent. It was well known that the Cornovians had not lifted a finger against Rome. Suspicions ran deep.

'I trust him,' said Caradoc with conviction. 'He has done much to aid our cause at great risk to himself and his people.'

'Then why have none of them suffered? All other occupied tribes have; why should his be so different?'

'Because we are not strong enough to fight,' replied Gwirocon. 'Pretending to befriend Rome was the only way. Caradoc knows well enough how much we strive to supply him with provisions and weapons at considerable risk to ourselves.'

'It is true,' confirmed Caradoc. 'And he gives me valuable intelligence concerning enemy movements.'

'But how does he get that intelligence?' asked Madrun. 'How do we know it isn't all a trap?'

'As I said, I trust him implicitly,' said Caradoc.

Gwirocon could sense his presence was affecting the proceedings. 'I will return to my hut,' he said, getting up. 'It is clear me being here will hinder free discussion.'

'Stay, my friend!'

'No, Caradoc. It is for the best. Invite me back when I am welcome. No doubt I shall hear what is said in due course.'

He looked vaguely but meaningfully in Tim and Caroline's direction as he departed.

'It will not do to offend Gwirocon, Madrun,' rebuked Caradoc after the door banged shut. 'He is not like other kings; he cares for his people and for Britain. It is a pity there are not more like him, else we should not be in this mess.'

'Let us continue the discussion,' said Venutius, king of northern Brigantia, changing the subject.

'Where is your wife, Queen Cartimandua?' asked Madrun, looking around. 'Why is she not here?'

Venutius shook his head.

'I'm afraid we cannot trust her completely,' he said regretfully. 'She has sided with Rome. The southern Brigantians will not help us.'

'Are we the only ones who continue the fight?' asked Ruticon, king of the Silurians. 'There aren't many of us.'

'Such is the damage caused by our enemies,' observed Caradoc.

'One good pitched battle will wipe them out,' said Madrun. 'I vote we should attack Castra Cornoviorum without delay.'

Caradoc shook his head.

'That will not work.'

'How do you know?'

'Because I have had more experience of their capability than anyone else here,' said Caradoc, ruefully. 'You are forgetting just how much I have witnessed. Why do you think I chose hit and run attacks?'

'I'd like to hear what happened from the time the invasion started,' said Venutius. 'Everything I've heard is second or third hand. It might help us decide on a course of action.'

Several others nodded. Without experiencing events for themselves, it would better their understanding of Caradoc's tactics and his success to date.

'When my father Cunobelin was alive, he made sure his own people did not suffer unnecessarily while at the same time maintaining good relations with Rome. He understood the power of diplomacy and I wish I'd had the sense at the time to follow his example. But I didn't. If anyone is to blame for exerting too much influence over me, it was the druids.'

He gave a long, hard stare at the several druids present. They said nothing, merely watched and listened; such was their way.

'Druids hate all things Roman. Consequently, when I was old enough, I sought to carve out my own kingdom. I banished King Verica and my brother Adminius from their lands; both were too friendly towards Rome and took bribes. Their people hated them for making their lives a misery.'

'Then Cunobelin died,' observed Madrun.

'Yes. And that was the start of our troubles. My eldest brother – Togodumnus – inherited Cunobelin's kingdom. Unfortunately, this was at the same time that Claudius was made emperor by the legions. Claudius needed a victory of one sort or another to gain the respect of the Roman Senate.'

'And he chose to invade Britain,' said Venutius.

Caradoc nodded. 'They made various excuses, as you'd expect, accusing us of harbouring rebel Gauls, like Cunorix here. We didn't think they'd have the courage to invade; Emperor Caligula's legions mutinied a few years earlier when he wanted to invade our shores. But this time was different. They landed on the coast above Cantiacorum under the leadership of Plautius. I tried to reason with him but he had his orders. Subdue Britain within a year!'

Loud laughter echoed around the hut.

'How many years is it now? Seven? Eight? Togodumnus and I assembled a combined army at a crossing on the River Maedwy. We vastly outnumbered the enemy and held them back for two days before we were forced to retreat. We fell back to the River Tamesis but some of our army deserted. The Romans were still heavily outnumbered but Togodumnus was slain and again our warriors were no match for the disciplined tactics of the enemy. I swore then I would never meet them again in a pitched battle, however advantageous the terrain.'

Madrun took offence at the last comment.

'Not fight a pitched battle?'

'No,' said Caradoc, emphatically. 'The British have the same problem with the way they fight as do their kings in their dealings with each other. All is mistrust. Warriors attack without thought; they are individuals trying to prove their bravery. They have no concept of fighting together as a single unit, nor do they take account of the enemy's own battle tactics. Britain is disunited; that is why the Romans occupy so much of our land!'

'If you hold us in so much contempt, why do you seek our help now?' demanded Madrun.

'It is not you I hold in contempt but our traditional methods of warfare,' said Caradoc patiently. He had to find a way of pointing out their deficiencies without antagonising them. 'I had wealth, palaces. Do you think I wanted to lose everything? It would have been easier to welcome Rome with open arms or at least remain neutral, like Cartimandua. No, I chose to fight with whatever resources I had and with whoever wished to join me. Like the Silurians. I think you will agree that I have been more than a little successful.'

Everyone nodded. There was no doubt about Caradoc's achievements, prowess or popularity. His fame had even spread to Rome itself.

'My men do as I say. Although they lack the discipline of the enemy, they have more courage. The Roman soldier is here because he is forced. He hates us, our land and our miserable weather. He fights to preserve his own life. He works as part of a highly organised team. Nevertheless, my attacks strike fear into his heart.'

'Is it true you have destroyed enemy forts?' asked Madrun.

'We have destroyed forts, advance camps, supply trains, patrols and foraging parties. We never strike in the same place twice. We know this land, its short cuts and hidden paths. When we campaign in an area, we are joined by warriors from the local tribes. After an attack, my men move on to another area and the local warriors return to their homes as if nothing had happened. Until now.'

'Scapula has weakened support in the occupied lands considerably,' observed Venutius. 'Which is why future resistance must take place in the mountains to the west. In Ordovician and Silurian territory.'

Madrun and Ruticon exchanged smiles.

'My people are scattered among the hills,' said Ruticon, 'but you can rely on my continued support.'

'And mine,' said Madrun. 'I have already set aside a hill fort for you. It's not far from here but will be difficult for Scapula to find. And it is near enough for you to harry his soldiers. I'll give you all the food you need.'

'What do you want from me?' asked Venutius.

Caradoc thought for a moment. 'Nothing.'

Several eyebrows raised.

'Brigantia will be my next line of escape if it is needed. You have enough problems with your wife and her subjects. It is better for you to appear neutral for the time being. But it would help if you could stir up anti-Roman feeling. And with Cartimandua's people, if that's at all possible. I'm sure the druids will be only too pleased to help.'

Venutius nodded. 'I'll do what I can.'

'When will you abandon this fort?' asked Ruticon.

'I'll see how things go. I'd like to teach Scapula another lesson before I move into Ordovicia.'

'Is there anything else we should do?' asked Madrun.

'Spread the word. The same goes for you druids. We need active support from as many warriors as possible. The Senate begrudges having to finance such an expensive enterprise. The longer the war drags on the better.'

'One final thing,' he paused to emphasise the point. 'My orders must be obeyed by everyone here, their warriors and tribesfolk. There must be no dissent. And that includes your opinion of Gwirocon. Trust him as much as you trust me!'

Remains of the fort on Caer Caradoc, as seen from the south-west. The Wrekin Hill lies in the far distance, left.

CHAPTER 10

Twice Bitten

Tim and Caroline were glad they'd had a decent rest before the discussions began. Caradoc and his guests spent most of the night talking, eating and drinking vast amounts of ale.

The meeting, once political matters had been completed, degenerated into reminiscences and boasting. It was incredible to see grown men behaving like children trying to make themselves seem more courageous than their peers. If their prowess in battle was to be believed, each king had been responsible for the total annihilation of hundreds of warriors from other tribes.

As more drink was consumed, the more outrageous the bragging became. Yet it was all taken in good humour. No one contradicted anyone's ridiculous claims and it soon became obvious to Tim and Caroline that this unseemly display of blatant one-upmanship was little more than a Celtic pastime. After what seemed hours, the revellers fell asleep one by one until they were all slumped in undignified heaps across the floor.

One aspect of the night's revelry which Caroline found particularly objectionable was the incredible amount of belching and breaking wind. It was almost as if there was a separate competition to see who could make the longest or loudest noise. Even though this was obviously considered acceptable behaviour, the air was so foul at times she expected someone to ignite. No one batted an eyelid, although several noses twitched when the fallout was spectacularly unmistakable.

The sky was just beginning to herald another dawn when Tim and Caroline stealthily returned to Gwirocon's hut. He lay fast asleep on the floor, curled around the remnants of the fire. Tim put some more kindling and wood on to revive it while Caroline gently shook the druid awake.

'Good morning,' he said, stretching his arms and yawning loudly. He rubbed his eyes. 'Well, what news?'

They recounted what they had heard but chose not to mention the bragging or wind-based competitions. They had just finished talking when the door opened. Caradoc entered.

He looked around the hut. He seemed puzzled.

'I thought I heard you talking to someone.'

'Probably myself,' said Gwirocon, amiably. 'Apparently I'm always doing it. So, how did the discussions go?'

Caradoc sat beside Gwirocon and prodded the fire with a small branch while appraising the druid king of what had been said at the meeting. Gwirocon was pleased that Caradoc's report agreed with the information given to him by Tim and Caroline. It proved Caradoc trusted him. It also proved that Tim and Caroline could be relied on to give accurate reports.

'I need you to keep on the right side of the Romans, whatever happens. I'll remain in this fort for as long as possible but at some stage I'll have to retreat further into the hills. Madrun has a fort ready for me.'

'I assume Madrun will provide food and arms?'

'He will, but the Ordovicians are scattered in the hills and their produce is not so plentiful as yours. Don't worry, we'll survive. We have to! But remember, do not give the Romans any reason to mistrust you!'

'It will be more difficult to help after you move,' observed Gwirocon. 'It'll be very risky.'

'I know,' agreed Caradoc. 'But I don't want your people suffering any more than they have to and I certainly don't want to lose you as an ally. You're one of the few people I can really trust.'

The door opened again. This time a youth about the same age as Tim and Caroline stood in the opening. Caradoc turned to see who was there. He smiled.

'Come in, Gerand.'

The boy entered.

'This is my son Gerand. Gerand, this is King Gwirocon.'

Gerand bowed respectfully.

'My father speaks well of you, King Gwirocon.'

Tim glanced at Caroline and rolled his eyes upwards. She had

That Look, usually reserved for pop idols. Smitten seemed such a small, inadequate word to describe her state.

'What do you want?' asked Caradoc.

'Forgive my curiosity,' Gerand said. 'But I wondered why King Gwirocon came here with three horses when one would have sufficed.'

'Doesn't he speak well,' thought Caroline. 'He's tall, handsome ... and the right age.'

Gwirocon seemed confused. What a stupid oversight on his part!

'Oh, the extra horses? I'm ... training them,' he said. 'Yes, training them.'

'Why? To do what?'

Silence.

'To do things without riders,' whispered Tim into Gwirocon's ear.

'Oh, just tricks. Without riders.'

Gerand seemed doubtful. So did Caradoc.

'You must show us,' said Caradoc.

'What? Now?' Gwirocon was somewhat taken aback. He must have a quiet word with Tim and Caroline. He disliked not being in control. The ghosts from the future could be a little too headstrong for his liking.

'No time like the present!' Caradoc led the way out. Gwirocon lingered while Gerand had followed his father outside.

'What am I supposed to do now?'

'Come on!' called Caradoc.

'Wait until we're mounted and just call out commands every now and then. Preferably in words no one can understand!' whispered Tim. 'C'mon Caroline. Don't disappoint your new-found hero!'

She glared at him. Her faced blushed crimson.

Gwirocon looked at her faint features for a moment, nodded and walked slowly towards Caradoc and Gerand. He waited until Tim and Caroline had jumped onto their horses' backs. It was fortunate that the sun had not yet managed to penetrate the dull, cloudy sky.

The druid raised his arms and shouted something incomprehensible. The two horses jerked their heads and proceeded to walk around in circles.

Caradoc was amused. Gerand was passingly interested but wanted to see something more dramatic.

'Is that all?' He sounded disappointed.

Gwirocon raised his eyes to the heavens, shook his head slowly from side to side (he couldn't believe he was doing this) and uttered another command. The horses reared up on their back legs. Another command and the horses jumped over a pile of firewood. And so the display continued. Word soon spread around the fort. In no time at all, kings, druids, warriors, women and children were standing around applauding.

Eventually, thoroughly tired out and stumped for ideas, Tim let go of the taut reins to let Gwirocon know he'd had enough. Although Caroline could have continued indefinitely, these exercises had stretched his riding abilities to the limit.

The druid clapped his hands as a signal for the horses to stop. He found it almost impossible to control the smile trying so desperately to break out across his weatherbeaten face.

'How did you do that?' asked Gerand. He was impressed.

'Patience and practice,' smiled Gwirocon with a twinkle in his eyes. 'And a little supernatural help.'

Gwirocon remained at the fort for the rest of the day. While he, Caradoc, the other kings and druids held further discussions and made plans, Tim and Caroline amused themselves wandering around the fort, eavesdropping on conversations and observing men and women doing their daily chores.

Although the everyday things Caradoc's people did were essentially the same as those done by the Cornovians, the hardships they had to endure were much greater. There was little in the way of permanence here; it was as if the inhabitants expected to abandon the settlement at a moment's notice and didn't want to be encumbered by unnecessary goods and chattels. They only required shelter, food and basic tools to maintain their weapons.

Caroline, of course, couldn't keep her eyes off Gerand. Tim noticed that, wherever they strolled, Gerand wasn't far away.

'It's no good,' he observed. 'He can't see you. He can't even touch you. You don't exist. So why bother?'

Caroline's eyes welled up. Her cheeks flushed.

'You just don't care!'

Tim realised his words had come out more harshly than he'd intended. He put his arm around her shoulders. She jerked away. He saw tears streaming down her face.

She stormed off back to Gwirocon's hut. Tim rushed inside after her and slammed the door behind him.

'Caroline, I'm really sorry. I didn't mean to upset you. Honest.'

She held her face in her hands, sobbing.

Tim felt awkward. He hadn't seen her like this since their grandad died.

'Don't push me away,' he said gently.

She looked into his eyes and saw how sorry he was. She threw her arms around him.

'Oh, Tim! What's going to happen to us? Gwirocon's the only one who knows we exist. I hate not being able to live normally and having to avoid the sunlight like a vampire! I want to go home, to our own time!'

'We will. One day. I don't know how, but we will.'

Caroline calmed down a little. Tim could be really cruel and inconsiderate at times but she knew he'd never let anything horrible happen to her if he could prevent it.

'I think we're here for a reason,' he continued. His voice sounded distant, as if talking more to himself than his sister. 'I believe people are put in unusual situations to serve some special purpose, and I think that's what's happened to us.'

'But what are we doing here? What's our purpose?'

'Perhaps it's to help Gwirocon save his people from tyranny. Or worse. I just don't know. But we must be sensible. I know you like Gerand a lot, but he's from a different time. If you were meant to have some sort of relationship with him, he'd be able to see, hear and touch you.'

'But he can't. You're right,' she wiped her eyes dry on the cuff of her anorak. 'I promise I'll try not to get too downhearted.'

Tim gave her another reassuring hug and breathed a sigh of relief. He hated having to seem strong and brave for Caroline's sake. He felt just the same as she did.

The door opened. Tim and Caroline froze, scarcely daring to breathe.

Gerand's head appeared.

'King Gwirocon? Are you there? I heard the door slam and wondered what was wrong.'

There was no reply.

Gerand peered into the gloom, shook his head and turned away. The door closed.

'That was close!' exclaimed Tim quietly.

'Isn't he gorgeous!'

'Oh, get a grip! C'mon.'

They sneaked outside and saw a small group of women and girls entering the fortress. But they didn't notice Gerand hiding behind a nearby hut, keeping watch on Gwirocon's door. He couldn't understand how the door opened and shut itself without anyone in sight. But he did notice the footprints appearing in the long grass. He decided to follow them. The footsteps stopped. So did Gerand.

One of the girls looked straight at Tim and smiled as if she was pleased to see him.

She was very pretty and not much younger than he was. Her flashing eyes were particularly attractive and full of humour.

Tim experienced a strange flutter in his stomach. His heart missed a beat. 'She's seen me!' he exclaimed.

'Who has?' said Caroline.

She followed Tim's eyes and saw the girl.

Caroline turned her head.

'You silly thing, she can't see us. She's looking at Gerand. He's behind us.'

Tim glanced over his shoulder. Caroline was right. Dismay wasn't the word to describe how he felt. Now he knew what his sister was going through.

Caroline saw the forlorn expression on his face. She put her arm around him.

'Tough, isn't it?'

Before they could move out of the way, the girl started running. Straight at Tim. Then through him. Right through him. It felt like a gentle breeze wisping through his body. He shivered. He could-n't believe what had happened.

Neither could Caroline. Her jaw dropped in astonishment.

They turned around slowly, shocked and amazed.

The girl stopped in front of Gerand and flung her arms around his neck. Tim, still stunned by his recent experience, suffered a fur-ther sensation of utter despair. The girl was already in love with Gerand! It was bad enough knowing he had no chance of striking up a friendship with the girl. It was even worse seeing someone else enjoying her affection.

He needn't have worried.

'Stop that,' said Gerand with a hint of feigned annoyance.

'If I can't hug my lovely brother, who should I hug?'

'Carys, hush,' said Gerand, somewhat furtively. He was staring at the ground where Tim and Caroline were standing.

Carys sensed something was up.

'What is it?'

Gerand whispered something into her ear. She was about to turn her head when Gerand's hand shot up and prevented her. He led her away to a quiet area at the northern end of the fortress. Tim and Caroline watched them disappear behind a hut.

'OK, they're brother and sister like us. What of it?' said Caroline.

'Is she older or younger than Gerand?' asked Tim. He was still in a daze.

'She could be a year either way. What difference does it make? Sorry, Tim. But his isn't the time or place for either of us to fall in love.'

'Who said anything about love?' said Tim, striding away from her.

'You didn't need to say it,' said Caroline, following him. 'You're so transparent.'

'That's the trouble,' he replied ruefully.

'Where're you going now?'

'Where do you think,' replied Tim testily. 'To see her. Carys.'

His sister shook her head in disbelief. She tugged his arm.

'After the way you lectured me? Well, pardon me, but I thought someone not a million miles away said something like *"can't see you, can't even touch you. You don't exist. So why bother?"* Or am I mistaken?'

Tim carried on walking. He didn't want her to see his pursed lips or the tear of frustration trickling down his cheek.

'Tim, just think about what you're doing ...'

'Shut up!'

'Don't you talk to me like that!'

Tim stopped abruptly. She almost ran into him.

'OK, I'm being stupid! I know nothing can come of it. It's just that I've never seen anyone like her before.'

'You've got it bad, haven't you?'

Tim nodded.

She noticed the tear and wiped it away with the back of her hand.

'It's horrible, isn't it? Can't get your breath, stomach churning, feeling desperate ...'

Tim nodded again.

'Can't I see her? Just for a few minutes?'

'Only if I can watch Gerand.'

Tim smiled.

'Do we have to do everything together?'

'We've always got to stick together,' said Caroline emphatically. 'Who else is going to look after us?'

Gerand and Carys were sitting on the wooden walkway behind the palisade, talking quietly together. Tim and Caroline sat down a few metres in front of them. They couldn't hear what was being said but Gerand seemed quite excited about something. Carys's eyes widened. She laughed and shook her head.

'Oh, Gerand, this is just another of your stories.'

'No, it's true, honest!'

She pretended to examine, with exaggerated movements, every

corner of that part of the fortress. She jumped down from the walkway and peered beneath the planks.

'No, no one here!'

'Look, I know what I saw. If you hadn't rushed over to me, I'd have caught them!'

'Oh, Gerand, I'm only joking!'

She gathered the skirts of her long dress and performed a short dance for her brother's benefit. After a short while, she stopped, sat down and folded her arms.

'Does that make you feel better?'

Gerand smiled.

'It certainly does,' whispered Tim to no one in particular.

Carys was sitting no more than a metre away from him. He couldn't resist the temptation. Before Caroline could stop him, he reached forward and gently touched Carys's hair.

She jerked sharply, running her own hand down the back of her head. Gerand saw and rushed over to her.

'What happened?' he asked earnestly.

'Something brushed against me.'

Gerand pointed at the ground where Tim and Caroline were sitting.

'Look! The grass is flattened! And there are the footprints I told you about!'

'So?'

'Can't you see? The footprints come from over there and stop here.'

The implication of what he said suddenly hit her.

'Now you've scared me! I'm not staying here to be haunted by ghosts!'

She ran away, through her invisible admirer, towards the centre of the fortress.

'Don't say anything about this to anyone!' called Gerand as he followed her after passing through Caroline.

She and Tim sat in silence for a few moments.

'They saw our footprints,' observed Tim. 'And ran straight through us.'

'Well, it's probably the closest we're ever going to get to them,'

110

said Caroline pragmatically. 'You were right; we don't seem to exist. How else could they walk straight through us?' She looked up at the sky. The sun was struggling to break through the cloud. 'We'd better get back to Gwirocon's hut.'

They left Caer Caradoc later that day and eventually arrived back at Wrockwardine, by which time the efforts involved in travel, spying and staying alert, together with hopeless feelings of love, had more than taken their toll.

While Gwirocon retired into his king's house to consider everything that had been discussed and agreed at Caer Caradoc, Tim and Caroline collapsed wearily in the relative safety of the druid's hut and fell into a deep, much needed, sleep. For once their dreams were happy ones.

But would they ever see Gerand and Carys again?

The church at Wrockwardine, built not far from the original Iron Age settlement where Gwirocon lived. Some believe this may have been a pre-Christian religious site, and that Wrockwardine was the location of the legendary city of Pengwern, destroyed by the Mercians c. 660.

CHAPTER 11

Exposed!

Having sampled the painful fruits of falling in love at first sight and not being in a position to savour them, Tim and Caroline suffered the listlessness and despair that is common among people with sensitive hearts. At least they hadn't been rejected by the objects of their affections. But even that didn't really compensate for the hopelessness of their situation.

They didn't discuss the subject. There wasn't any point. In a similar way to the Cornovians, they had to stick and work together to ensure their survival, both emotional and physical.

Of course, they hadn't mentioned anything to Gwirocon about their near-discovery at Caer Caradoc. It's not that he wouldn't have understood – he was far too experienced and wise – but the truth was they felt more than a little embarrassed at the way they had taken advantage of their invisibility to stalk and spy on innocent people. And they'd noticed that embarrassment was very rarely displayed by anyone they met in this harsh world.

Spying on the enemy was a different matter entirely. In fact, they quite enjoyed listening in on conversations inside Castra Cornoviorum and in the open countryside where Roman patrols frequently took place. It was also interesting to see how some of the Cornovians, encouraged by the lack of hostility shown to them by Scapula's soldiers and with Gwirocon's permission, made regular visits to the fortress to trade ale and other goods, particularly fine enamelled jewellery. Information gleaned during casual banter by these traders was passed on to Gwirocon.

Scapula began to develop plans to catch Caradoc. He knew the rebel leader's fortress was somewhere to the south but didn't know exactly where. So far his men had only ventured a mile or two south of the river crossing. The time had come to explore further.

He knew, from information supplied by merchants and the

Rome-friendly Dobunni tribe (who occupied land in the Droitwich area), there was an existing trade route southward through Ordovician land to Silurian-held South Wales. His strategy was for part of the Twentieth Legion to forge a way northward from Glevum, up the Wye valley and eventually to Castra Cornoviorum; the rest of that Legion would secure Siluria.

At the same time a portion of the Fourteenth at Castra Cornoviorum would march south. The two contingents were to join up somewhere along the route and thus extend the frontier westward beyond the river Severn.

With luck, Caradoc's followers would be trapped between the Severn valley and the new frontier created by the Twentieth Legion. The worst that could happen was for Caradoc to retreat into the hills further west.

At the very least, Scapula stood to increase the territory held by Rome and hem the rebel forces in even more.

Gwirocon was annoyed to find Scapula had been observing the surrounding hills during the winter months and noticed bonfire smoke appearing more frequently on one particular hill than any other, apart from Caer Gwirocon. An expedition was to be mounted to investigate that hill which was, of course, Caer Caradoc.

A scouting party was to gather information at first hand (Scapula knew he couldn't rely totally on the opinions of merchants), whereupon sufficient men would be deployed to capture the fort. It was imperative for the hill to be taken because it overlooked the proposed route southward and could prove to be a thorn in the side if it was not destroyed.

Scapula even asked Gwirocon about it. The druid king, aware that his standing with the Roman governor was always on a knife-edge, confirmed that, although the hill lay within his territory, it had been abandoned by the Cornovians many years ago and was used occasionally by neighbouring tribes and itinerants.

Gwirocon had to warn Caradoc. He arranged for further supplies of food and weapons to be collected from various settlements around Caer Gwirocon and taken by a few of his trusted people to

Caer Caradoc. Knowing that his instructions would be faithfully executed, he set off with Tim and Caroline, following the same route as before.

Both Tim and Caroline travelled the arduous journey with mixed feelings. They longed to see Gerand and Carys again, yet were apprehensive about how they would cope with the inevitable frustrations another meeting would bring. They were also frightened at the prospect of being caught up in a battle. They'd both seen the horrors of war in television programmes and films but it was extremely doubtful that they would be in any way prepared for witnessing those horrors at first hand. Fear of the unknown gnawed at their insides; much worse than sitting exams.

Gwirocon sensed their disquiet but, because he did not know of their feelings towards Gerand and Carys, put it down to the prospect of witnessing death by violence. He promised to keep them out of harm's way as much as he could and reminded them that, provided the sun did not shine brightly, they should remain virtually invisible. He also advised them not to watch the fighting in case it proved too traumatic.

As soon as they arrived at Caer Caradoc, Gwirocon was taken to the same hut as before and allowed to have a brief rest before joining Caradoc. There was no sign of Gerand or Carys.

'How long can you stay?' asked Caradoc.

'A few days,' replied Gwirocon. 'Scapula will be too busy overseeing his campaign to notice my absence.'

'What are his plans?'

'To send a scouting party in this direction with a view to attacking your fort.'

'How many men?'

'For scouting? Probably a few centuries. Many more for the attack.'

'So, not the whole legion to start with.'

'I shouldn't think so, no.'

Caradoc smiled.

'We'll outnumber them. As you know, I won't risk everything in a pitched battle or defending this fort, but I can mount a surprise attack while they're on the march. When will they arrive?'

Gwirocon shrugged his shoulders.

'Not sure. No more than a day or two. I've arranged for more supplies to reach here no later than midday tomorrow.'

He paused.

'You do realise that when you ambush the scouting party Scapula will send a larger force to attack you almost straight away? Castra Cornoviorum is only about ten miles distant.'

Caradoc nodded.

'We're ready to abandon our position here. Remember, Madrun has another hill camp waiting for us in Ordovician territory.'

Gwirocon opened his mouth to speak. Caradoc guessed what was on his mind.

'Don't worry, my friend! I know it'll be very difficult for you to provide me with more supplies when we leave. Madrun will look after us.'

'I hope so ... although I have doubts about his promises. At least you won't be trapped behind the frontier if Scapula succeeds in extending it.'

'Extend the frontier? How?'

'The Twentieth Legion is split into two at the moment. Some Fourteenth Legion soldiers stationed at Castra Cornoviorum are to march south down this valley and join up with a contingent from the Twentieth already moving northward.'

'This is bad news.' A deep frown creased Caradoc's brow. 'Leave me to consider and consult my warriors. We'll continue our talks tonight.'

It only took a few minutes for the population of Caer Caradoc to assemble around their leader. Caradoc raised his arms and called for silence. He recounted everything Gwirocon had told him and explained that an attack would be made on Scapula's scouting party as soon as they were within a mile or two of the hill. There were plenty of trees and undergrowth to provide hiding places. He'd fill them in on the details after he'd had a chance to devise a plan of attack.

In the meantime, the warriors must put in some combat practice while the womenfolk packed everything ready to make a quick getaway after the ambush. Finally, he sent a messenger to advise Madrun that they would soon retreat to the safety of the promised camp in the hills to the west.

A mixed atmosphere of expectation and foreboding hung over the whole fort. Everyone who followed the charismatic Caradoc did so willingly, yet none relished the frequent upheaval of travelling from one safe haven to the next. And combat inevitably gave rise to injury and even death. Not all their loved ones would return from the skirmish.

Tim and Caroline, pleased to see their respective heart-throbs in the assembled crowd, retired to the hut and joined Gwirocon. It was best if they kept out of the way while everyone went about their business. As he entered the doorway, Tim paused to observe the methods of combat practiced by the warriors. He frowned and shook his head.

'What's the matter?' asked Gwirocon.

'The way the warriors fight. They use their long swords as if they were axes or hammers,' he replied.

'So?' said Gwirocon. 'Isn't that how they should be used?'

'As soon as they attack, the Romans will regroup to form a testudo.'

'What's a ... testudo?' said the druid, mystified. He had little knowledge of Roman battle techniques.

'All the soldiers bunch up and make a wall and roof around themselves with their shields. It's called a testudo because the formation looks a bit like a tortoise shell.'

'What of it?'

'It makes it almost impossible to penetrate. Warriors can hit the shields as much as they like, but they won't break through. But the Romans can use their shorter swords to stab Caradoc's warriors from behind the safety of their shields.'

Gwirocon considered what Tim had said.

'I'm sure Caradoc knows what he's doing. He hasn't lasted this long without learning how the Romans fight.'

Tim wasn't satisfied. He'd read that warriors tended to do their own thing in battle and weren't trained to fight as a single unit. Individual bravery and skill were all they could rely on. Every man for himself.

Caroline understood what he was thinking.

'Tim's right,' said Caroline. 'We'll have to think of something.'

'I don't want you to get involved in the fighting,' insisted Gwirocon. 'It's far too dangerous.'

'I can't see how it'll be dangerous for us,' insisted Tim. 'We can't be seen, can we? Or touched. So how can we come to any harm?'

'What if the sun shines and you are seen? How do I explain that? All my efforts to persuade Scapula that I can be trusted will be ruined. What will happen to my people then?'

Gwirocon rarely displayed anger. Tim glanced at his sister. She saw his look of determination and shook her head imperceptibly. He took the hint.

'Fine. I won't lift a finger.'

Gwirocon was visibly relieved.

'Unless I can come up with a cunning plan.'

Gwirocon buried his head in his hands. When would they learn not to interfere? Gathering information was one thing; trying to change tradition was something else entirely.

Just then they heard a rumpus outside.

'Leave me alone, you bully!'

It was Carys.

Tim leapt to the door and flung it open. He saw a youth pulling Carys's hair and forcing her to the ground. The boy was in his late teens and much taller than Tim.

'Just because your dad's a king doesn't mean you're better than the rest of us! You don't have to live on short rations!'

'It's not my fault,' cried Carys. 'You don't know what it's like, always on the move and trying not to let my dad see I'm scared most of the time!'

Tim had seen and heard more than he could handle. He burst out of the doorway and gripped the boy in a Judo hold. The youth went flying across the ground.

He gathered himself together and stood up. He was in a foul mood. He advanced menacingly towards Carys.

Tim stood resolutely in the way. The boy charged straight through him and raised his arm to strike Carys, who lifted a hand to protect her head.

Tim, confused that he had been able to manhandle the boy yet couldn't prevent him passing through him, grabbed hold of his long hair and again hurled him to the ground.

'Leave her alone, you coward!'

Both Carys and the boy looked around, startled, their mouths wide open.

'Who's there?' he said, struggling to stand up.

'Clear off and don't lay a finger on her ever again!'

The boy looked at Carys.

'Is this some kind of trick?'

She shook her head.

'I said, go away!' ordered Tim, pushing the boy's chest. Scared, he ran away. He didn't look back.

Tim helped Carys to her feet. She tried to back away. She looked terrified.

'Don't be afraid, Carys. He won't bother you again.'

At that moment, a shaft of sunlight burst through the cloud. Carys saw the almost transparent features of Tim's concerned face changing into something clearly visible. She stepped back in alarm.

'Who ... what ... are you?' her voice faltered.

Realising he had been seen yet wanting to savour this precious moment, Tim kept a gentle hold on Carys's shoulders.

'I'm just a friend,' he said reassuringly. 'I'm not a ghost so don't be alarmed. I'm called Timothy. Tim.'

He desperately wanted to hold her, to comfort her. But that wouldn't be fair. It's not every day you meet a friendly wraith. He gazed into her dark brown eyes for the briefest of moments and saw they no longer showed fear. She smiled.

'Thank you for saving me,' she said quietly. Hesitantly, she put her arms around him and hugged him gently.

Tim gasped. He could feel her touch! He could feel her head resting on his chest! He could even smell her hair! How was this possible? He didn't want the moment to end but it wasn't safe to prolong matters now that he was visible to all and sundry.

'I must disappear,' he said, very reluctantly. 'Please keep this a secret. Just between the two of us.' He was aching to kiss her.

He let her go just as a cloud blotted out the sun.

'Where are you?' she said, her voice trembling. 'Will I see you again?'

'I hope so!'

He watched her walk slowly away. She turned and glanced in his direction but he'd disappeared from her sight.

Tim went back into the hut. Both Gwirocon and Caroline were livid.

'Do you realise what you've done?' demanded Gwirocon.

'I couldn't just stand by and watch her get hurt!' shouted Tim.

'This is precisely why I don't want you to get directly involved! Now she'll tell Caradoc and I'll have to explain where you came from and what you're doing here.'

'I don't think so. Who's going to believe her?'

'What if the boy says something?'

'He won't. How would he look if it came out that he was beaten by a girl much smaller than himself? No, his pride will keep his mouth shut.'

'I agree with Gwirocon,' Caroline said. 'You had no business interfering.'

'Oh, and I suppose you wouldn't have stepped in if Gerand was being hurt by someone! Yeah, right! You're just jealous!'

Caroline was about to yell back at him but the druid beat her to it.

'Keep your voices down!' he urged. 'This is getting us nowhere! We'll have to hope Tim is right and that neither of them will speak of these events.'

'I'm sorry for shouting like that,' apologised Tim.

'Let the matter drop,' said Gwirocon. 'Argument achieves nothing except ill feeling. Now, what was it you said about Caroline defending Gerand? What's he got to do with all of this?'

'You and your big mouth,' said Caroline, shoving Tim with annoyance.

'Well?'

The druid couldn't see them but heard their feet shuffling on the straw-covered floor. He sensed their guilt.

'This isn't the first time you've been seen, is it?'

'What makes you say that?' said Tim, sheepishly.

Gwirocon was getting frustrated.

'Just give me a straight answer! Have you or have you not been discovered by anyone before today?'

'Well, sort of ...' Caroline looked at Tim for help.

'What happened?' said Gwirocon, sighing heavily.

'We weren't seen exactly,' began Tim.

'Huh! Even I cannot see you exactly!'

Tim tried hard to find the right words.

'It wasn't our fault!'

'What wasn't?'

'Tell him,' said Caroline. 'There's no point in keeping it secret any more.'

'Gerand noticed our footprints in the grass,' admitted Tim. 'He followed us. We didn't realise until it was too late.'

'So, what happened?'

'Nothing. Gerand told Carys and she didn't believe him. She thought he was making it up as a story to frighten her.'

'And?'

'That's all. He definitely didn't see us, and neither did she. Until today.'

Gwirocon mulled things over for a few moments. After what seemed ages, he spoke.

'I accept you meant no harm by protecting Carys, but you must take great care not to be seen or, it now transpires, heard! And I have to say I am very disappointed you kept Gerand's discovery a secret from me. I thought I could trust you!'

'You *can* trust us!' insisted Tim and Caroline in unison.

'We didn't think it was so important,' said Tim. 'Gerand couldn't prove anything.'

'But rumours spread and cause mistrust,' said Gwirocon. 'Promise you will tell me everything in future.'

'We promise,' said Tim.

'Don't be angry, Gwirocon, you've been very good to us and you know we only want to help,' said Caroline.

The druid smiled. 'Then let us say no more about it. None of us is perfect, we can only do our best. I'm going for a walk.'

'We'll stay here.'

'Good. Make sure you do.'

As soon as he had shut the door behind him, Caroline gripped Tim's arm.

'Well? What was it like?' she demanded. 'Holding Carys?'

Tim heaved a great sigh.

'Great! Absolutely wonderful!'

King Caradoc, as drawn by Mrs Dale from a description given by Tim.

CHAPTER 12

Caratacus!

Mindful that Scapula's men would soon be coming towards them, Caradoc instructed his followers to prepare to leave. To encourage them, he ordered unused huts to be set on fire so that the Romans might think the camp had already been vacated and the urgency of their advance delayed until his new whereabouts were discovered, as they must surely be; remaining huts would be set ablaze when evacuation was almost complete. Caradoc's plan was thwarted after a very short while; black, ominous clouds scudded swiftly from the west. Further outdoor activity was pointless.

Incessant torrential rain and thunderstorms forced everyone to remain indoors except when calls of nature or a quick scuttle to a partially packed cart was necessary to retrieve something essential. Enforced confinement in very cramped surroundings was far worse here than it ever was for Cornovians during the winter months spent on Caer Gwirocon.

Anxiety showed on every face. They hated being in a state of limbo and wanted to leave the fort and move to the safety of the hill camp promised by Madrun before the Romans arrived. Thankfully, the rain stopped during mid-morning of the next day.

Both Tim and Caroline were relieved to see that it was still very cloudy, which meant they could stretch their legs outdoors without risk of being seen. They did so while activity to resume packing continued with extreme haste. Gerand and Carys worked as hard as everyone else; they'd obviously had a lot of experience in hasty departures. It couldn't be much fun living a life so full of uncertainty and danger.

They didn't have to wait long for news to reach them that a large contingent of Romans had already set out from Castra Cornoviorum and was moving steadily towards them. Their progress had been surprisingly fast.

One of Caradoc's men appeared, in an extremely wet and bedraggled state, and breathlessly reported that the enemy had already covered over two thirds of the distance between their fort on the River Severn and Caradoc's camp on the hill. Caradoc immediately exhorted his people to continue packing with increased vigour. He knew it was going to be a slow process for heavily laden carts to make their way down the hillside into the valley below, and the route to Madrun's promised camp was likely to prove difficult, especially after the recent rainfall.

In spite of his misgivings, Gwirocon agreed to let Tim and Caroline ride towards the Roman advance, on the strict understanding that they kept themselves and their horses out of sight and hurried back to him if they discovered anything Caradoc ought to know.

As they rode slowly towards the northern gateway, they saw women and children still gathering their belongings and piling them into wagons and small carts. A few men were helping but most were busily honing their weapons or daubing their faces with dark blue, creamy-looking paste, which Caroline took to be woad. They obviously expected trouble; if the Romans were so close, they might reach the migrating Britons before they could all escape.

No one raised an eyebrow when Gwirocon's horses wandered through the northern defences; by now it seemed quite natural for these remarkable animals, with a mind of their own, to do as they liked. Even Gwirocon didn't seem to have full control over them, nor had he tried to stop them, so why should they? Caradoc's followers were far more concerned with evacuating the hill while they still had time.

Leaning backwards in their stirrupless saddles, Tim and Caroline rode their mounts gingerly down the wet and steep grassy bank, aware that Gwirocon was watching with a frown etched deeply into his brow.

It only took them a few minutes to reach the woodland at the base of the hill, whereupon they turned sharply west to join the main trackway which led southward from Castra Cornoviorum towards Glevum. Doubtless a contingent at Glevum was, at this very moment, marching northward to meet up with Scapula's own soldiers of the Fourteenth Legion. Heavy rain didn't prevent any Roman from following orders.

Tim and Caroline turned northward. The track, although reasonably well trodden and obviously an important route for merchants distributing their wares, was quite narrow in places. Deep ruts had been left behind by traders' wagons and there were considerable stretches where cattle hooves had churned up the mud. Branches from small trees occasionally overhung the path, but not enough to slow them down. Tim thought it weird that the path was the equivalent of a modern-day main road.

It wasn't long before noises up ahead made them stop dead in their tracks. They dismounted and tied the horses to a thicket some distance away from the path before creeping stealthily towards the noises. They heard men joking and cursing in Latin. Finding themselves at the top of a hummock a few metres away from the track, Tim and Caroline sat down with their backs against a large oak tree and quietly observed the activity taking place in front of them.

They were fascinated by what they saw. The soldiers worked like a well oiled machine. It was obvious their job was to widen and improve the road while at the same time making sure they were protected against possible attack.

Two mounted scouts rode very slowly for some two hundred metres, carefully looking around and listening for signs of the enemy. Satisfied that all was clear, one raised an arm motioning the soldiers forward.

A centurion issued a command, whereupon eighty men stacked their shields and spears upright in piles in the middle of the widened track, laid their cloaks and provision sacks next to them and drew their short swords. With helmets dangling from straps around their necks, they began to hack away at the undergrowth in front until the overgrown verges were cleared to about ten metres wide. Mules, ropes and saws were used to remove every tree standing in the way; branches and roots were thrown in heaps a short distance away. The men worked tirelessly, sweat pouring profusely from their brows and bodies. It was hard going.

Another century of soldiers stood behind the road-widening contingent in two straight lines along the edges of the track which had already been widened. Their job was to keep watch for any signs of attack from the sides and rear.

Although they joked and chatted quietly with their comrades, they clutched their spears nervously. Their centurion strolled backwards and forwards between the two lines, occasionally barking words of sarcastic criticism or bellowing brief orders to keep the men alert.

Several heavily-laden supply wagons with drivers, about twenty-five mules and an officer stood at the end of the two lines of guards, whose centurion nodded to the officer every time he returned along the line. It didn't take very long before the contingent of track wideners reached the scouts. Their centurion yelled a command and the men formed four rows across the full width of the road, facing the way they had come.

Another command. Tim and Caroline almost laughed out loud when the men shuffled and stamped their feet, flattening the ground to firm the road surface until they reached the lines of guards. The soldiers then took turns to douse their heads and drink mouthfuls of water from leather gourds strapped to the backs of the mules before replacing their helmets.

Their centurion bellowed again, exhorting them to retrieve their shields, spears, cloaks and sacks. When they had done so, they formed into ranks between the two outer rows of guards, whose centurion gave an order. His men turned to face the stretch of new road. Another order: they marched briskly until they reached the scouts. Another command: the two lines of guards exchanged places with the men in the middle who had widened this part of the road; it was now their turn to hack away at the undergrowth after the scouts had surveyed the next stretch while the others took a breather and kept their eyes open for trouble. The supply wagons, mules and officers also edged forwards until they reached the guards.

And so the highly efficient process continued. Because there had been no attempt made to surface the road with cobbles, and some stretches required very little work, it was obvious that the intention was simply to create a temporary road in the shortest possible time and, as a consequence, trap Caradoc's rebels before they could escape into the uncharted hills to the west.

As the day wore on, Caroline realised it would not take the Romans very long to reach Caer Caradoc. This peculiar system of track widening (as opposed to road building) seemed highly unorthodox and rather silly and, as far as she could recall, wasn't mentioned in any of the history books she'd read. It was as if the young commander was trying out a new idea, just to impress Scapula back at Castra Cornoviorum and make a name for himself. Certainly, judging from the soldiers' fleeting looks and shaking heads, this was not normal procedure.

If only the woodland along the track had been thicker, progress would be that much slower. At this rate, the Romans would reach Caradoc's people and their slow moving wagons before nightfall. A battle of some sort seemed inevitable, and it wouldn't be easy for the Britons to fight if they had a long line of children, women, animals and vehicles to protect.

'C'mon,' she said. 'Let's get back to Gwirocon.'

Tim stood up. He tripped over a root and tumbled down the hummock. Fortunately, he didn't cry out.

'You OK?' asked Caroline, anxiously.

Tim picked himself up and nodded, rubbing his shin. They walked back to their horses.

'I've just had an idea to slow the Romans down,' Caroline said, thoughtfully. 'It'll take some persuasion, but it might just work.'

Tim listened intently while she explained. His eyes widened in disbelief.

'And you think Gwirocon and Caradoc will swallow it?'

'Why shouldn't they?'

Gwirocon met them at the northern gateway of Caer Caradoc; the camp was empty apart from Caradoc himself and a few warriors. They were busy setting fire to the remaining huts, which was proving rather difficult because the thatch and timber were still damp after all the heavy rain.

The height of the hill enabled them to see the activities of the Romans on the one side and the slow moving train of British wagons heading into the valley on the other. The warriors left the fort when the last hut had been ignited successfully.

There was no doubt the Romans were getting closer. Fortunately, the scouts could not see the retreating Britons, whose progress was severely impeded by boggy ground. If Caradoc's idea to burn the huts was intended to delay Romans pursuing him, he was very much mistaken.

Caradoc was short of options, which may have been why he reluctantly agreed to Gwirocon's far-fetched idea, hastily explained by Caroline to the druid a few moments after she and Tim returned. They had taken the druid behind a smouldering hut so that no one would see Gwirocon apparently talking to himself. He emerged a short while later, rubbing his leg as if he had fallen over and hurt it.

'This plan requires a lot of trust,' Caradoc said. He sounded very doubtful. 'And how can I, let alone my men, put my faith in your horses?'

'Just look at your people,' replied Gwirocon, pointing to the wagons below. Yet another set of wheels sank in a muddy patch. 'It won't take long for the enemy to see what an easy target they have in front of them. Your losses will be great if you try to defend the indefensible. The warriors want a fight. Attack, and you have the initiative. All I'm saying is that my horses will give you an even greater advantage, but you must do exactly as I have said! Timing is vital!'

He and Caradoc looked deeply into each others' eyes, as if searching for proofs of honesty and trust. After what seemed an age, Caradoc spoke.

'I wouldn't take this sort of risk for anyone else,' he said, grimly. 'But you and your steeds have powers I just don't understand.'

They shook hands.

'Good luck, my friend,' said the druid.

'I'll need more than that!' replied Caradoc. 'I'll send word when we reach Madrun's camp.'

'It'll be very difficult to send supplies once the enemy controls the road,' said Gwirocon.

'I know,' replied Caradoc, sighing. 'You have been more gener-
ous than I dared hope. You're a good man, Gwirocon, but don't
worry. Madrun has promised help.'

He mounted his horse and began the slow descent down the
slippery southern slope to rejoin to his people.

'This mad plan had better work! Take extreme care!' said
Gwirocon to Tim and Caroline. He still couldn't get used to con-
versing with thin air. 'I'm going home before the Romans catch
me!'

He walked his horse through the swirling smoke towards the
northern gate.

'We'd better get a move on,' said Tim.

The sky, with weak glimmers of evening sunlight piercing breaks
in the cloud, hinted that dusk was approaching.

The Romans had almost finished the last stretch of road widening for the day. Some had already begun pitching their leather
tents. A few soldiers, who would normally be standing guard, had
been called upon to clear a small patch of ground alongside the
road; others were unpacking tents from the mules and wagons.
The scouts, deciding they no longer needed to keep watch (they
hadn't seen a soul all day), were helping to unload provisions.

The centurion in charge of the road widening party gave an
order. Relieved, his men sheathed their swords and assembled into
ranks ready to shuffle and stamp their way back to the camp site.
They were each looking forward to a long, thirst-quenching drink
and refreshing wash before erecting their tents. Rest and relax-
ation, that's what they needed.

They had barely covered half the distance when someone
shouted.

'Look! Behind you!'

Several soldiers turned to see two horses galloping towards
them. They laughed.

'Scared of a couple of horses?'

'Try to catch 'em! They'll be worth a bit.'

Their amusement rapidly faded. A horde of British warriors, stripped naked to the waist and covered in swathes of blue paint, were riding at break-neck speed towards them, a few metres behind the two riderless horses. Caradoc, standing proudly in a lightweight chariot driven skilfully by Cunorix the Gaul, led the attack.

'Run!'

The road workers dashed toward their neatly stacked weapons. It might have helped, on this occasion, if they had not been so well trained. Unfamiliar with the concept of panic, they refrained from yelling or screaming. Consequently, a few vital moments passed before soldiers of the other century realised something was amiss.

The Romans were in disarray. A few hurled spears over the heads of the two riderless horses, hoping to hit the enemy or at least slow them down.

The officer shouted, 'Testudo! Testudo!', but soldiers trying to obey his order were hindered by others desperately grabbing the first stacked shield and spear that came to hand.

No one paid much heed to the riderless horses; the Romans were more concerned with the enemy bearing down on them. And, of course, they couldn't see the invisible rope, nor the invisible riders urging the horses to stay on opposite sides of the newly widened road.

The invisible rope bounced along the ground. The unseen riders braced themselves, keeping their heads down in case a lucky spear hit them. They managed to maintain their speed even after the rope tripped up the first fleeing stragglers.

Carefully avoiding soldiers rushing from the camp site to the centre of the road, the horses continued to gallop forwards, leaving behind them a trail of fallen men and equipment, tripped or tipped over by an enemy they couldn't see and pounced upon by vast numbers of Britons yelling 'Caratacus! Caratacus!'. Those were the last words many of them heard before emptiness filled their minds and everlasting darkness descended.

The two horses came to a sudden halt a little further along the road and turned around, snorting blasts of hot steam through flared nostrils. They shook their heads as if they had enjoyed the exciting run and couldn't wait to go again.

The scene in front of the horses was terrible to see. The Romans had been caught completely off guard. Almost all discipline had evaporated into thin air as soldiers darted about like headless chickens.

Some instinctively ran to their comrades' aid without considering the consequences and were hacked down mercilessly by long Celtic swords. Others were stunned by hard smacks from British shields before being trampled to death under hooves or stabbed while trying to defend themselves.

A few snatched spears but, scared in case they hit one of their own men in the fray, cast them aside after a moment of indecision and grabbed a nearby shield instead before sprinting as fast as they could in a desperate attempt to assemble around the officer.

Many didn't make it; they were cut off by circling warriors, slashed or dismembered by swords or impaled on spears and left to die, writhing and screaming on the mud-churned ground.

Caradoc and Cunorix were a formidable pair. Immediately after the warriors had engaged the enemy, Cunorix guided the chariot effortlessly around the unfinished camp site, chasing stragglers and avoiding partly-erected tents and startled mules.

Caradoc showed no fear as he ran along the narrow pole connecting the chariot to its two horses until he stood between their heads. From this position, he was able to slash any Roman stupid enough to run in front of him. Between hits he ran back along the pole and stepped over a low wooden strip into the platform of the chariot until Cunorix, turning the vehicle sharply this way and that, caught sight of another victim.

After what seemed ages but was, in reality, only a few minutes, the fighting stopped. But not because the warriors had won, far from it. About fifty Romans had managed to assemble themselves into a makeshift testudo and were moving slowly, resolutely, from the camp site towards the centre of the road where the ground was more even.

Muffled shouts came from somewhere inside the solid walls and roof of bright red shields. Only fidgeting, shuffling legs below the knees were visible. The area around the testudo was littered with the dead and mortally wounded.

It took a few moments for the warriors to realise the tide of events had turned against them. They knew from past experience that attacks on testudos, however small, led to high casualties among attackers.

A Briton advanced gingerly towards the walls, only to be met by a short sword rapidly thrust out between a crack in the shields. He retreated to join the others who had gathered around Caradoc's chariot, waiting for instructions, shouting and waving their swords, spears and shields angrily.

'Wait!' commanded Caradoc. 'Stay back! They're not going anywhere!'

He was right.

The testudo had stopped moving. The Roman officer was thinking as fast as he could. There were too few men left to launch an attack. There was little prospect of reinforcements arriving. He had been stupid to think so few men could have undertaken road-widening duties; he had honestly believed there was little chance of an attack and mistakenly believed the smoke rising from Caer Caradoc meant the rebel king had long since left the area, having set fire to the huts to stop anyone else occupying them.

The testudo couldn't shuffle forwards: there was nowhere to go. The only option seemed to be to return slowly – too slowly – to Castra Cornoviorum. But it would soon be dark and his men wouldn't be able to see to defend themselves against an unseen enemy. The situation was hopeless.

Caradoc sensed indecision within the enemy ranks. He quickly surveyed the scene before looking up the road towards the two horses who had led the ambush. He motioned to Cunorix, who flicked the reins. The chariot moved slowly towards the riderless horses and came to a halt a few metres in front of them. Caradoc jumped out of the chariot.

'Gwirocon was right; you led us into battle,' he said gently, stroking the horses' manes. It was as if he was talking to Gwirocon himself rather than two dumb animals. 'But what are we to do now? We could attack on our own, but I fear many of my men will die before the Romans are crushed. We could wait until nightfall, but my men are too impatient. Can you do the same again? Or does Gwirocon's magic only work once?'

Caradoc shook his head and chuckled to himself.

'By the gods! What am I doing? As if you could understand! I must be going mad!'

He hopped back into the chariot. Cunorix flicked the reins again and gave Caradoc a sidewards glance which implied the king had lost his mind.

After assessing the situation for a few more moments, Caradoc quietly gave his men instructions, whereupon they spread out, encircling the testudo.

He was about to raise his hand to signal the attack when all eyes turned back along the road. The riderless horses were galloping towards the testudo.

No one noticed a solitary Roman soldier behind a nearby tree. It was Marcus, the man who had been stabbed by evil Ludo. He'd been engaged in relieving himself of a particularly vicious bout of diarrhoea and stomach cramps (army rations sometimes had that effect) and, fortunately for him, missed all the action. But he had witnessed everything from the partial privacy of his makeshift latrine.

He saw the two horses charging towards the testudo and suddenly realised that they had somehow played a vital part in the ambush.

Without a second thought, he ran forward and, with every ounce of strength he could muster, hurled his small latrine shovel as hard as he could. It narrowly missed one of the horses' heads but seemed to hit something before it bounced back onto the ground. He couldn't believe his eyes and stood rooted to the spot, his mouth wide open with astonishment.

A moment later, a large, round pebble hit Marcus sharply on his brow. He slumped to the ground without a murmur. Eagle-eyed Cunorix had spotted him lurking in the trees; an empty sling dangled in his right hand. He smiled; Gauls were expert marksmen with slingshot.

No one except Marcus had seen the spade bounce off thin air.

And no one at all could see Tim's body, not even Caroline. She was too busy urging her horse forward towards the testudo, doing her best to ignore writhing or motionless bodies scattered over the ground.

The flying shovel had struck Tim hard and knocked him off his horse. He thudded to the ground and rolled into a ditch, blood gushing from an angry gash across his forehead.

He wasn't moving.

Ambushed Romans struggle to form a testudo.

CHAPTER 13

The Second Caer Caradoc

While the massacre had been in full swing, Tim and Caroline sat in stunned silence on their horses. They'd seen men die many times in films and on television but nothing, nothing could prepare them for the grizzly action taking place in front of them now. They both felt numb. Bile rose from their stomachs into their dry mouths, leaving a nasty taste.

When Caroline had mentioned her plan to Tim, all she had thought would happen when the invisible rope dragged along the ground was that the Romans would be delayed long enough for Caradoc's people to avoid being trapped on Caer Caradoc. Even Tim, in the excitement of thinking their action would be rather amusing, had not considered the consequences.

Gwirocon had, of course. He had not managed to survive so long without giving very careful thought to the consequences of any of his decisions. His unspoken concern had been whether or not his invisible helpers could cope with the trauma they would suffer when they witnessed a vicious battle first hand.

Caradoc had made his name by inflicting devastating defeats on Roman soldiers for several years; his success depended on him showing no mercy. He took no prisoners unless there was some advantage to be gained. It was not a matter of enjoying cruelty, it was simply a case of survival. Caroline and Tim, until they heard those first death cries after their horses tripped soldiers striving to defend themselves, had not appreciated that silly pranks can have dire consequences.

People do desperate things to preserve their lives and avoid injury. Common decency and consideration has no place on the battlefield. The overriding need to survive makes folk do unspeakable deeds. Death is forever; there is no glory.

Actors killed on screen pick themselves up and walk away. They feel no pain, no suffering. Viewers are seldom able to appreciate the gnawing sense of loss. It wasn't like that for Tim and Caroline. After they had made their first run, they calmly turned the horses round to see the chaos they had caused.

Their exhilaration was short lived. They sat, transfixed, while men from both sides hacked, stabbed, speared, concussed, mutilated, murdered. Bodies and limbs twitched uncontrollably, blood gushed from ugly wounds; even the bravest men screamed in agony, begging someone to end their pain, to put them out of their misery. And all because Caroline had devised a simple plan, taking advantage of the fact that neither they nor the rope could be seen.

The initial onslaught had taken but a few minutes yet caused untold devastation. When Caradoc had approached their horses and asked for help, it was as if his voice came from miles away; their ears, like their minds, were trying to block out what they had caused and witnessed. Caradoc's words had been spoken gently, with some humility, a tone unexpectedly out of place with the turbulent mayhem of the past few moments. As soon as the king turned to rejoin his expectant warriors, Tim and Caroline woke up from their involuntary reverie.

'Tim, what can we do? If we trip the testudo, everyone will be slaughtered!' Her voice was almost inaudible.

'They'll die anyway,' Tim replied matter of factly. 'They don't stand a chance. Remember Ginger, our cat? When he was so ill, the vet said nothing could be done to make him better.'

'The best thing was to put him to sleep straight away?'

Tim nodded. 'It's the same here. If we do it, it'll cause less suffering in the long run.'

'I can't. I just can't!'

'But what shall we do? We can't just sit here!'

Suddenly, without warning, his horse reared and lurched forward. Caroline's followed. Neither rider could stop them, despite tugging hard on the reins. They charged towards the testudo. Several warriors stepped back to let them pass and pounced onto tripped Romans as soon as they fell over, like a pack of ravenous wolves.

Before reaching the end of the testudo, the head of Caroline's horse jerked sharply to one side; the animal fell to the ground, legs kicking wildly as it tried to right itself. The rope had caught beneath the falling bodies. Caroline was thrown out of the saddle when her horse struggled desperately to escape the carnage.

She leapt forwards, fumbling with the rope tied around its neck while soldiers and warriors collided with her or passed straight through her body. Suddenly, the rope worked loose and the terrified horse sped away southward down the track.

Caroline made a move to follow it but her jaw smacked against someone's elbow. She fell backwards in a daze; it took a few moments to recover her wits, whereupon she sat up and reluctantly let her eyes wander over the bloodstained ground.

Men of the testudo lay in a contorted heap a few metres away. Warriors searched bodies, removed helmets, cloaks, swords, daggers, coins, rings and brooches and anything else worth taking. Anyone with a fatal wound was quickly and, from a soldier's point of view, mercifully dispatched.

After what seemed an age, Caradoc called his men to leave the area. He led them, and the captured mules laden with sacks of provisions, southward to rejoin the rest of his people.

Caroline felt sick. She looked around for Tim, but couldn't see him anywhere, nor his horse! She jumped up, trying to shake off the dizzy feeling in her head. Tim was nowhere to be seen! She didn't know what to to. Had he seen her fall, assumed she'd been killed and run off because he couldn't stand the idea of seeing her dead? Had he gone back to Gwirocon? Or had he followed Caradoc?

She decided to go south. It was, after all, the direction her horse had bolted and she wouldn't get very far without it.

After one last look around the sickening scene she had been responsible for and would never, ever, forget, she staggered along the ancient track.

Dusk was descending rapidly.

She felt so alone. Neither Tim nor the horses were anywhere to be seen. Behind her lay the results of her despicable stupidity, men who would be mourned by wives, children and comrades. She tried to console herself by arguing that these same men would have thought nothing of slaying the women and children, let alone the warriors, in Caradoc's band of rebels. The Romans had no right to invade Britain and they must accept the consequences.

But it was no good; she had no right to be there either. It wasn't her problem but she had taken advantage of her (and the rope's) invisibility, and look what had happened.

Where was Tim? And why was it that sometimes people could walk through her and and at other times hit her, actually making physical contact? It just didn't make sense. Nothing made sense. Had Tim been hurt – or worse – and could he still be lying, unnoticed, on the battlefield? And what would happen to him if she returned to her own time without him? After all, she was the one wearing the talisman pendant, not him.

She burst into a fit of uncontrollable, inconsolable, sobbing. It was fully dark now and even the moon peering out from gaps between drifting clouds didn't do much to light her way. Not that more light would have helped a great deal; her eyes were so full of tears. She could hear herself wailing, weeping, sniffing. She didn't know where she was going, but did it matter? All she knew was that her horse had gone in this direction. With a bit of luck she might find it.

Her legs were so tired, she felt so weary, miserable, cold and scared in case she encountered a wolf or wild boar. She heard something ahead. Muffled sounds. Voices! She stopped crying immediately. Help was not far away. Perhaps Tim was there!

Spurred on with hope, she summoned the energy to quicken her pace. Low branches whipped her face, roots tripped her up, but she didn't care. She deserved the pain as a punishment, and she needed company.

The noises became louder and louder, nearer and nearer. There they were! Not far now, just a few more metres.

'Who's there?' someone shouted, menacingly.

Caroline stopped abruptly. She was shivering, she didn't know whether it was the cold or fear. She held her breath and remained rooted to the spot.

'Only an animal,' another voice called. 'Carry on!'

Caroline waited a few moments until she thought it was safe to continue. She soon caught up with the tail end of a long train of people, winding their way along the track for as far as she could see. Some men on horseback held brightly burning torches aloft to show the way.

The ground was very muddy beneath her aching feet. It was easier to walk on grassy tufts at the edge of the track. She walked a little faster, alongside the wagons and carts, hoping for a glimpse of someone familiar, perhaps even Tim. She hurried a bit further and there, sleeping soundly in a heavily laden wagon, were Gerand and Carys. And her horse was tethered to the back!

Relief swept over her like a bracing wave at the seaside. She'd made it! These were Caradoc's followers! Tim must be here somewhere! She ran eagerly to the front of the train, which had veered off the main trackway and was now winding its way along a much narrower, more uneven, path, frantically looking at everyone she passed.

Tim wasn't there. Her heart sank. Holding back a replenished supply of tears, she tried to think clearly. Tim wasn't here, but her horse was. She hadn't a clue where the train was going but it must be on its way to Madrun's fort. The best thing would be for her to stay with Caradoc's people.

She decided to hide in the back of a wagon and get some sleep. She'd be more alert in the morning. And she needed a rest.

Caroline didn't sleep at all well, despite her exhaustion, although the gentle lurching roll of the wagon felt quite pleasant. It was a mixed blessing: every time she dozed off, troubled dreams were filled with terrifying images of the dead and screams of agony from the dying. Her brow was plastered with sweat each time she awoke; she just couldn't get these horrible images out of her mind.

Morning came, much too early for the way Caroline was feeling. Bright sunshine contrasted sharply with the gloom of the last two days and she longed to escape from the cramped and uncomfortably hard floor of the wagon but realised she'd have to keep out of sight. As the day wore on, the heat generated beneath layers of thick woven blankets under which she lay hidden became almost unbearable. It was only through sheer desperation that she begrudgingly took a sip or two of warm water from the small amount remaining in her plastic bottle. Her empty stomach grumbled almost as loudly as the timbers of the wagon creaked on its laborious way.

It was late afternoon when the wagon reached its destination. The last hour or so had been even more uncomfortable while the wagon crawled up steep-sided slopes before coming to a sudden halt. Caroline heard voices shouting directions.

She lifted the blankets slightly and saw they had reached a hill camp full of ramshackle huts. Some people stood around in angry groups, obviously unhappy with the quality of the buildings. Others, realising the site was better than nothing, had already begun to unpack and were busily carrying goods from the carts and into the huts. While she surveyed the scene, more and more people arrived.

'Gather round!' Caradoc's voice was unmistakable. Caroline saw him standing in his chariot with Cunorix, as usual, clutching the reins. Making sure no one was near and everyone had their backs turned on her, she slipped out of the wagon and darted in the shadows from hut to hut until she had a better view of the king. He didn't seem at all happy. Folk mooched around with downcast faces. Even the captured mules seemed miserable.

'My people! Welcome to our new home! I know some of you are disappointed with the amenities ...' A few laughed sarcastically. '... but we have to make do with what we are offered! Madrun assured me that food will arrive in a day or two, so we will have to ration what we have at present. Your British fighting spirit served you well yesterday and today. Don't be disheartened by our new surroundings! Unpack your things and relax ... we'll be staying here for some time!'

Only a few people cheered. Many looked downright disgusted. Everyone was exhausted from the battle and by the time and effort spent travelling. They hadn't enough energy left to argue with Caradoc. They knew he had led them here in good faith. Resigned to the present situation, they set about settling in.

Caroline remained out of sight, watching. It took far less time to unpack than she had thought possible and it was not long before small fires had been lit to cook meals. It began to get dark. Spirits were lifted when a couple of men burst into song, encouraging others to join in. It reminded Caroline of Guide camps she had been to, where the warmth and cheeriness of a flaming fire and a community sing-song took your mind off all discomfort and misery.

While everyone was preoccupied with eating and entertainment, Caroline helped herself to water and small amounts of food from under their noses, taking care to keep in the shadows cast by the firelight. Refreshed, she decided it was time to stretch her legs.

Shafts of moonlight revealed the hill was surrounded by many others and the valleys in between were covered with trees. Glancing around the compound, Caroline understood why its new occupants were feeling so disgruntled; while the fort might be well hidden, its huts were grouped very close to one another and much smaller and far more dilapidated than the ones they had left in such a hurry the day before.

Horses and mules were grazing happily in the long grass. She noticed her own horse tethered by a long rope at the rear of Caradoc's hut. Overjoyed, she ran over and flung her arms around its neck, taking pleasure in stroking and patting it. Undeterred by not being able to nuzzle up to her (its nose, as usual, kept passing through her body), it seemed to appreciate her presence. Unable to stop herself, Caroline spoke words of comfort into its ear.

'Who's there?' A voice called, uncertainly, behind her.

It was Carys, holding a burning torch aloft. She came cautiously nearer, peering into the dim light cast by the flickering flames. Fear flashed across her face when she saw the ghost holding the horse. She turned sharply on her heels, about to rush to her father.

'Don't go!' called Caroline. 'Don't be afraid! I'm Tim's sister!'

Carys turned around, trying to get a better look.

'Timothy Tim, the spirit who protected me?' she said, her voice faltering slightly.

'Yes,' replied Caroline. 'But his name's Timothy, not Timothy Tim, but I call him Tim.' She knew this sounded stupid, but carried on talking. She didn't want Carys to leave. 'Have you seen him?'

Carys shook her head. 'I only saw him that once. Why? Have you lost him?'

'Sort of. I haven't seen him since the ambush.'

'You were there?' Carys asked incredulously. 'Were you riding Gwirocon's horses?'

Caroline nodded.

'What was it like? The fighting, I mean.'

'I don't want to talk about it. It was horrible.'

'I've never seen an ambush. Dad says it's too dangerous, not like pitched battles where there's plenty of time to escape if things go wrong. Dad prefers ambushes, says it gives him an advantage. Are you a wraith, like Timothy Tim ... Tim?' she asked.

Realising Carys had lost all fear, Caroline sat down and beckoned to Carys to join her.

'We're not wraiths,' said Caroline. How was she going to explain things?

'But I can see straight through you!'

'Well, it's like this. Tim and I come from the future.' It sounded like she lived in the next village. 'About two thousand years from now. Yes, I know it sounds impossible, but that's the truth. We don't know how it happened, nor does Gwirocon.' She knew she shouldn't have said that.

'Gwirocon knows?' gasped Carys. 'Does dad?'

'No,' said Caroline. 'And he must never know. Nobody must! It has to be kept secret, otherwise Gwirocon and the Cornovians will be in serious trouble with the Romans.'

'That's what dad said. He trusts Gwirocon. He must do, else he wouldn't have followed your horses into battle. Don't worry, I won't say anything to anyone, not even dad. But where's Tim now?'

'I don't know,' said Caroline, crestfallen. 'We got separated during the ambush. I haven't seen him or his horse since.'

'I haven't seen his horse either. Yours came galloping along the road and we managed to catch it. Dad knows it belongs to Gwirocon and won't let anyone else near it. Says he'll return it as soon as it's safe. Don't know when that'll be, though,' she added doubtfully. 'Dad says it's unlikely we'll see Gwirocon again now we're out of his territory. We won't get any more supplies from him, it's up to Madrun now, although dad doesn't seem to trust him all that much.'

She looked thoughtfully at Caroline.

'I don't understand why I can't touch you, but Tim actually held me in his arms. It was great!' she added coyly. 'Look.'

Carys moved her hand through Caroline's head. In response, Caroline touched Carys's cheek.

'See?' said Carys.

'Move your hand towards mine. I'll move mine towards you at the same time,' said Caroline.

They did. Carys gasped. They held each other's hands, fingers intertwined!

'That's it,' exclaimed Caroline. 'You can't feel me if I don't move, but you can if I'm moving towards you! That's how I got hit during the ambush!'

'You were hit?'

'Yes, when Tim and I were riding at the Romans. I fell off the horse and was hit several times before I could get out of the way!'

'But you're all right now? You're not hurt or anything?'

'No, I'll be fine, except that I'll never forget how horrible it was to see all those men killed. Were any of Caradoc's men hurt?'

'No, only a few scratches. Didn't you hear them bragging earlier on? Men! That's all they ever do, boast. You'd think they'd killed a whole legion!'

'I wish I knew where Tim was,' said Caroline.

'He'll be fine,' said Carys. She tried to put an arm around Caroline's shoulders. 'It can't be easy having no one to hold you.' She smiled. 'It was nice when Tim held me ... I think I wanted to, well, you know, kiss him.'

'I know he wanted to kiss you!'

They laughed.

'Do you like my brother?' asked Carys. They say he's quite good looking ... for a boy!'

'Do I!' said Caroline. 'But I don't stand much chance if he can't see me! He doesn't even know I exist. Well, sort of exist.'

'Oh, yes I do!'

Gerand was standing a few metres away. He walked over and sat down beside Caroline, as if it was quite normal to mingle with supernatural beings.

'I heard everything. Well, nearly everything. Who's this Tim character?'

'My brother. We're twins.'

'And you've lost him.' It was a statement, not a question. Caroline nodded. She was aware that Gerand couldn't keep his eyes off her. His eyes were dark, like his sister's. Their eyes met. Caroline blushed. Gerand was equally embarrassed.

'Er, is there anything I can do? Um, do you want anything?' he asked hesitantly.

'Only you,' thought Caroline. 'Clear off, Carys!'

'No, I'll be fine,' she murmured, aware that her voice had dropped an octave and sounded almost like she was purring.

'Can't be easy for you,' said Gerand, squeakily. He should have cleared his throat before attempting to speak. 'Being away from your own time and family, I mean.'

'No, it's very lonely, even with Tim around.' She felt tears welling up.

Gerand noticed her unhappiness. He moved towards her. She moved towards him. They held each other tightly. Caroline could feel herself melting like warm ice cream.

'Pardon me!' said Carys, tactfully. 'I know when I'm not wanted!'

She left, taking the torch with her.

Shortly before dawn, while the sky was a beautiful dark blue and the first blood-red layers of sunlight were beginning to form on the distant horizon, Gerand gently awakened Caroline and escorted her inside Caradoc's hut.

Caradoc, his wife Branwena, Cunorix and Carys were soundly asleep on roughly heaped straw mattresses. Dying embers of a fire smoked languidly in the centre of the floor.

Gerand beckoned Caroline to hide on the ground by the rear wall where it was darkest and then lay down to make it look as though he had been there all night. Caroline, knowing she could not be seen and feeling far more relaxed than she had done for ages, closed her eyes and drifted into a delightful slumber.

Several days passed. Caroline sensed an overwhelming annoyance with Madrun and the failure of his promised supplies to arrive. Caradoc, while making light of the situation and inventing reasons for the delay, was inwardly incensed. Only the faithful Cunorix was privy to his leader's true feelings.

For once, Caradoc, who had, until now, largely been in control of his own destiny, felt isolated. There was such a great difference in the help he had been given by the trustworthy and honourable Gwirocon and the unrealised promises of Madrun. That he would have had to evacuate his last fortress anyway was an indisputable fact, but he expected much better treatment from another king and ally.

Unfortunately, Caradoc did not know the layout of the land surrounding his new camp. Nor did he know where the nearest stores of food lay: supplies were running out at an alarming rate. It would be ironic in the extreme if his people were forced to disband or surrender simply because they had no food after he had led the rebellion for so many years.

Despite the fact that Madrun, a few skinny cattle and a modest supply of food arrived at the camp after almost a week, Caradoc was filled with foreboding. Madrun's excuses had been less than believable ('*forgot which camp you were in*' and '*wasn't so much grain as I thought*').

The future seemed bleak.

Caroline, Gerand and Carys spent as much time together as they possibly could. There was still no news from Gwirocon or of Tim.

Perhaps Caroline's intuition made her sense that Tim was in no immediate danger. Resigned to the fact that it was stupid to go searching for him on her own and she didn't, in any case, know the way back to Gwirocon's village, Caroline decided it was better to remain where she was, at least for the time being.

This didn't reduce the anxiety she felt for Tim's safety but at least she was being well, if covertly, looked after.

The Wrekin Hill from the south-west. Caroline and Tim saved Marcus after Ludo's attack in the woods in front of The Little Hill; at that time, woodland covered the whole area at the bottom of this photograph.

CHAPTER 14

A Stroll in the Dark

A deathly hush filled the air, disturbed only by an occasional owl hoot. Tim opened his eyes and saw the moon peeping out from a gap in the clouds. His head hurt; he brushed a hand across his forehead. It felt sticky, but at least he was alive.

He tried to sit up. The throbbing in his head increased. He lay back again, trying to remember what had happened and why he was lying in a ditch in the dark. He felt awful.

Tim rolled onto his side and struggled to remove his backpack. He fumbled for the bottle of water and took a long, refreshing swig before lying down again.

In spite of the pain, he could remember charging along on his horse towards the testudo; then millions of stars flashed before his eyes and everything had gone black.

He took out his torch and shone it around. He winced. There were dead bodies lying all over the place, as far as the beam reached. Small details caught his eye: contorted faces, a severed hand, pools of blood soaking silently into the ground. He thought it odd that only a few bent spears and broken swords lay scattered between the bodies. And no warriors. Caradoc must have won! His men had stripped the corpses of anything useful or valuable.

He felt ashamed at his momentary elation; the beam fell on a jumbled heap in the middle of the road. That had been the testudo, packed with men. Two centuries worth of living, breathing men. Now look at them! He felt sick. This was not make-believe, this was the real thing. At least there was no sign of Caroline, nor her horse. She must have missed him lying in the ditch and ridden to Gwirocon for help.

Something rustled in the undergrowth a few metres away. He heard a groan. Tim switched off the torch and held his breath, straining hard to hear further noises while trying to shut out the relentless pounding in his head which resembled the bass beat of a heavy metal band.

Something was walking slowly towards him. An animal. A big animal. A big animal which snorted. Against the light of the moon he caught sight of ... his horse!

Tim staggered to his feet and gave a whistle. Recognising the sound, the horse ambled uncertainly in Tim's direction. It sensed someone familiar was there but couldn't see who it was.

Tim switched his torch back on.

'Over here, boy,' he called gently, his voice a little croaky.

The horse stopped in front of him. Greatly relieved, Tim patted the animal and ran the torchlight over him to make sure he was OK. There were no signs of injury and the rope still hung around its neck. Tim untied the rope, coiled it and slung it over his head and shoulder.

'Who's there?' growled a voice behind him. He heard a sword being unsheathed. 'Turn round. No funny moves, mind!'

Tim turned around to face a silhouette backlit by the moon.

'I said turn around!'

'I did!' insisted Tim.

'Well, I can't see yer!'

Tim noticed the shape of the man's helmet. Roman! He quickly switched off the torch.

'Oh, no! C'mon, play fair! I've had more than I can take for one day! Where are yer?' The voice didn't seem threatening, more fed up and sorry for itself.

'Look,' it continued, 'I'm weak and feel ruddy rotten. I've put me sword away now. Please help ... uhh!'

The man's knees gave way and he crumpled to the ground.

'If yer can understand me, either help me or put me out of me misery. Let me join me comrades!'

Tim didn't know what to do. He was still feeling a bit groggy himself. The man heaved a long gasp of frustration.

'Oh, don't mess about! Get it over with!' he pleaded.

Tim switched the torch back on and walked over to the man. Sure enough, the sword was back in its scabbard. He shone the torch into the man's face. There was a lump about the size of an egg on his forehead. Bruising had given it a wonderful range of colours: yellow, green and deep purple.

'Marcus!' Tim almost dropped the torch.

'Eh? Who's that?'

'Never mind,' said Tim. 'Where do you hurt?'

'Isn't it ruddy obvious, numskull!' he retorted, pointing to the lump. 'Got a drink?'

'Only water.'

'Huh! That'll have to do.'

Tim took out the bottle, unscrewed it and put it to Marcus's lips.

'Thanks. Anything to eat?'

Tim produced a chunk of stale bread. It was all he had. He tore it in two and gave half to Marcus. They munched away until it had all gone. They took another swig of water.

'Thanks again,' said Marcus. He paused. 'What're yer doin' here? You a warrior or what? You ain't no Roman, or an auxiliary, that's for sure.'

'No, I'm not a fighter,' replied Tim.

'Just passin' through, then?'

Tim smiled. 'Yeah, passing through.'

'Bit young to be travellin' alone, though. Stayin' here long?'

'No longer than I have to. It's, er, difficult to return home.'

'Know what yer mean, what with the war and everythin'. Difficult to travel anywhere safely these days, whichever side yer on. Can't trust anyone, not even yer own.' He winced, recalling the pain where Ludo stabbed him.

'What's that in yer hand? A lamp? Never seen one like that before. Gives a good light.'

'Yeah, a sort of lamp.'

'Shine it up. Let's see what yer look like.'

Tim turned the beam on himself. Marcus gasped.

'Nasty cut yer've got there!' He raised a hand.

'Don't touch it!' exclaimed Tim.

But it was too late. The soldier's hand had already reached Tim's head and the fingers were fumbling with thin air. Marcus's response was superbly matter of fact.

'You a ghost or spirit? Only I've had dealings with `em before.

Seem a friendly bunch o' untouchables. Helpful like.'

Tim laughed.

'Yeah, we're spirits, sort of.'

Marcus looked around sharply.

'We? There's more?'

'Not here. My sister's disappeared.'

'Hardly seems the right word, seein', or rather, not seein' as yer not exac'ly solid flesh. Here! How'd yer know me name?'

'We saved you from Ludo.'

'That was you?'

'And my sister Caroline.'

'What's yer name?'

'Tim.'

'Well, er, Tim, pleased t' meet yer ... again.' He extended his hand. Feeling stupid, he was about to withdraw it when Tim grasped it firmly.

'Can't tell yer how grateful I am. Would have died. Mind you, I've taken some stick from the lads since. Spirits, indeed. Didn't believe me. To be honest, I didn't believe mesel'. But now I know I wasn't dreamin'. I'll tell them!'

'You mustn't do that!' said Tim, earnestly. 'No one, absolutely nobody, must know about us! Do you hear? Nobody!'

Marcus was taken aback.

'Pity. I was lookin' forward to showin' yer the boys. Could've had some fun. Whose side are yer on? Brits or us?'

'Neither.' He hoped Marcus didn't make the connection between his horse and the ambush.

'Just 'ere to help, like.'

'Yes. We saved you after Ludo stabbed you, didn't we?'

'I said I was grateful!'

'Cool it,' said Tim.

'Nasty bit of work, that Ludo.'

'What happened to him?'

'Scapula ... yer've heard of him, our governor?' Tim nodded. 'He was right angry. Ludo had a fair, well, fairish trial. Found guilty, of course. He was cudgelled to death.'

'Cudgelled?'

'Yer. That's what happens to soldiers what've attacked their comrades. Body thrown int' river. For all I know, he might have met up with the Twentieth at Glevum.' He chuckled at the thought. 'Don't suppose he'd be much use to them, though. Nasty way to go. Serves him right. Doesn't do to go killin' yer own. Leads to mistrust, see. Can't rely on them when yer need to.'

They sat in silence for a few moments. Marcus was thanking his lucky stars that this spirit had come to his aid. Tim was reflecting on what a violent time this was. War was a complete waste of time and effort. So many people, civilians as well as soldiers, died just to satisfy a ruler's greed for land and power. He looked closely into Marcus's eyes. This wasn't a killer, just a man following orders so that he could survive in an unjust world.

'Why did you become a soldier?' asked Tim.

Marcus shook his head.

'No choice, really. Me dad, rest his soul, was a small king in southern Gaul. I don't mean he was short, just that there wasn't many folk in the tribe an' we didn't have much land. He tried to make a pact with the other kings when the Romans came, but there was no love lost between 'em cos we'd been at each other's throats for years. No trust, see. Couldn't even arrange marriages without a fight.'

'Same thing here,' said Tim.

'Tha's right,' agreed Marcus. 'Brits are useless when it comes to allying wi' folk they've been fightin' for decades. That's why we've done so well here.'

'What happened in Gaul?'

'Romans just walked over us. Dad was killed, and my uncle. I was captured an' taken to Rome as hostage. Given a choice of enlisting in the army or dyin'. No choice at all, was it? Joined the auxiliary an' eventually they transferred me into the Fourteenth. Shouldn't have, really, I didn't stric'ly qualify cos I'm not a Roman – me real name's Marek, but they call me Marcus now – but they had to make up the numbers after the Maedwy battle, see. That was years ago, when we first set foot in Britain. Only time I saw Caratacus. Until yesterday. Brilliant fighter,' he added, showing great respect for his enemy. 'Still going strong in spite of us.

Slippery, yer know, like an eel. Attacks when yer least expect it. Like here.' He waved a hand vaguely over the battlefield.

'Why were there so few of you here?'

'That's officers for yer! Ain't got the sense they was born with, some of 'em!' He shook his head. 'We set off with half a legion. Rest was left behind to protect the fort. We was only supposed to widen the road as far as Caratacus's hill. Then we saw all that smoke comin' from the top. Julianus, our Officer in Charge, bit of a wimp really but his dad's in the Senate an' pulled a few strings to make a man of him, decided the enemy had vacated the camp an' there wouldn't be any danger. Sent the rest back. He's always had it in for my century, and the other one lyin' over there. Ruddy fool. Basic trainin', see. Always take as many men as yer can into alien territory. Can't be too careful. The prat wouldn't listen.'

He spat as if to emphasise his disgust. The spittle shot through Tim and landed with a plop on the ground behind.

'Sorry!'

Tim pretended to wipe the phlegm off his chest. Marcus grinned, feeling a little embarrassed.

'Have you met Claudius?' asked Tim.

'The emperor? Only the once. He graced us with his presence when we took Camulodunum. Brought a load of ruddy elephants over with him. Scared us more than the enemy.'

'What's he like?'

'Oh, I dunno, just a bloke who's managed to survive, an' that's saying something! His family were a right bunch, I can tell yer! Not all there in the head, if yer get me meanin'. Murdered, stabbed, poisoned each other, just for power. You name it, they did it. And Caligula! Well, a real nutcase, that one. They say he ate his own sister!' He shook his head. 'Can't understand how we've got an empire at all! Mind you, Claudius can't be all that stupid. Knockin' on a bit now, but got all his marbles. Not a bit like the others. Got a sense of justice an' fair play. How's yer head?'

'Still throbbing.'

'Mine too. Better clean that wound, don't want it festerin'.' He stood, still a little unsteady. 'There's a stream near here. C'mon.'

He reached his hand out. Tim held it tightly and pulled himself up. Guided by the torch, they soon found the brook. The water bubbled along, boosted by the recent rain. Tim refilled his bottle with water while Marcus tore some cloth from a nearby corpse. He dipped the cloth into the brook and wrung it out before handing it to Tim, who couldn't help noticing the dripping water was tinged with red. He reluctantly took the cloth and dabbed the dirt from his wound. He washed the cloth and ran it over his face before giving it back to Marcus, who also used it to refresh himself.

'How'd you feel?' asked Marcus.

'Much better, thanks. You?'

'Better than I was. Head still bangin', though.'

They fell silent, not knowing quite what to say or do next.

'I suppose you'd best get back to Castra Cornoviorum,' suggested Tim.

'Nothing to keep me here, is there?' replied Marcus. 'Which way's yer's?'

'I'll come with you.'

'Does yer live near the fort?'

'Not really,' said Tim. 'I'm just ...'

'Passing through,' they said together. They laughed.

'Well, best get going,' said Marcus. 'That your horse?' he added, jerking his head backwards.

'No,' lied Tim. He didn't want Marcus to link him with the attack. 'It seems to have taken to me.' He gathered the reins and walked northward with Marcus. They were both about the same height but Marcus was much more solidly built.

'What happened to you back there?' How come you weren't killed with the rest?' enquired Tim.

'Dunno. I was having a crap behind a tree an' all hell broke loose. By the time I'd hitched me britches, it was almost all over.' He frowned, trying to remember exactly what had happened next. 'I remember seein' a couple of horses heading for me comrades and thinkin' they had sommat to do wi' the attack. I threw me bog spade at them ... it bounced off thin air! Next thing it was dark an' I had a sore head. You wasn't ridin' them horses, was yer?'

'Me? No. Whatever makes you think that?' So he'd been struck by Marcus's toilet spade!

'Dunno. I've seen some strange things recent, what with spirits and attackin' horses.'

'I don't think you'd better mention the horses to Scapula.'

'Dunna worry, Tim! I knows when ter keep me trap shut! They'll think I've gone barmy if I tell them I saw riderless horses attacking us! No, I'll just say I was ... er ... indisposed when the attack began and was hit with somethin' when I ran to help.'

'Which is true, isn't it?'

'They'll believe me as long as I've got this lump on me head.' He touched it gently, just to make sure it was still there.

'Don't worry, I'll give you another one if it's gone by the time you get back!'

They walked on in silence. Tim found the going quite easy along the newly widened and levelled road and felt reasonably happy. He assumed Caroline had returned safely to Gwirocon and Caradoc had escaped, uninjured, with his followers to wherever Madrun's promised hill fort lay. At least they'd be safe from Scapula for a while longer. And as for Marcus, well, he was quite a good guy really. Rough, but not bad company. More to the point, he felt sure he wouldn't say anything about him, Caroline or the horses to anyone.

The first signs of daybreak were slowly lightening the sky. Although Tim didn't know it, Caroline was, at that very moment, still travelling on her bumpy journey to Madrun's fort.

'All those men killed because of a ruddy road,' said Marcus, for no apparent reason. Like Tim, fleeting thoughts had been crossing his mind for some time.

'Where was the road supposed to end?'

'The Twentieth are on their way up from Glevum to join us here,' replied Marcus. 'Scapula wanted to catch Caratacus unawares an' trap him in his camp an' cut him off. That's why Julianus had orders just to go as far as the southern end of the hill. Scapula was expectin' to fight it out so's the Fourteenth could get some glory – we've bin a bit short on victories recent – before the Twentieth arrived on the scene. Stupid, ain't it? If they'd left it a few more days, the Twentieth would've been here an' we could've had a combined attack. But no, some idiot boy who thinks he knows best leads us right into a massacre. Probably learned all about tactics from a scroll. They just dunna want to listen to experience! Scapula would've had his guts for sandal straps if he was still alive. As it is, he'll probably get a posthumous award for bravery on the field of battle.'

'What will happen now?'

'Oh, they'll ask me loads of questions, send men to recover the bodies – gotta give 'em a decent burial; most of the poor sods paid in advance for their funerals – and then ... then, when the Twentieth arrive, send every man they can to hunt Caratacus down. And kill him! Then our troubles will be over and we can all go home!'

'I don't think so,' thought Tim. 'There'll be a lot more fighting for years to come.' He decided against giving Marcus a history lesson; it would be too depressing for him, especially while he was in this state.

'What makes you think you'll be able to catch Carad– ... Caratacus?'

'Scapula reckons he'll make for the hills in the west cos there's nowhere left for him to hide in the east.'

'Won't the hills make it more difficult for you?'

'Well, a bit, but if anyone can track Caratacus down, we can. It's just takin' a while longer than we thought.'

Tim caught sight of the ramparts of Castra Cornoviorum a short distance away. They were approaching the wooden bridge over the river Severn.

'Not far now,' said Marcus, following Tim's gaze.

'No,' replied Tim. 'Marcus, I'd better leave you. I don't want to be seen by the sentry on the bridge.'

Marcus was about to say Tim couldn't be seen at all when a shaft of sunlight burst unannounced over the eastern horizon. Marcus was grinning from ear to ear.

'Nasty cut yer've got there!' he smiled.

'How can you ...?'

Tim looked down at himself and realised he was completely visible. Marcus tried to pat him on the shoulder. He patted the air instead.

154

'Well, at least I know what yer look like complete!' he beamed. 'Strange clothin'. Well, thank yer again, Tim. I'm very grateful to yer.'

'That's OK,' said Tim.

'How's me lump?' asked Marcus, pointing at his forehead.

'Almost as big as your head!' laughed Tim, shaking the soldier's hand. 'Goodbye, and good luck!'

'Goodbye, my friend. Now, go and find yer sister, and thank her for helpin' me last time.'

He raised a hand to salute Tim and strode towards the bridge.

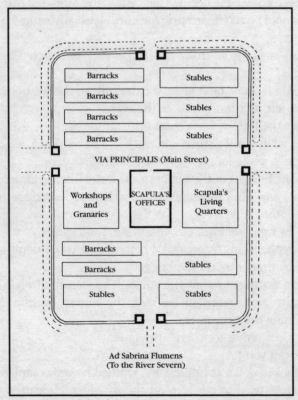

Tim's plan of the Roman fort at Uriconium.

CHAPTER 15

Strategies

Gwirocon was furious.

'She could be lying there dead! Did you wait until daylight to look for her? No! You were more concerned with your own safety! So much for brotherly love!'

'It wasn't like that! I told you, her horse wasn't anywhere to be seen and I assumed she'd come back here.'

'Well, she didn't! I just hope she's got more sense than you!'

Tim didn't say anything. He knew Gwirocon would cool down eventually. He'd explained everything that happened in great detail and was taken aback by the druid king's reaction. What else could he have done in the circumstances?

Gwirocon continued mixing paste in a small clay bowl but Tim could tell his mind wasn't on the job. Most of the paste splattered randomly on the floor of the druid's small house in the village. The flickering flame from a candle stump eerily lit Tim's features.

'No, you're right. I shouldn't have lost my temper,' Gwirocon admitted quietly after further thought. 'She's not here, that's all there is to it. I don't suppose I'd have done any different.'

'I think she's safely hidden somewhere. Perhaps her horse got injured. I'm sure I'd know if any harm had come to her.'

'Oh, that twin thing,' said Gwirocon, doubtfully. 'I'm not convinced. Nevertheless, there's not much I can do. We'll have to see if Caradoc sends word of his new quarters. She may be hiding there although no one will be able to see her ... unless she does something stupid. I hope it's not a family trait.'

'I could look for her myself.'

The druid glanced up at him. He wore an expression normally reserved for the simple minded.

'And just where, exactly, would you search? Do you know, precisely, where Caradoc's new camp is? I have no knowledge of

Madrun's territory. The Ordovicians are not great friends of ours. Here.'

He held out the bowl. Tim reached inside and scooped out the grey-green paste. It smelled awful, like sweaty socks.

'Smooth it over the cut, then tie a cloth around to hold it in place.'

Tim did as he was ordered. The cut smarted. He winced.

'Keep it there for a few hours. It'll clean the wound and help heal the broken skin.' He spoke just like a doctor, in a matter-of-fact sort of way. 'A latrine shovel, you said? That's a new one.'

Gwirocon rinsed out the bowl and laid it upside down on the table to dry. His penetrating eyes looked directly at Tim, who felt very uncomfortable, for several, very long, minutes. It was as if his mind was being probed.

'I honestly don't know what to do.' He shrugged his shoulders, completely at a loss. 'All we can do is wait and see what turns up.'

Tim had also been racking his brains and reluctantly had to agree with Gwirocon.

'Fingers crossed.' said Tim.

'How is that going to help?'

'It's just an expression. It's like wishing for good luck.'

'Luck has nothing to do with it! Fortune, yes. But not luck. There is a difference.'

Tim shook his head. He wasn't ready for an academic discussion. His head still throbbed, although not so badly. More like a distant drum beat.

'Marcus said part of the Twentieth Legion was on its way here?' mused Gwirocon, stroking his beard thoughtfully. 'Any idea how long it'll take?'

'Only a few days, perhaps a week. The track won't take much effort to widen; it only took Marcus a day to reach Caer Caradoc.'

'It would help if we knew what Scapula's plans are ...'

Tim understood what the druid was getting at.

'Let me get my head back to normal first.'

Gwirocon smiled. 'No rush. Tomorrow will do.'

So much for not putting Tim under pressure!

It took Tim almost two hours to get inside Castra Cornoviorum. The sun was shining brightly and he had to wait for drifting clouds to blot it out for moments at a time so that he could scramble a few more metres before lying face down again in the long grass. Things became more difficult the nearer he got to the walls of the enlarged fortress; sentries seemed more numerous than they had ever been before and were watching every centimetre of the surrounding countryside.

Once inside, Tim sensed a strange atmosphere among the troops, a mixture of anger, sorrow and fear.

'It's not right or proper,' he overheard one of the soldiers say as he made his secretive way towards the centre of the fort. 'We should've brought the bodies back here and given them a decent burial. I wouldn't want to be thrown into a communal grave.'

'Nor me,' agreed his comrade. 'But you can see Scapula's point. It would have taken us ages to bring them all back on wagons, dig individual graves and hold a separate funeral service for each one.'

'Doesn't make it right, though. There's no headstones, and I know for a fact that at least thirty paid the stone mason in advance. And he won't hand over the money to the relatives, will he? No, he'll pocket it for himself. Disgusting, ain't it?'

'Yeah. There'll be no trace once the grass grows. And nobody seems to know what happened. Pity Marcus couldn't tell us more.'

'At least he hasn't gone on about supernatural beings saving him again, like he did last time!'

'No, but he's keeping something back. Sure of it. Lucky sod!'

'Ain't he just! Mind you, I'm glad Julianus sent us back.'

'Serves him right. Got no idea, no idea at all. I've always said officers shouldn't be allowed to buy their way in. Proper training in the ranks, that's what they need. Experience. Old emperor Augustus knew that.'

'Ah, now he was a real good general. My grandad served with him way back. Never had a bad word to say about him.'

'What do you reckon to Scapula?'

'Bit harsh, but fair. I overheard him saying he hated being in Britain but he'll stick it out to the end, you mark my words, despite his poor health. Worries too much, but not a quitter, oh, no. Too quick to take action for his own good, though. Bit manic about gettin' Caratacus, if you get my drift. Affects his judgement. That's why the Twentieth have been on the go all this time without a rest. Chasing shadows, if you ask me.'

'Better not cross him then.'

Tim reached Scapula's office and loitered outside until the door opened and he was able to creep in.

Scapula was in a foul mood.

'All dead except Marcus! Whatever possessed that idiot Julianus to leave himself undermanned and unprepared! I'll have to write to the emperor and his father and spin them some story to say how courageous he was. It'll be easier for them to take bad news if I mention it was Caratacus. Have to give Julianus an award, of course. Arrogant young fool!' Scapula calmed down a little. 'Marcus doesn't seem to know much, but he's alive. Again. By the gods, I wish all my men had his luck!'

'Do you think it's wise to promote men from the auxiliary?' asked Quintus, tentatively.

'Not a great deal of choice, is there? We have to replace the men Julianus lost from somewhere and everyone in the other legions is stretched. Claudius made it very clear there was no way he'd transfer anyone from anywhere else in the empire; the Senate would make a meal of him if we asked for more resources. Have to make do with what we've got.'

'The men think it's a waste of effort chasing after Caratacus all the time. It's costing too many lives. I've heard he's being hailed as a hero, back in Rome.' As soon as Quintus said it, he knew he should have kept his mouth shut.

'Can't understand it; he's nothing more than a rebel and troublemaker! The men will do as they're told! The emperor made it very clear that Caratacus had to be dealt with, whatever the cost in terms of my men or time! That's exactly what I'm doing! He won't get away from me for much longer. And as for treating him like a hero, well ...' Scapula couldn't find the right words to say how disgusted and frustrated he felt that success against his sworn enemy was not coming easy.

'He has lasted far longer than we expected ...'

'I'll get him! I'll chase him round this blasted country until I drop rather than give in now! Quintus, I'm surprised at you. I expected better.'

'I'm concerned about your health, sir. You've hardly slept a wink for months and this pursuit is beginning to look like a personal vendetta rather than a military objective.'

'What if it is? I have my orders. So have you.'

Scapula thumped the table with his fist. He was getting quite worked up. Quintus thought it would be a good idea to accept the inevitable and discuss new plans to pursue Caratacus.

'Have you any thoughts about what to do next? Judging from the tracks leading from the hill near the massacre, Caratacus seems to have headed south.'

'In that case, he'll run up against the Twentieth on their way here. He's more likely to go west into the hills; I shouldn't think he'd be so stupid as to stay behind our frontier line.'

'Should we send out scouts to check?'

'Now that we've buried our dead, yes. Whose territory is it down there?'

'Could be Silurian, but it's more likely Ordovician. The border between the two isn't very well defined.'

'Have you made contact with the Ordovician kings?'

Quintus shook his head.

'No; so far we know virtually nothing about them, only pieces of information taken from merchants.'

'So, they're not on our side.'

'Definitely not. We won't get any help from them.'

Scapula sighed heavily.

'And I suppose their territory is hilly, like Silurian?'

'Worse. The mountains are apparently much higher and the valleys longer and deeper. Any campaign there will be harder than the Twentieth have experienced so far in Britain.'

Scapula thought long and hard. He ran his fingers absent mindedly over the rough map lying on the table. The map had very little detail. Tim could see where new bits of information had been added from time to time, presumably gleaned by interrogating traders and scouts.

'There seems to be a route from here to this island.'

Tim saw the governor's finger pointing at 'Mona Insula' – Anglesey.

'It could be the road traders follow to get to Hibernia.'

Tim remembered Hibernia was the Roman name for Ireland.

'Mona Insula rings a bell.'

'It's where the druids have a religious centre. Apparently there's a college there.'

Scapula's eyes narrowed.

'The druids have a lot to answer for. They support everyone who fights against us.'

'Uirocon's a druid,' observed Quintus.

'Yes, but he's also a king who does not want to bring harm to his people.'

'What I meant was, if he's a druid, he must know something about the route to Mona Insula.'

Scapula mulled over his words. 'It's possible ...'

'I think we should ask him.'

'I'll ride out to him later.'

He scrutinised the map again, then looked up at Quintus.

'When the men from the Twentieth arrive, I want them to stock up with supplies and follow the tracks left by Caratacus; they should still be visible. And they must keep following him, wherever he goes. And I want them to send messengers twice a day to keep me informed. Make sure they have a map maker assigned to put as much detail on this as he can.'

Quintus looked at the map.

'There's a chance Caratacus will be able to escape from Ordovician territory and hide in Brigantia.'

'Queen Cartimandua is our ally; he won't go there.'

'She may be, but her husband Venutius sympathises with the rebels.'

'Then we'll have to cut off Caratacus's retreat. The Fourteenth will begin to explore and secure the route to Mona Insula without delay.'

'To trap Caratacus between the Twentieth Legion in the south and the Fourteenth to the north?'

'Precisely.'

For the first time in months, Scapula smiled.

Tim only just had time to tell Gwirocon what he'd heard when Scapula arrived with his bodyguard. One of the soldiers handed the governor a long scroll.

Gwirocon invited the governor inside his king's roundhouse and gave him a beaker of ale. Scapula sipped it and tried not to pull a face. He really didn't like this British brew; he preferred mead or sweet wine, but he didn't wish to offend his host. He needed information.

'Ostorius Scapula, welcome to my humble dwelling,' said Gwirocon. 'Is there a problem with the supplies I gave Gaius Mannius Secundus, your collector of taxes?'

'No, King Uirocon, everything is in order.'

'Terrible news about your soldiers,' said the druid king, with just the right note of sympathy. 'Have you caught Caratacus yet?'

Scapula took another sip and winced, both from the taste of the ale and Gwirocon's question.

'Not yet, but we will.'

'I hope you don't think my people had anything to do with the ambush. You know we value your friendship.'

'No, I'm sure you had nothing to do with it. It looks as though Caratacus has retreated westward. Which is why I've come to you. I need some information.'

'What do you want to know?'

Scapula unrolled the scroll and laid it on the floor near the open door where the light was better. It was the map Tim had seen earlier. Gwirocon and Scapula knelt down to examine it.

'This is wonderful!' said Gwirocon, who had never seen anything like it before. 'Is this Britain?'

'Yes,' said Scapula. 'These are Cornovian, Silurian, Ordovician, Brigantian lands ... and down here we have Camulodunum, Londinium, and many other towns and settlements. Here's Castra Cornoviorum.'

Gwirocon marvelled at the sight and suddenly realised the

strategic importance of the map. It enabled the enemy to plan campaigns and keep track of Caradoc's movements.

'I think Caratacus is somewhere in this area.'

Tim saw him pointing vaguely at mid-Wales.

'My men will try to find him. But I'm more interested in this area, between here and this island.'

Gwirocon was thinking as quickly as he could. He could see very clearly what Scapula's intentions were but didn't want to give any more help than was absolutely necessary to keep his enemy's confidence. Much depended on what, precisely, Scapula asked.

'What do you know about the island?'

'I went to the druid school there.'

'Are there many druids there?'

'I don't know ... most druids go back to their own lands after training. There were only a few actually living there permanently.'

'But presumably there are trainee druids there now.'

'I really don't know. Since your people came to Britain, many druids have been killed and haven't been replaced.'

'Hm. How easy is it to cross from the mainland to the island?'

'Dangerous. The shore is riddled with shifting quicksand. Many have perished. Many more have died trying to cross the strait; the sea currents are extremely turbulent and there are very few safe landing places.'

'Do you know where they are?'

'No; I was blindfolded when I went there. The resident druids take precautions to guarantee their safety.'

'What about the route there? From here.'

'I was very young, in my teens, when I was taken there and can't recall much. It seemed a very long journey. It was quite easy to start with, low hills and a decent road. Well, decent by British standards.'

Scapula nodded. He well knew the state of the roads, and so did his footsore men.

'Go on.'

'Then it became harder. Very high mountains, long valleys, constant rain, very low clouds, freezing cold and almost completely uninhabited. The road became no more than a stony track.'

Scapula nodded again.

'That's what traders have told me.'

'Good,' thought Gwirocon. 'At least I haven't told you any-thing new.'

'What about the Ordovicians? Do you know their king or where there main settlements are?'

'Their over-king is Madrun; I have never met him. I know next to nothing about his under-kings, nor where they live,' he replied with just a hint of apology. 'I'm afraid Cornovian relations with the Ordovicians are, shall we say, strained. They continue to steal our cattle, in spite of your protection, although they are willing to trade for the salt we produce in our northern parts.'

'My men can't be everywhere, as I'm sure you appreciate,' said Scapula, also with a hint of apology. 'We have more pressing prob-lems at the present time.'

'Is it your intention to invade Ordovicia next?'

'It would seem the next logical step,' mused Scapula. 'And we could kill two birds with one stone. Occupying Ordovicia would put a stop to their cattle rustling and at the same time cast the net around Caratacus. Are you sure you don't know where Madrun's fortress is?'

Gwirocon shook his head again.

'No. He may have more than one. Bearing in mind the nature of the terrain, he may spend some months in the higher ground and others in the drier valleys. Remember, his people rear cattle and probably migrate to where the better feeding grounds are according to the seasons.'

'But they must grow wheat and other crops, which would imply more permanent settlements somewhere.'

'If they do, I'm afraid I haven't a clue where they are.'

Scapula took a full mouthful of ale before realising what he had done. He gulped the foul brew down, turning his twisted face away from Gwirocon. Tim saw it and almost burst out laughing at Scapula's discomfort.

Scapula stood and rolled up the scroll.

'Thank you, King Uirocon. You have been very helpful.'

He bowed and left the building.

'I sincerely hope not,' said Gwirocon, when Scapula was well out of earshot.

'What are you going to do?' asked Tim.

Gwirocon shrugged his shoulders and shook his head.

'I can't send Caradoc a message because I don't know exactly where he is and we don't know how near the soldiers of the Twentieth Legion are to him. But I can send a warning to one of Madrun's people to pass on. Let's hope it arrives in time!'

Mr Dale's 1940's aerial photo of the inner Iron Age fort on The Wrekin Hill.
Heaven Gate is bottom left, the Needle's Eye towards the top.
Evidence of roundhouses can be seen in the centre.

CHAPTER 16

Chasing Shadows

Caroline was having rather a good time in Madrun's fort. Carys and (more to the point) Gerand spent almost all their spare time idling the hours away with her.

She couldn't help feeling sorry for them. Most of their lives had been affected by the war. Gerand had vague memories of living in a large wooden palace with rich furnishings and hot and cold running servants. Carys, being that little bit younger, couldn't remember much at all about the good times her family had enjoyed before the Romans arrived.

Since then, not only had they been forced to flee from one place of safety to another, but had also constantly suffered the uncertainty that their father would return safely from an ambush.

As the years rolled by, their lodgings had become more and more shabby, food scarce and boringly similar from one day to the next, and the children of loyal followers blamed them for the miserable lives they, too, were forced to lead. In some ways they were in the same isolated position that Tim and Caroline were, except that Tim wasn't here.

The amount of time Gerand and Carys were able to spend with Caradoc varied. Sometimes he was away for days at a time; at others he was kept busy by constant streams of messengers delivering the latest news. Whenever he was wounded, he put on a brave face and pretended he was fine, but the numerous scars on his arms, legs and chest told a different story.

He seldom spoke to anyone about the way his war was going. Although he knew overall victory was extremely unlikely, he had become a symbol of hope to every tribe who valued their liberty. Despite retreat after retreat, men and, sometimes, their families travelled great distances to join him after their own settlements had been destroyed or their kinsfolk slain. Caradoc was the only leader who stood any chance of victory against the ruthless Romans. The fact that he was still alive and seemingly invincible provided the only light at the end of a very dark tunnel. Surely the Roman Senate would not allow such an expensive war to continue indefinitely?

Branwena was a faithful wife to Caradoc and a wonderful and patient mother to Gerand and Carys. She had probably suffered more than anyone else in Caradoc's band of rebels.

This life of constant worry and wandering was not what she, the daughter of a Belgian king, had expected. Nevertheless, she had adapted well to the hard and miserable life she now led and was the only one in whom Caradoc confided his darkest fears. But if she was being entirely honest, she enjoyed being with her children for so much of the time and took immense pleasure playing with and talking to them between the times set aside for their education, irregularly provided by a steady stream of itinerant druids.

It didn't, however, stop her worrying about what the future held for herself, her husband, Gerand and Carys.

They had not been at their new camp for many weeks when Madrun reappeared with a small group of warriors and a druid.

'The Romans are not far away,' he said, grimly. 'Soldiers from the Twentieth Legion reached Castra Cornoviorum and retraced their steps until they found the tracks made by your folk when they came here. They're setting up a permanent camp at the junction.'

'How many?' asked Caradoc.

'About a thousand soldiers and perhaps another two thousand auxiliaries.'

A mass of anxious faces quickly assembled around the two kings. They sensed something was wrong because Madrun had not brought any supplies with him.

'What's happened?'

'No food ... again!'

'I knew we couldn't trust him! At least Gwirocon never let us down!'

'Quiet!' shouted Caradoc angrily. 'What King Madrun has to say is far more important than food!'

The crowd quietened down apart from a few disgruntled murmurs. Caradoc resumed his conversation with Madrun.

'Once the enemy has established a base it won't take long for them to get here. You must move out. I have another fort a few miles south-west of here. It's not an easy route, though; you'll have to ditch the larger wagons and put as much as possible in carts and on mules.'

'Then we have to thank the Romans for providing us with suitable transport!' Caradoc chuckled. He stopped when he saw so many dismayed faces around him. 'Come now! Where is your sense of humour? Our foes have regularly supplied us with everything we need to survive; I'm sure Governor Scapula is very pleased to know we don't waste anything his men let us take!'

Caroline was fascinated to see how the mood in the camp changed. Caradoc certainly knew how to raise their spirits with a few well chosen words.

'I don't have to remind you of everything you have suffered; isn't that why you're here with me, keeping the torch of freedom alight? Your countrymen are proud of your sacrifices! So am I! Thanks to you and your courage, we are alive! And free! But freedom comes at a price, of that you are all well aware. We don't want to give up now, do we?'

The crowd erupted.

'Long live King Caradoc! Death to the Romans! Britain for the British!'

Caradoc raised his hands; the crowd, feeling much better, fell silent again.

'King Madrun and I have things to discuss. Prepare to leave. Remember what he said: only take what is essential! It will make travel easier.'

The crowd dispersed.

'I have men keeping an eye on the enemy camp; the patrol has already set out.'

'I couldn't see much in the dark on the way here; are there any places good enough for an ambush?'

Madrun shook his head. 'Not for horses.'

Madrun's druid stepped forward. He had been following their conversation very closely. Normally, druids didn't get involved with warfare, but times had changed.

'There is but one place. Where the track crosses the stream; it is always flooded there and the mud will slow the enemy down. There are many trees and much undergrowth in the vicinity, sufficient to hide your men.'

'I know where you mean. The sides of the valley are quite steep there. Caradoc, you won't be able to launch a full attack, but your men will be able to fire arrows and slingshot onto the enemy below.'

'Which would slow them down.'

'Yes. And your men will be able to escape from the scene without fear of pursuit.'

'As long as they don't linger,' agreed the druid.

'Dad, can I come with you?' asked Gerand, who was standing nearby. 'Please.'

'No,' said his father. 'I've told you before, it's too dangerous.'

'But the druid said ...'

'I said no!'

'Your father's right,' said Madrun. 'You are not experienced enough.'

'Other boys my age fight,' Gerand protested.

'They grew up fighting. It is in their nature. You are the son of a king and, one day, will become king yourself. Kings are leaders, they have to use their heads more than their hands.'

'You do!'

'Not from choice, Gerand.' He ruffled his son's hair, much to his annoyance. Gerand sensed Caroline was watching and didn't want her to see him treated like a child. 'I need you to look after your mother and sister: I can't lead the attack and do that as well. Their safety is just as important.'

'It's not fair,' Gerand muttered to himself before disappearing inside a hut to help his mother and sister pack their meagre belongings yet again.

The first heavily laden mules descended the hill a little over an hour later, led by some of Madrun's warriors and the druid. It didn't take long for the fort to be evacuated now that so many wagons and belongings had been dumped.

Although the people were still in a buoyant mood after Caradoc's stirring speech, they didn't realise their lives were about to become much more difficult than they had ever been before. Even the cloudy sky didn't dampen their spirits.

Branwena took the reins of a small cart with a wobbly wheel while Gerand and Carys held on to its thin timber frame. Caroline followed on her horse, which was tied to the rear of the cart along with a mule packed with all the family's worldly goods. There wasn't much in the sacks. It made her realise how much Caradoc had been forced to sacrifice for his people when he could have taken the easy option and accepted Roman rule with open arms, and been rewarded well for doing so.

Caradoc and his band of warriors took the opposite route, back along the track towards the enemy camp. They were all on horseback and lightly armed with bows, arrows, slings and shoulder bags filled with carefully selected round pebbles collected from the stream at the foot of the hill.

It wasn't long after Caradoc's men disappeared that Caroline saw Gerand fiddling with the rope pulling her horse behind the cart. It fell to the ground and Gerand discreetly motioned with his hand. Caroline understood; he wanted her to take the horse away from the moving train. She pulled the reins to one side and directed the horse towards the trees on the side of the track.

'Mum! Gwirocon's horse has escaped!' called Gerand, jumping from the cart before his mother could stop him. 'I'll catch it!'

He ran after the horse; it turned its head and trotted into the undergrowth. It stopped as soon as it was out of sight. Breathless, Gerand caught up.

'Caroline, are you there?'

'Of course I am, silly. Why did you untie the rope?'

'I want to see the ambush! C'mon, give me a hand up!'

'Are you sure? I don't really want to.'

'Oh, go on! I'm dying to see what it's like.'

Reluctantly, she hauled Gerand into the saddle.

It was a very odd feeling. Caroline held the reins and directed the horse while Gerand shared exactly the same spot in the saddle. Every now and then he could feel her arms brush against him. It felt good. Strange, but good.

The horse ambled downstream for several miles while they chatted in whispers. Gerand knew his father would be extremely cross if ever he found out but there was something about Caroline that made him feel perfectly safe, even if she wasn't completely real.

A flock of birds shot up into the sky a short distance in front. Something had disturbed them. Gerand pointed upwards to the right.

'Up there!' he said quietly. 'Go up there!'

She saw where he meant; a small area where the trees were less dense. Before long they had a clear view of the narrow valley below and could see warriors hiding behind trees and bushes. They could also see the muddy pool mentioned by Madrun's druid.

A Roman scout appeared at the far end of the pool. He paused and looked around before calling to someone behind.

'This way! The track crosses here!'

More soldiers reached the pool. They were auxiliaries, not legionaries. It was common practice to send auxiliaries up front in case there was trouble and to use legionaries for more serious combat. Auxiliaries were disposable.

After lifting their weapons well above their heads, the auxiliaries began to wade through the muddy pool. One fell into the water. Several of his comrades laughed and shouted insults at him. Another fell under. Then another. The laughter stopped abruptly.

'Ambush!'

Several more men fell into the water. Many standing along the track preparing to cross the pool groaned when arrows plunged into their chests or pebbles smacked into their faces.

'Back! Back!'

Mayhem and panic took over. Those retreating for their lives were hampered by comrades who hadn't realised anything was amiss. There were many more casualties during the short but effective onslaught which came to an abrupt end as soon as the auxiliaries had retreated a safe distance away.

'I think we'd better leave,' said Caroline. She should have known better. Dead and dying bodies brought back terrible memories of her previous encounter.

Gerand nodded. Like Caroline, he felt sick at what he had witnessed. He now understood why his father hadn't wanted him anywhere near.

They caught up with Branwena and Carys only a short time before Caradoc and his men also arrived. Gerand was told off in no uncertain words by his mother, who had been worried sick. She made sure Gwirocon's horse was very securely tethered to the cart before moving on.

Caradoc was pleased with the result of the ambush and knew, from past experience, that the enemy would be delayed for quite some time before continuing their pursuit. By then his people would be well away from danger.

Caradoc was wrong.

Scapula was livid when he received news of the attack and sent a terse message telling them to take more care while hunting down his arch enemy. He'd received another letter from the emperor demanding to know how much longer the campaign against Caratacus was going to take.

Members of the Senate were getting more and more irritated by the popular reputation the troublemaker had gained among ordinary citizens. It made Claudius, the ruling classes, Scapula and his legions look like incompetent fools.

Scapula began to explore the northern portion of Ordovicia, this time deploying large numbers of auxiliaries attached to the Fourteenth Legion.

Having heard what had just happened to the auxiliaries of the Twentieth Legion, Marcus was understandably relieved to remain on guard at Castra Cornoviorum. Although he was no coward, it was safer to be a regular legionary than an auxiliary, who made an easy target for an unseen adversary.

Both Gwirocon and Tim were becoming more and more frustrated because they didn't have a very clear picture of what progress was being made in the hunt for Caradoc or how he and his people were managing to evade the Romans.

Although Tim's brief excursions into Castra Cornoviorum were almost a regular daily routine, he wasn't getting much information about how Scapula's campaigns were going.

It was also taking a long time to send messages to Madrun and they couldn't be sure whether vital information was reaching Caradoc himself.

Only one thing gave them some consolation; a messenger reported he'd seen Gwirocon's horse; apparently Caradoc had forbidden anyone to ride it because it had special powers, although the king's son had been seen on it several times.

Tim took this information as proof that Caroline was alive and well, although Gwirocon was still not convinced.

'She must be there,' Tim had said. 'I'd know if anything had happened to her. How else would Gerand be able to ride the horse? He must be riding it with her!'

'Tim, my boy,' Gwirocon said, with great sympathy and understanding. 'Much as I'd like to agree with you, you mustn't raise your hopes. She may well be safe, at the moment, but you must be prepared for the worst. Gerand may simply have befriended the horse and it lets him ride it.'

Tim knew the druid king was right; he couldn't argue. If only there was a way of finding out for sure. But that was impossible. Roman patrols were all over the place and Caradoc was having to keep on the move all the time.

Caradoc's followers were having a bad time. For almost three months they'd been pursued relentlessly all over the hills and valleys of central Wales.

No sooner had they settled into another of Madrun's numerous hill forts than news came through that the enemy had picked up their trail and was steadfastly marching towards them. Impromptu ambushes and raids were taking place almost every week but still the Romans continued to pursue them. It was like a nightmare; however much they tried to shut it out, it kept coming back.

Everything seemed to be going wrong. More and more warriors were being killed or seriously wounded during the ambushes. Food supplies were running short because Roman patrols made it increasingly difficult for goods to be transported without being confiscated.

It had reached the point where Caradoc's people were reluctant to unload their belongings whenever they arrived at a new refuge. They'd even had to resort to eating some of the mules in an effort to keep a few cattle alive: their milk was an essential part of the rebel diet.

It was now late summer. Madrun, who was still regarded with more than a hint of suspicion by Caradoc's warriors despite the fact that he and his own tribesfolk were suffering similar oppression, had done his best to keep Caradoc one step ahead of the enemy.

New safe havens were becoming more difficult to find. Cader Idris and other high mountains in the west were totally inhospitable; high rainfall and virtually no food meant there was nothing to be gained by going in that direction. Further retreat to the south was ruled out because of the Twentieth Legion.

Soldiers of the Fourteenth Legion, whose auxiliary campaign to occupy land on either side of Sarn Wydellin to Mona Insula was well under way, were almost in a position to start their own campaign against Caradoc. Hopefully (from Scapula's point of view), the rebel army would soon be sandwiched between the Fourteenth to the north and the Twentieth Legion in the south.

Both Caradoc and Madrun had realised several weeks before that the situation would only get worse. They didn't, of course, mention this to anyone else in case the knowledge spread fear and despondency to loyal supporters who still held some hope for a better future.

Nevertheless, their followers weren't oblivious to the reasons behind their suffering: constant moving from one temporary shelter to another, the gradual loss of property caused by the need to travel ever lighter ... and their meagre supplies of food dwindling by the day. But they were freedom fighters. Britons throughout the land depended on them to harass their foreign enemies until they gave up and left their shores forever.

Belief in Caradoc gave them the strength to carry on against all odds.

But they couldn't go on like this indefinitely; something had to give.

And soon.

Caradoc's band of rebels was pursued relentlessly by Scapula's army, which chased them around the hills of southern Shropshire (above) and mid-Wales. The terrain was inhospitable, heavily wooded with narrow pathways.

CHAPTER 17

Cornered!

Tim missed Caroline more than he would have thought possible. He hadn't seen her for over four months and, even though no definite word reached Gwirocon, he still believed she was moving around the Shropshire or Welsh countryside with Caradoc. He had never been separated from his sister for so long but he felt sure they would be reunited soon, whatever Gwirocon said.

Caradoc's situation was undoubtedly getting worse. It had been more than a month since the last messenger told Gwirocon the band of resolute rebels was having to keep on the move almost constantly. Casualties were still relatively low but it had become impossible to carry severely wounded warriors; if they couldn't keep up, they were left behind, often with their wives and children, to fend for themselves. Abandonment was accepted as inevitable; no one bore Caradoc any malice or resentment. In fact, they felt they had let their leader down, such was their loyalty to his cause.

Tim couldn't imagine what it must be like for them. His own life had become rather dull in recent weeks. Of course, he paid frequent visits to Castra Cornoviorum but the thrill of going there had long since gone; it was now part of his routine, almost like going to work at the same place, at the same time, seeing the same old miserable faces and hearing the same old grumbles from the same old soldiers.

Because he was no longer able to deliver weapons to Caradoc, Gwirocon's metal workers, scattered around in sheltered clearings in the woodland in and around the Severn Gorge, were continuing to make swords and axes but now sold them to tribes who had been disarmed after Scapula's edict months earlier.

Anti-Roman feelings were still running high, feelings that druids throughout the land were only too willing to encourage.

One day, perhaps one day soon, the whole country would unite and retaliate. They had to be prepared for that moment, whenever it came, however long it took.

Gwirocon's farmers were also reaping the benefits of trade with the mass of soldiers stationed at Castra Cornoviorum, Uxacona and Bravonium, the fort created by the Twentieth Legion at the start of this latest campaign against Caradoc.

Surplus food not taken by Gaius Mannius Secundus in taxation was sold, with the result that payment in coins began to replace the traditional Cornovian system of barter. Small shanty villages sprang up short distances away from the forts; they became centres of adult entertainment and gambling as well as local market places.

Skilled metal workers were able to make highly sought after enamelled brooches when they were not producing illicit weapons. Ale was becoming more popular, especially since it had a stronger flavour than the usual watered down sour Italian wine: drinking it had some interesting side effects, although it wasn't always possible to remember what they were the morning after. Despite their differences, Romans and Cornovians were learning to live together in peace.

Gwirocon observed these changes with fascination. On the one hand, his people were still involved in underhand activities against the invaders. On the other, they were learning to co-exist – and profit – from the enemy.

Now that his own involvement in supporting Caradoc had ended, there was less chance of someone saying the wrong thing to the wrong person and getting him into trouble.

'The present turn of events will bring two other benefits,' Gwirocon said to Tim. 'If the Romans eventually manage to gain full control over Britain, the allegiance and support I have given them should put me and my people in a favourable position.'

'But what if the Britons are successful?' asked Tim. He knew it wouldn't happen.

'Even then we win. If it comes to the point where Claudius and the Senate withdraw the legions because the war becomes too expensive, the Cornovians shall be remembered for the way they supported Caradoc. Either way, we can't lose.'

For the first time in years, Gwirocon felt as though there was some hope for the future of his tribe.

Tim listened to what Gwirocon had to say but didn't pass any further comment. He had seen Scapula's map too many times in recent weeks. It had far more detail than it had a few months ago.

As it was so late in the campaign year, Scapula and Quintus examined the map much more closely. There were very few gaps left in the Welsh area; they tended to be along the central and northern coastline and from half way between Castra Cornoviorum and Mona Insula. The most noticeable blank spot was almost smack in the middle of Wales.

'We only have a few weeks left before autumn,' mused Scapula. 'Not enough time to finish taking the road to Mona Insula.'

'No,' agreed Quintus. 'But I think we can afford to leave that until next year. It's unlikely Caradoc will be able to cross our lines and escape to Brigantia unless he struggles to cross these mountains.' His finger pointed at the Snowdon range. 'It must be getting harder for him to move.'

'He has to be somewhere here,' Scapula said with an evil, almost triumphant grin. He looked more closely at the small area of uncharted territory. 'Have we tracked down King Madrun's stronghold?'

Quintus shook his head. 'Not yet, assuming he has one. So far the largest things we've found are a few very small villages and abandoned hill forts. Most Ordovicians seem to live in isolated farmsteads, many only with women, children and old folk.'

'Then the men must be with Madrun. Somewhere here.'

'In that case ...'

'Time is marching on, and so must we!' said Scapula. 'Instruct the Fourteenth's auxiliaries to fortify positions along the road to Mona Insula; leave enough men to occupy them over winter. The rest are to withdraw ...' he scrutinised the map again. '... here!'

He indicated Oswestry, on the border between Cornovia and Ordovicia.

'I see there's a British camp there. Well stocked with grain pits, if I recall.'

'Then what?' asked Quintus.

'Well, let's see. Give the men a couple of days rest, then march them south-west. You take command. There seems to be a path in that direction. I'll lead the men stationed here due west. Our forces should meet up somewhere here.'

'And the Twentieth?'

'Take them a copy of this part of the map.' He vaguely indicated the area of central Wales where his enemy was thought to be. 'I want them to stop following Caratacus and press on westward for a few miles, then circle back towards our meeting point. I'm convinced Caratacus is in that area somewhere. With a bit of luck, the Twentieth will flush him out straight into our hands!'

'And if they don't?' Quintus rolled the map up to take to the camp cartographer.

'We strengthen whatever positions we gain and wait until spring. Don't worry, Quintus. I'm certain we'll get him this time!'

Quintus didn't share the same conviction. Caratacus had been and still was a slippery customer; nothing Scapula had said gave him cause to change his mind.

Caroline was shattered. Gerand and Carys were used to life constantly on the move and took frequent upheaval in their stride. But Caroline just couldn't get used to spending so many hours almost every day in the saddle or, to give her backside a rest, walking alongside Branwena's cart. Furthermore, hiding beneath hot blankets on sunny days was equally unbearable. She had never felt so tired, nor suffered so many aches and pains. The longest time the freedom fighters and their families had spent in any one place was a mere six days.

Yet, in spite of all their hardship and the tears shed when yet another family had to be left behind to take care of a wounded husband, son or father, the survivors were in good heart. Heavy rain, treacherous paths, sickness, limited food and the constant threat of attack did nothing to dampen their spirits.

Victory would not come easy. All this suffering was necessary for a better future. It had reached the stage when the arrival of another messenger telling them to move on was greeted with enthusiasm. The longer they could keep on the move and inflict a few more casualties on their enemies, the better. If they were having such a bad time, just think what the Romans were going through. Months and months without a victory and the constant threat of ambush had sent already ebbing Roman morale plummeting.

Only Caradoc and Madrun knew the truth. They were running out of places to go. There were still several weeks left before the Romans would stop their campaign for the winter. And a lot could happen between now and then.

Friction between the two kings had been brooding for some time. Madrun had kept his promises, as best as he could in the circumstances, to provide refuge and food for Caradoc's army but the unrelenting pursuit and advances made by the Romans was not something Madrun had catered for. His own people were scattered throughout central and north Wales. It was becoming increasingly hard to obtain regular supplies of food and there was a limit to the number of suitable hidden valleys and hill forts left unused.

Caradoc, aware that the situation was getting worse, maintained that his policy of hit-and-run attacks was best. It slowed enemy progress down. It demoralised soldiers by increasing the fear of possible attack and having to bury dead comrades. It raised doubts in the Senate about the mounting cost of the campaign, and for what? Britain had still not revealed the treasures it believed were there for the taking. And very few of its inhabitants could be trusted not to rebel against Roman rule at the first opportunity, not even those who willingly took advantage of the enemy's generosity by apparently welcoming them with open arms.

The question was, could Caradoc hold out for the rest of the campaign season?

If so, he stood a remote chance that more warriors could be persuaded to join his cause ... but only if he managed to avoid capture (or worse) for the rest of the year, and still had the support of a sufficient number of warriors to make his resistance worthwhile. And that was becoming increasingly more unlikely.

'We cannot go on like this!' insisted Madrun for the tenth time in as many days. 'Our people are weary. They need to put an end to all this wandering and get back to their normal lives.'

'I've told you before, Madrun. I will not risk everything in a pitched battle. We hold the upper hand!'

'There are Romans all around us!'

'Not yet, they're not. Be patient. If we can hold out for just a few more weeks, it gives us all winter to prepare ourselves for next year.'

'How will that help? We'll still be here. And weaker.'

'Venutius says he's gaining support in Brigantia. He hopes to join us with his own followers.'

'Next year.' It was a statement, not a question.

'Yes.'

'We need more than promises from a king who has no power in his own country.'

'You are forgetting. Brigantia belongs to Cartimandua, his wife. She rules, with Rome's support. But many of her people are restless. They see how we resist and want to help. Venutius will deliver, you'll see. I can trust him.'

'But you won't trust me!'

'Of course I trust you, Madrun! But gambling everything on a single battle will not win the war.'

'Of course it will! If we defeat Scapula's army, the whole country will revolt. His legions won't stand a chance!'

'And if we lose? What then?'

'At least we will have tried!'

'The country's eyes watch our every move. Each week we remain at large gives hope. We represent freedom and the right to defend ourselves, to live our lives the way we have always done. Not as slaves. Not as a storehouse for others to plunder.'

'I agree with what you say; my people agree with me. But ambushes are for cowards! Real men fight in battles, where the enemy can see our strength before they suffer under our blades!'

'Real men fight in order to live, not die with glory! A corpse has no honour, no future!'

'My men do not like it! They have already sacrificed too much. They need to return to their homes before their crops wither; you know what hardship that will cause next year when their families have no food to eat. And if they have no food for themselves, they can't be expected to support you! Can they?'

'You may be right, Madrun, but I beg you. Support me for a few more weeks.'

A rider galloped into the camp.

'Romans! The enemy is coming!'

Caradoc was more than a little dismayed to discover the Romans had made so much progress in such a short time. Not only had the Twentieth Legion increased the vigour of its wanderings around central Wales it but no longer bothered to follow his tracks.

For once the enemy seemed to be using some intelligence, trying to anticipate his next move and circling round to cut off his line of retreat. They'd even gone as far west as the coast near Aberystwyth in an effort to stop him escaping to the south.

News of Scapula's activities in north Ordovicia was also met with disbelief. Madrun had been convinced that the Fourteenth Legion would continue the campaign to reach Mona Insula before inclement weather set in. He was very much mistaken.

It was obvious to Caradoc that Scapula had pulled back as many men as possible with the sole intention of trapping him before the campaign season came to a close. Doubts were ever present in his mind. It would take a stroke of luck to keep the enemy at bay long enough, and Madrun's constant criticisms didn't help. If only Venutius had been able to rally support sooner!

Caradoc's worst fears were soon realised.

His army of road-weary followers had managed to stay in the same place for four peaceful, worry-free days until Gerand and Carys noticed something unusual while they were feeding Caroline's horse one morning. A few miles away, in almost all directions, they could see smoke gently swirling above the treetops in distant valleys. They ran to tell Caradoc.

'Fetch King Madrun,' he said grimly.

Madrun arrived at his side within moments. He, too, surveyed the scene in silence.

'Well?' said Caradoc. 'What do you think?'

'I think we've got a problem. A big problem.'

They scanned the horizon again, searching for a possible escape route.

'We can't all go south, that's for sure. Nor west. Eastwards is a possibility: the fires aren't so close together there.'

'East is no good. We're bound to run into enemy patrols.'

They turned around. There was a narrow gap between the bonfires.

'North-west?' said Caradoc.

Madrun shook his head. 'Difficult. Very difficult. We'd have to cross those mountains. It would be too slow, take far too long, considering how many folk we have to move.'

'No doubt the scouts will have told Scapula,' agreed Caradoc. 'He must be feeling pleased with himself.'

'A battle, then?' said Madrun. He took no pleasure from his words.

'Let's take a ride first.'

Before setting off, several volunteers were sent to spy on enemy positions in all directions, just to get a better picture of how they were deployed and how many there were at each location.

Caradoc and Madrun rode northward. This time, Gerand had been allowed to accompany his father on Gwirocon's horse, occupying the same space in the saddle as Caroline. Carys, begrudgingly, stayed behind with her mother.

Progress from one hill top to the next was slower than they had anticipated. The valleys in between were not only steep but full of trees and undergrowth as well as rushing streams, boulders and rocky outcrops.

By noon the two kings had come to the same conclusion. Soldiers of the Fourteenth Legion had spread out so far across the area that escape for the rebel army seemed almost impossible.

'Are you sure the mountains aren't feasible?' asked Caradoc.

Madrun shook his head.

'No, Caradoc. I'm not just saying that to force your hand, but it really would be too difficult unless you want to abandon the women and children.'

'And we know what the Romans would do to them.'

'Exactly.'

'Well, Madrun, it looks as if you'll have your battle after all!'

'But not as I would have hoped,' replied Madrun.

Caradoc surveyed the surrounding hills.

'We need a strong defensive position. With a good line of retreat in case ...' his voice tailed off. He didn't want to consider the possibility of defeat.

'Why not this one, dad?' said Gerand.

Caradoc smiled.

'The slopes are not steep; the Romans could attack us on all sides. And it's too small; we couldn't get all our people on here.'

'I think I know just the place,' said Madrun. 'Follow me.'

He led them further northward. Two hours later they reached the top of yet another hill. But this one was different to any they'd seen earlier.

It was a long, wide plateau. The southern side was bounded by dense woodland and sloped gently into the valley below. Grass-covered eastern and western slopes were fairly steep with a few outcrops of rock. More to the point, the grass was slippery and would be very difficult to climb, especially by Romans wearing full, heavy, armour. And it would be impossible for mounted cavalry to even attempt an attack from those directions.

'This is a good spot,' said Madrun. 'Warriors can hide in the woods in the valleys on either side to stop anyone reaching the southern slope. The enemy will have to attack from the north.'

'Show me,' said Caradoc.

Gerand's horse shied when it came to the edge. It took a few moments for Caroline to bring it under control.

'Well done, Gerand! I had no idea you were such an accomplished rider!' beamed his father.

The drop in front was almost vertical for at least twenty metres. Piles of loose, slippery scree lay beneath jagged outcrops of rock which formed the northern edge of the plateau. Large stones were littered all over the scree. But what Caradoc also noticed was that the scree reached as far as a wide, meandering river. Even though the ground on the opposite side was quite flat, bulrushes and other plants indicated wet marshland. Not the sort of place from which anyone liked to launch an attack.

'If we have to stand and fight, Madrun, this is probably the best place we're likely to find. Let's get back. We have a lot to do, and very little time!'

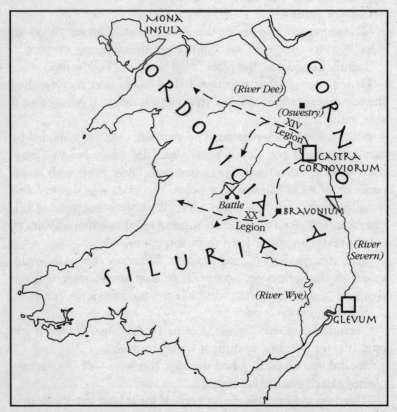

The entrapment of Caradoc and site of his last battle.

CHAPTER 18

The Last Battle

It was evening by the time Caradoc, Madrun, Gerand (and Caroline) arrived back at the camp. The two kings had discussed and agreed a plan of action during their return journey..

While Caradoc's followers prepared to evacuate the camp, he and Madrun gathered the Ordovician warriors together and gave them very precise orders. They were chosen because they knew the layout of the land far better than any of Caradoc's people. Once instructed, a small group of them rode south towards the bonfires lit by soldiers of the Twentieth Legion.

They were to sneak through enemy lines and attempt to draw the soldiers away from the area so that there was little chance of them meeting up with Scapula's Fourteenth Legion. Caradoc knew one legion would be more than enough to cope with.

The camp was evacuated early the following morning, apart from another small group of Madrun's men who stayed behind. Their task was to build large bonfires and cover them with damp grass to make sure they generated vast clouds of smoke.

If the Twentieth Legion, for one reason or another, came in that direction, the bonfires would be lit to attract attention and divert the enemy away from Caradoc's chosen battleground on the plateau. The Twentieth would believe the camp was occupied, thus delaying them long enough for a battle to take place without them taking part.

Preparations for the battle began as soon as everyone else arrived at the plateau.

One group of men clambered down to the river and built a high wall from boulders in the scree to plug gaps where the northern slope was less steep and easier for the enemy to climb.

Another team hacked down trees at the southern end of the hill. Stripped branches were heaped in piles and the trunks stacked in pyramids above the northern cliff edge. Children scoured the bank of the river for rounded, smooth pebbles while huddles of women made arrows.

The few small carts, chariots, horses, mules and cattle remaining were sheltered under the trees at the southern end of the plateau, well out of the way in case the Romans managed to scale the cliff and break through the defences.

Women and children traditionally accompanied warriors preparing for battle and remained nearby to help tend the injured. A small band of travelling druids, carrying copious supplies of poisons and drugs, appeared from nowhere to help fatally wounded warriors on their way into the next world. Like vultures, they seemed to know instinctively when fresh corpses were imminent.

Caradoc and Madrun gave orders, often looking nervously towards the hills and valleys where Scapula's bonfires had been the day before.

'We need to attract his attention in this direction,' said Madrun.

'Yes. The sooner he gets here, the better. The longer we delay, the more chance there is of the Twentieth attacking from our rear.'

'A fire should do the trick,' said Madrun. He went off to organise one.

'Plenty of smoke until nightfall,' called Caradoc after him. 'And bright fires at night!'

'Of course!' Caradoc did state the obvious at times.

An hour or two later, the muted sound of a distant horn punctured the air. Gerand and Carys, who had been keeping a watchful eye out from the edge of the plateau, shouted for their father to come and see.

'Romans! There!'

Auxiliaries led the way from woodland into the open land alongside the river. Behind them came the cavalry, followed by the standard bearer and infantrymen of the Fourteenth Legion with a train of heavily laden mules and wagons trundling along at the rear.

There were thousands of them, marching like regimented ants as far as the eye could see. Another blast from a horn gave the signal for the men to fall out and prepare to set up camp for the night. While they did so, two men dressed in highly ornate uniforms slid off their horses and stood at the river's edge.

'At last we've caught up with him,' said a gleeful Scapula, rubbing his hands together. 'I told you, follow the bonfires!'

'Strong position,' observed Quintus, ruefully. 'I don't suppose there's another approach.'

'Send scouts out to check the side valleys. I'd prefer a three-pronged attack if possible.'

'And I'll send word to the Twentieth.'

'That won't do much good. It'll take the best part of a day to get a message to them; they'd never get here in time. If we wait, Caradoc will escape. I'm not having that. I've waited years for this!'

Ten men waded in waist-high water across the rapidly flowing river. Caroline saw them divide into two groups holding shields aloft to protect them from missiles heading in their direction from the top of the plateau. One group circled to the left, the other to the right. The ground was extremely boggy underfoot.

Each group made its way into one of the narrow valleys. Moments later, two soldiers reappeared from the entrance to the left valley, and only one from the right. Caradoc had been prepared for this and positioned archers and slingers in the woods to prevent the enemy from approaching from those sides. He needed the Romans to attack from the steep northern slope and allowed a few scouts to escape so that they could report back to Scapula.

There was nothing more the Britons could do but wait until the attack began.

Night in the open was cold and uncomfortable, but at least it hadn't rained; even the grubby, dilapidated huts at Caradoc's last camp would have been better than nothing.

No one slept very well; the woods were full of suspicious sounds, and not just of men sharpening their swords for the umpteenth time. Everyone wondered what the outcome of the battle would be and who would survive. Even the fires, burning brightly as they did in the darkness, gave little comfort.

Caroline, Gerand and Carys sat at the edge of the cliff until well after darkness fell, watching the enemy sentries patrolling between the tents on the other side of the river. Every now and then they caught a fleeting glimpse of something darting past the fires, possibly a wild animal scavenging for food. Eventually they decided to try to get some sleep.

The next day would be long, tiring and dangerous.

Dawn came, far too soon. Caroline kept well out of the way while everyone prepared themselves for the big event.

Every face clearly was etched with fear and anxiety. A few could remember what had happened the last time Caradoc had fought the Romans in a pitched battle, but that was eight or nine years before. The human mind has a habit of shutting out dreadful experiences but memory also has a habit of dragging them back again. The reality of those memories was unsettling.

Caradoc and Madrun ran tirelessly from one group to the next, making sure their warriors knew what was expected of them.

Meanwhile, across the river, the Romans were also getting ready. A few auxiliaries tossed small items into the river as bribes for their gods to protect them during the battle.

Quintus and Scapula were examining innumerable spears whose long metal ends had been bent into U shapes, making them totally useless; they didn't seem very happy.

Woad-painted warriors, with hair tied into topknots to make them seem taller and more daunting, taunted the enemy from vantage points above the crags, beating swords and spears against shields. They made an incredible din.

Scapula and Quintus gave orders to their company officers. Standard bearers stood silently in front of the men in their platoons, ready to lead when their group was ordered to attack: it was a great honour to be chosen for this job; unfortunately, it was a job with no guaranteed long term prospects. Standards had to be held high at all times so that generals knew where each company was at any given time and how well (or badly) they were performing. Fallen standards led to confusion; the enemy knew that and so standard bearers became prime targets.

Scapula walked along the full length of his massed army, shouting words of encouragement to each and every one of his men. It was almost impossible for his voice to be heard above the din descending from the plateau.

'Some of you will die today,' he yelled. 'If we win, we shall earn great honours for ourselves and for Rome. Caratacus has been a thorn in our side too long! This is your chance to avenge your dead comrades and crush him once and for all. Victory shall be ours! For the honour of Rome, fight as you have never fought before!'

He nodded to a horn blower whose instrument looked like a large curved brass trumpet. As soon as it issued its resonating mellow sound, a contingent of auxiliaries stepped into in the murkily turbulent waters of the river.

High on the hill, Caradoc was also finishing a speech to his warriors.

'Fight for your honour and your families' futures! Do you want to live in slavery?'

'NO!'

'Do you want to spend the rest of your lives as outlaws?'

'NO!'

'This may be our last chance to expel the Romans from Britain! Fight for your freedom!'

'Long live Caradoc! Death to the Romans!'

'Light the bonfires! Take up your positions!'

Caradoc noticed Gerand and Carys standing behind him.

'This is no place for you! Join your mother in the trees; it's safer there. Before you go ...' A look of intense concern crossed his brow. He put his arms around them. 'This may be the last time I see you. If anything happens to me, flee with your mother to Gwirocon. He'll take care of you. Now go! I love you both!'

Caroline saw tears in his eyes. She turned away to look over the edge towards the river.

The first auxiliaries had already crossed the river but countless casualties were floating face down with arrows and spears firmly embedded in their bodies.

Something caught her eye near the long line of stationary Roman soldiers on the far bank. A horse was making its way slowly across the river. Surely it couldn't be? Yes! Yes! It was Tim's horse! It stumbled several times in the clinging mud before reaching the other side. It trotted into the wooded valley on the right.

Caroline ran back to the trees and leapt onto her own horse. Before she could leave, Gerand ran over. 'Caroline? Are you here?'

'Keep your voice down!'

'Where're you going?'

'Tim's horse is on its way here. At least, I think it's Tim's! I'll be back soon!'

She galloped away, down into the valley where several warriors were still hiding in the undergrowth ready to shoot any enemy attempting to attack that way. Tim's horse came trotting towards her.

'Caroline?'

'Oh, Tim! I've missed you!'

'Ditto. We can't stay here. Take me up to the camp.'

They rode up the valley; bemused British faces watched the two riderless horses disappear behind the trees. Caroline pulled her reins, stopping her horse out of sight from prying eyes and ears.

'Let's talk before we go up,' said Caroline.

'No time. The battle's started!'

'I know. But how did you get here?'

'Followed Scapula. Knew he'd find Caradoc eventually and I felt sure you wouldn't be far away.'

'Why didn't you come over last night?'

'I spent most of the time bending spears, chucking arrows on fires and damaging catapults! You should've seen Scapula's face when he found out!' He grinned from ear to ear. 'Thought it would help Caradoc. Pity I didn't have time to do more damage! Mind you, I've cut and blistered my hands something terrible. Look.' He held out his hands, palms upwards. They were covered in dried blood, numerous thin cuts and red blisters. His skin seemed green.

Caroline winced.

'Yuk! Why's your skin green?'

'I rubbed in wild marigold leaves. The juice is supposed to be good for cuts. At least, that's what Gwirocon told me once.'

'I think he was having you on. Did it work?'

'Seems to. They're not smarting as badly as they did a few hours ago.'

'Good. So that was you last night! We saw something darting behind the fires!'

'Yeah! Nearly got caught once or twice ... What do you mean, 'we'?'

'Gerand and Carys. We were watching you.'

'They know about you?'

'They know about us! How do you think I've survived? I'd be lost without them!'

'Look, we can't stop here. They may need us on top.'

Caroline was not in a hurry to return.

'I don't want to kill people again, Tim.'

He could tell from the tone in her voice that she was having problems coming to terms with the outcome of the Caer Caradoc ambush.

'We didn't kill anyone; the warriors did!' insisted her brother. 'We may even have saved a few lives by interfering! And we might be able to do the same now! C'mon! We're wasting time!'

Reluctantly, Caroline felt he was right but it didn't dispel the guilt. Her stomach began to churn at the thought of what she would see once the Romans reached the top of the plateau. She led the way back.

After dismounting and making very brief introductions to Carys and Gerand, who had to take it for granted that Tim's voice came from a real invisible person, Caroline and Tim dodged their way between warriors to a vantage point on one side of the plateau.

Auxiliaries continued to surge across the river, using fallen comrades as stepping stones and holding shields aloft to protect themselves from the steady deluge of arrows, spears and slingshot.

The Roman attack concentrated on the hastily constructed wall of boulders above the scree. Desperate hands tore in fury against this formidable obstacle. Unless it could be removed, and quickly, the number of casualties would be unbelievable. And there was no other way to reach the enemy at the top of the slope. Progress was hindered by having to haul the dead out of the way and by the piles of burning branches hurled down from above, setting fire to their clothing. Agonised screams echoed around the hills.

Dogged persistence in the face of adversity eventually paid off. But the Britons were not beaten yet. No sooner had the wall been demolished and the auxiliaries began scrambling, clawing, their way desperately up the slippery stone scree amid a constant barrage of missiles than the warriors above introduced a new weapon. Massive, sturdy tree trunks thudded loudly as they bounced off rocks before knocking the soldiers over like tenpins at a bowling alley.

A horn blasted a different tune. The auxiliaries slowly, carefully retreated across the blood-stained river and regrouped. Almost a third of their number had perished and lay scattered across the mud-churned ground or floated silently, peacefully, downriver.

Scapula viewed the wildly cheering horde on the plateau with disdain. The auxiliaries, expendable as they were, had achieved their objective; breaking through to the top would have been a bonus but you can't have everything. The next stage of the attack could begin. He gave an order to the horn blower, who blew the signal to attack.

Shield-bearing soldiers of the Fourteenth Legion wound their way to the crossing point like elongated centipedes with hundreds of legs only just visible beneath its scaly body. Their standard bearer, holding the legion's proud and precious steel eagle aloft, led the way.

An officer, with sword outstretched, yelled orders. As if by magic, the whole length of soldiers silently transformed itself into numerous testudos.

The standard bearer waded into the water. He felt very vulnerable and knew his days were numbered. Several arrows pierced his armour before he reached the other side. He fell, squirming in agony until the feet of comrades crushed his body into the mud where he lay still, unseen and forgotten in the heat of battle.

Another soldier fumbled for the legionary standard in the churning water and took up his position, leading metal-studded, leather-soled, regulation army-issue sandaled comrades over the uneven surface of mud, stones and bodies on their disciplined, relentless way forward.

More tree trunks and burning branches rained down, more men were sent flying backwards into their comrades, more clothing burst into flames. The first testudo scattered, only to be replaced by the next. And the next. And the next. Each fresh group, in spite of all that came their way, made a little more progress. And every time the eagle fell, it was raised with renewed determination.

A Roman hand clung to a rock at the top of the slope, only to be viciously severed by a British longsword. Its owner's screams faded away as he bounced downwards from shield to shield until he lay, lifeless, face-down in the mire; by that time, several of his former comrades were already fighting hand-to-hand with the enemy. The defences had been breached!

While Scapula nodded with approval from across the river, Caradoc's worst fears were becoming very real.

The Romans, having broken through, fought desperately to reform testudos and create a protective wall between the warriors in front and the soldiers following up behind.

Little by little, walls of impenetrable shields pushed the defenders back further, creating more space for others to join them. Warriors threw themselves at the walls, some even leapt onto the shields forming roofs; they tried everything to break through. Small successes were countered by even more defeats. The Romans were gradually gaining the upper hand.

'We cannot hold them much longer!' yelled Madrun to Caradoc. 'We must retreat!'

Before Caradoc had a chance to respond, Madrun signalled his men to retreat into the woods. Caradoc's heart sank; why couldn't Madrun have waited a little longer? Even some of his own men fled. It wouldn't be long before the rest followed.

'Fall back! Regroup!' he yelled, straining to shout above the noise of battle.

His warriors did as they were ordered and formed a deep line across the full width of the plateau. The Romans, glad to be offered the chance for a brief rest, stood their ground. Caradoc realised, too late, that more and more Romans were arriving. In only a few seconds, a long, solid wall of shields stood before him; it grew deeper by the minute.

'I'll tell the women and children to flee,' said Cunorix quietly.

Caradoc nodded. 'I think this may be the end,' he said, grimly.

The Gaul made his way behind the warriors, who had resumed their shield-bashing and yelling with renewed vigour, and ordered the onlookers to flee as quickly and silently as they could. He returned to Caradoc's side.

'Good luck, my friend! I'll meet you later. Either here or in the next world!' They shook hands firmly.

A horn sounded again from behind the Roman front line. Hundreds of spears whooshed into the air, over the line and thudded into unlucky warriors or their shields; very few actually landed in the ground. The horn sounded again and soldiers began to beat a rhythm with swords on their shields. It was slow, in unison, menacing. They moved forward, stepping in time to the relentless beat.

Caradoc was powerless to prevent his men lurching forwards, hurling themselves against the wall with little effect. Many fell back, blood gushing from well-rehearsed stabs thrust out from gaps in the shields which immediately closed up after inflicting lethal damage.

Despite their greater numbers, the Britons were too closely packed together to wield their long swords. And their arrows, spears and slingshot had no effect on the advancing shields.

The warriors were forced backwards, metre by metre, their fallen comrades crushed beneath advancing sandals.

Only the silent druids were allowed to pass through the enemy line; they knelt beside one dying warrior after another, pouring sweet poison into screaming mouths to put a rapid end to agonising suffering.

Caradoc, realising the battle had now been lost, had two choices; order a retreat or fight to the bitter end and die with his men.

'Retreat,' advised Cunorix. He knew how his master's mind worked. 'Retreat, and we can fight another day. We'll be slaughtered if we stay here! And what for? Rome will rule all Britain! Curse Madrun for fleeing too soon!'

'What's done is done,' said Caradoc. 'Order the retreat.'

Panic spread throughout the defenders. From now on, it was every man for himself. They turned on their heels, making straight for the cover of the woods.

Caradoc felt as though everything was conspiring against him. His way was blocked by slow-moving carts, womenfolk, children and frightened animals. Branwena and her children desperately struggled to push their way through the fleeing horde. They got nowhere fast.

Caradoc fought his way through the confusion and grabbed hold of the horse pulling his wife's cart. Trees and terrified folk rushing this way and that blocked the way; escape would only be possible by turning the cart back towards the open ground in front of the enemy line and circling round the trees to where his own small chariot was parked. It would be extremely dangerous.

The Roman horn sounded again, giving the signal for soldiers to break ranks and pursue the enemy. They did so with relish; everyone who stood in their way was hacked down mercilessly. Some misguided, bloodthirsty warriors determined to avenge dead comrades put up a strong fight. It was to no avail, but at least it delayed the enemy advance for a short time.

Branwena's cart trundled towards the battlefield, Gerand and Carys clinging to its sides. The wobbly wheel thudded against a tree; its spokes shattered. The cart lurched over, tipping everyone out in a heap. Caradoc rushed to their aid.

A soldier saw what happened and sprinted towards them. Gwirocon's horses blocked his way. Cunorix ran to Caradoc's side, sword raised high ready to strike. Branwena, Gerand and Carys stood terrified behind them.

'Cunorix!' The Roman exclaimed in astonishment.

Cunorix turned round, equally surprised. 'Marek! Is that you?'

They stood, staring at each other, dumbfounded. Other soldiers were slowly slashing their way towards them.

'Marcus, this is Tim!' shouted a voice from nowhere. 'Let them go! Before it's too late!'

Marcus was not the only one taken by surprise.

'Spirit Tim? Is that you?'

'Yes. Let them go!'

Gwirocon's horses stood resolutely between Marcus and the others. Marcus didn't know what to do. Friendship said let them escape. Duty told him to attack. His future had to lie with duty; there was no choice. He tried to get past the horses; they blocked his way again. Perhaps he was wrong. He gave in.

'Cunorix, it was good to see you again, but get the hell out of here! Take Caratacus with you!'

'I can't leave my family!' yelled Caradoc.

'There's not enough room in your chariot for them all! Go now, while you have the chance!'

'Gerand! Give me your hand!' screamed Caroline. She yanked him onto her horse and trotted out of the way.

Soldiers were heading in their direction.

'Yes, go my husband, before it's too late!' Branwena gave Caradoc a quick kiss and looked lovingly into his frustrated tear-filled eyes. 'This good man will take care of us. Go! Go!' She pushed him away.

Cunorix leapt into the chariot, all but hauled Caradoc in after him and flicked the reins, Caradoc looked back at them with a terrible expression on his face. They disappeared into the trees.

'Carys, come here!' yelled Tim, holding his arm out. Carys was confused. She heard his voice but couldn't see him. Unlike Gerand, who had been helped onto a horse by an invisible rider several times, she didn't know what to do.

A short sword whacked Tim's horse hard on its backside: it shied and ran off in Caroline's direction. Tim tugged the reins as hard as he could to go back, but it was no use.

Marcus turned and saw he had been joined by three of his comrades. He dithered; humbled on the one side by this beautiful, brave woman and her daughter, and hounded by men from his own legion on the other. He glanced around, suddenly feeling disgusted at the sight of his comrades hacking down other women and children. After all his years in the army, it dawned on him that slaughtering the innocent was cowardly and totally unnecessary.

Unfortunately, his comrades were not so enlightened. Seeing Marcus apparently doing nothing to the rebels cowering before him, they ran up to him, dripping swords at the ready.

'What's up, Marcus? Lost your bottle?'

'Leave them alone! It's Caratacus's family!'

'So what?'

They tried to dodge past. Marcus stood in their way. They moved again. So did he. He wondered how long he could keep this up for. Branwena and Carys were still cowering silently on the ground. There was no hope now that Tim and Caroline had gone.

'Spirits deserted you, Marcus?' One of the men sneered. 'Got to look after yourself for a change? Are you with us or against us?'

Fortunately, Scapula appeared.

'Marcus! You again! Who have you there?'

'Caratacus's wife and child, sir. Thought it best not to kill them!'

'Well done!' He rounded on the others. 'Use your heads, idiots! Don't kill everyone, take prisoners; we can sell them for slaves! Well, what are you waiting for? Get on with it!'

Tim, Caroline and Gerand watched in dismay while Branwena and Carys were bound by Marcus and led away. Nothing could be done to save them now.

'Let's get out of here,' said Caroline. 'Gwirocon will know what to do.'

'I ought to go to my mother and sister,' said Gerand. 'Give myself up. Dad will never forgive me for deserting them!'

'You didn't desert them,' insisted Caroline.

'I hope Carys will be all right,' said Tim. His voice was barely audible. If only she'd grabbed his hand. 'Follow me; I know the way back.'

Caradoc and Cunorix managed to escape the battlefield moments before Roman cavalry entered the valleys on either side of the plateau. They were now safely out of harm's way.

'Where to?' asked Cunorix.

'To Brigantia,' replied Caradoc. 'See!'

He pointed at the low front rail of the chariot. Someone had scratched something in Latin with a dagger.

It read: 'AD CARTIMANDUAM ITE. IAM!'

'FLEE TO CARTIMANDUA. NOW!'

Caradoc's chariot.

CHAPTER 19

Traitors and Travellers

'You did well to get here without being caught,' said Gwirocon. 'But what do we do now?'

'Rescue Carys and mum,' said Gerand, hopefully. If anyone could do it, surely Caroline and Tim could. Perhaps he was hoping for the impossible.

'I don't see how. Have you any ideas?' said Gwirocon, talking to the barely visible faces sitting near the candle on his table.

'Not without causing trouble for the Cornovians,' answered Tim reluctantly.

Caroline shook her head.

'And Caradoc said you were to come here if anything happened to him?' asked Gwirocon: he sounded very concerned.

'Yes, sir,' replied Gerand glumly.

'Well, he hasn't been caught yet, as far as I know. So he may try to send word to me.'

'Everyone fled in all directions after the battle. Those who survived, I mean,' said Caroline.

Silence reigned for a short time while they each reflected on the hundreds slaughtered on – and off – the battlefield. And those put to sleep by the druids. Strange the Romans didn't kill them as well, considering how much Scapula hated druids. He must really respect their supernatural powers; being superstitious, he probably respected anyone who stood between Men and their gods.

'Anyone any idea where they may have gone?'

Tim looked away. Caroline noticed but didn't say anything. Gerand shrugged his shoulders. 'Madrun didn't say anything about meeting up somewhere, did he?' he asked.

Still no one said anything.

'This is like talking to the dead!' Gwirocon was exasperated. He needed straight answers!

'Don't say that!' implored Caroline. 'I never want to see another dead person as long as I live!'

Gerand tried to put an arm around her. He gave up and felt a little jealous to see Tim succeed where he had failed.

'Scapula may send out search parties as soon as he gets back,' said Caroline. 'To look for Caradoc or Gerand.' She couldn't resist giving her heartthrob a smile over Tim's shoulder. Gerand blushed. Gwirocon noticed and turned away discreetly. Really!

'Do any of you have any idea where Caradoc may have gone?'

'We'll just have to wait and see what happens,' said Tim. There was something in his voice which made Gwirocon raise an eyebrow, but he let it pass. 'I'll go to the fort in two or three days' time. Scapula will be too busy to get back much before then.'

'It's late. Get some sleep.' Gwirocon sensed he would get no more information for the time being. 'We'll talk again in the morning. You can have my bed, Gerand. I'll sleep in the king's house next door.'

He left, deeply troubled, without uttering another word.

Gerand lay on the bed. Caroline blew out the candle.

'We're going outside for a few minutes,' said Caroline, grabbing Tim's arm and pulling him towards the door. 'I want to have a private word with my brother.'

'I can take a hint. Don't be too long.'

Caroline dragged Tim until they were well away from the roundhouses in the village.

'What do you know that I don't?' she asked tersely.

'How'd you mean?'

'Back there. When Gwirocon asked where Caradoc had gone. You know, don't you?'

'Not for sure, no.'

'But you've got some idea!'

'OK, so he may have gone to Queen Cartimandua.'

'To Cartimandua? You must be joking! She'd hand him straight over to Scapula!'

Tim didn't respond.

'Why Cartimandua? Why not one of his friends, like Venutius?'

Tim still didn't say anything.

'Tim, talk to me! What makes you think he's gone to her?'

'I scratched something on Caradoc's chariot.'

'What?'

'Flee to Cartimandua. Now.'

Caroline was gobsmacked.

'You prat! Do you realise what you've done?'

No reply.

'Let's hope he didn't see what you wrote.' It was a forlorn hope.

'That's why I said I didn't know for sure. But if he did, he may think it was a message from the supernatural and do as he was told.'

'The supernatural? No, he wouldn't be so superstitious.'

'Why not? He'd just heard me yelling at Marcus, remember? He must have realised something odd was going on.'

'But why Cartimandua, of all people?'

Tim was very reluctant to explain. She'd go ballistic!

'You've got to tell me! We're in this together!'

'Look,' he said eventually. 'Madrun's warriors have scattered all over the place and Caradoc didn't know where they'd gone. Venutius is in no position to help ... yet. Cartimandua seemed the best bet.'

'But why her? She'll kill him!'

'No, she won't! Caradoc's more use to her alive; she's already in Rome's pocket and will try to get some sort of reward from Scapula. All she thinks about is her own luxurious lifestyle.'

'But wouldn't Caradoc have been able to get the Brigantians to side with Venutius?'

'No, but they will if Cartimandua hands him over to Scapula. They'll hate her for handing over a national hero.'

This time it was Caroline's turn not to say anything. She couldn't argue with what Tim had said but she still thought he'd done the wrong thing.

'That's the way it is in the history books,' Tim continued. 'OK, so Scapula was prepared to kill Caradoc on the battlefield because he wouldn't have had much option. But if Caradoc's caught alive, Scapula'll be able to hand him over to Claudius. The Senate will love him!'

'And what about Caradoc and Branwena? And Carys and Gerand?'

'I know what dad's history books say. We'll just have to make sure they're right without giving too much away to Gwirocon, and certainly not to Gerand.'

'What do you mean?'

'Trust me. You'll see.'

Gwirocon still wasn't sure what to do for the best. Although it was unlikely anyone, apart from this Marcus character, knew what Gerand looked like, if Scapula discovered he was harbouring the son of his arch-enemy, all the druid king's efforts to keep the Romans happy would be undermined.

Wraith Tim knew something, of that he was sure. The candle-light might have been dim and his eyes could have been playing tricks but he was certain the boy had purposely not answered his questions. It had been the same throughout the two days after they'd returned. Try as he might, Tim had evaded direct questions. If only Gwirocon could find out why.

While Caroline and Gerand remained in the druid's hut, Tim visited Castra Cornoviorum on his own shortly after dawn. The atmosphere there was much more positive than it had been at any time before in the fort's brief existence; soldiers went about their daily chores in a jubilant mood; several even whistled merrily. That in itself was a novelty.

Everyone, that is, except Scapula and his prisoners.

From what Tim overheard from the soldiers, every prisoner able to stand and hold a shovel had been allowed to bury the British dead while druids chanted over the graves and guards stood near-by. At the same time, Romans gathered their own dead and laid them in a communal grave; there were far more Roman casualties than British, a sobering fact not overlooked by Scapula.

At least the revolt had been crushed; that was some consola-tion. But the elusive Caratacus had managed to slip through his fingers yet again! As for that Marcus, well, he'd kept Caradoc's wife and daughter alive which, for a bloodthirsty Gaul (all Gauls were bloodthirsty in his opinion, only good for battle fodder), showed a commendable degree of forethought. Not like the rest of his moronic army, who'd kill everything that breathed. He now had something Caratacus wanted. Badly.

The journey back to Castra Cornoviorum, although less than thirty miles, had been slow going. Over two hundred prisoners had been captured, including more women and children than Scapula had hoped. Most of the captured warriors had minor injuries and would survive to suffer whatever punishment he decided to impose. Much depended on how well they co-operated.

The prisoners were crammed into a fenced-off, heavily guarded compound behind the governor's residence inside the fort. They were brought to Scapula, one by one, for questioning.

He didn't get very far: no one knew to where Caradoc, Madrun or any of the escaped warriors had fled, nor where Madrun's stronghold lay if, indeed, he had one. Tim watched prisoner after prisoner enter Scapula's office and leave a few minutes later. He'd scoured the group of miserable captives while the interrogations progressed but couldn't see Carys or Branwena anywhere.

'Bring Caratacus's wife to me!' Scapula ordered a soldier.

Tim followed him to a small workshop not far from Scapula's office. A sentry stood outside. Tim darted in when the door was opened to let Branwena out. Carys was left inside, chained firmly to the wall. She'd been crying.

'How are they treating you?' whispered Tim once the door closed behind him and a bolt shot into place.

'Tim!'

'Hush! Keep your voice down!'

He sat beside her and put an arm around her shoulders.

'Oh, Tim! Where's Gerand? Is he safe?'

'He's with Gwirocon and Caroline, but don't tell anyone, not even your mum. Scapula mustn't find out!'

'At least he's free! Do you know where dad is?'

'No,' he said. He wasn't really lying; he didn't know for sure whether Caradoc had gone to Cartimandua or not. 'Gwirocon doesn't know what to do for the best. He's worried in case Scapula finds out he's hiding your brother. Gerand misses you terribly.'

She began to weep. Tim held her tightly. He knew exactly how she felt. They sat quietly together. Tim kissed her hair and cheek several times. By him moving slightly towards her, she was able to hold him and get the sort of love and comfort a mother just cannot give.

The bolt shot across. Branwena returned.

'I'll have to go!' Tim gave Carys a quick kiss on the lips; she barely had time to respond, but it was enough. 'I'll be back!'

Several more days went by. Tim and Caroline paid regular visits to the fort, not all of which were satisfactory because they couldn't get in to see Carys without arousing suspicion.

Gwirocon had given up trying to squeeze information of out Tim and had to be content with reassurances that 'something will turn up'. Fortunately, Scapula was too busy to be bothered with visiting Gwirocon, so Gerand's presence there, for the time being at least, didn't cause a problem.

It was during one of their visits that Caradoc and Cunorix were hauled in chains before a delighted Scapula. Their arrival was greeted by the soldiers with an interesting mixture of ecstatic enthusiasm and subdued awe. So this was the man who had caused them so much grief!

After despatching a cartload of amphorae of wine and spices to Queen Cartimandua, as a sign of Rome's appreciation for the betrayal of a fellow Briton, Caradoc was dragged into Scapula's office. The door slammed shut before unseen visitors could slip inside, so Tim and Caroline sat in the shadows watching Cunorix.

'Cheer up! Yer still in the land of the livin'!' said a cheery voice.

Cunorix looked up. A smile broke across his careworn and dejected features.

'Marek!'

'Shame about getting caught!'

'I knew we shouldn't have gone to that ... that bitch!' responded Cunorix bitterly.

'Look on the bright side: yer still alive. Surely that's worth something!'

'But for how long?'

'No brother of mine is going to be executed,' said Marcus.

So, Cunorix and Marcus were brothers!

'I can't see how you can prevent it, Marek. Slavery or death; that's what happens to rebels, isn't it? Let's change the subject. You seem to have done well for yourself, even if you are on the enemy's side now. I haven't seen you since our father was killed.'

'I didn't have much choice when they caught me. Join the army or die. I chose to live: seemed the better option at the time. At least it gave me a future. Bit risky mind, but it's not that bad.'

Cunorix remembered what Caradoc had said to Madrun: 'Death is forever. There is no glory'. Perhaps he had a point. Death was the end, no sun on your face. Cunorix liked the outdoor life. He didn't want to enter the next world just yet.

'Have you gone mad?' demanded Gwirocon. 'Give Gerand up? Have you the remotest idea what Scapula would do to him?'

Tim nodded.

'It's for the best. Look, Gwirocon, he needs to be with his sister and parents, he's sick with worry. I know he wants to rejoin them. He's said as much to Caroline. And there's no way we can rescue Caradoc.'

Gwirocon fixed him with a hard stare.

'What is it you're keeping from me? You knew where Caradoc had gone and that he'd be betrayed by Cartimandua, didn't you?'

'Yes! No! I didn't know for sure.'

'Whyever did he even think of going to her? He's not stupid!'

'I scratched a note on Caradoc's chariot.'

'But why to Cartimandua, of all people?'

Tim didn't answer. Gwirocon calmed down.

'There's more to what you're not saying, I can sense it. You know what's going to happen, don't you?'

'Not definitely. Oh, Gwirocon, I know what's supposed to happen!'

'What?'

'I can't tell you!'

'Why not?'

'Because it could affect what you and the Britons do in the future.'

'But how do you know? Surely you and your sister being here has a purpose? And don't talk to me about changing the course of history! You've been interfering ever since you came!'

'This is different. Caradoc's life is at stake. And his family's.'

Gwirocon sat in silence for a few minutes. His eyes lit up.

'Then can't you give history a nudge in the right direction?'

'How'd you mean?' Tim was intrigued.

'With your knowledge, couldn't you, well, suggest something?'

'Perhaps.'

'It's just that it doesn't seem right that King Caradoc should be executed after all he's been through. He deserves better. As do his family. They've suffered a lot since the Romans invaded.'

Tim nodded. He could see the sense of Gwirocon's proposal.

'OK. But you must do exactly as I say.'

'What's oak hay got to do with it?'

'Never mind. Just listen.'

It took hours of heart rending, soul searching, discussion before Gerand agreed to give himself up. After hearing Gwirocon's reasons, he had little choice but to follow the druid king's advice.

Caroline understood it was probably the best course of action for him to take: he belonged with his family, whatever the outcome, and Caroline's future couldn't possibly be with him. It hurt her to have to admit it.

Tim remained silent and refused to join in the conversation.

He had other things on his mind.

Gwirocon led Gerand, who held his head high and did his best not to appear frightened, to the fort. A sentry challenged them.

'I have urgent business with Governor Ostorius Scapula. Take me to him immediately!' commanded Gwirocon.

The sentry led the way; Scapula was standing near his office.

'Welcome, King Gwirocon! These are happy days indeed! Who's that?' he added, noticing the grubby youth at the druid king's side.

'This is Gerand,' answered Gwirocon in a matter of fact sort of way. 'The son of Caratacus.'

Scapula's eyes lit up.

'He arrived at my door last night. He's decided he should rejoin his family. Whatever the outcome.'

Scapula looked at Gerand thoughtfully.

'You're either very noble or extremely stupid,' he observed.

'Sir, I didn't want to cause any trouble. I just want to be with my family.' He burst into tears.

'Don't overdo it,' thought Caroline.

'How've you been feeding yourself?' Scapula hoped the boy would disclose Madrun's whereabouts.

'I didn't eat anything until I found King Gwirocon,' he whined.

'You there! Marcus, isn't it? Take the boy to his mother. Gwirocon, you come with me.'

Caroline followed Scapula into the office. Tim went after Marcus and Gerand. He grinned when cries of joy came from behind the bolted door of Branwena's cell.

'Marcus,' said Tim when they were out of the sentry's earshot. 'It's Tim. Can we go somewhere quiet to talk?'

Marcus turned a corner as if he hadn't heard and went into an empty stable.

'What is it, Tim?'

'Cunorix is your brother, right?'

'Yeah. What of it?'

'You want to save him?'

'Not much chance of that. Why?'

'Speak to Scapula. Tell him the facts. Be honest. Tell him you'd like him to be given another chance, with the auxiliary. If he objects, say that it doesn't seem a good idea to let a brave fighter and excellent slinger be sent all the way to Rome either to be executed or given the opportunity to join the auxiliary anyway. Say you'll vouch for him.'

'I'll have to ask Cunorix first; he may not agree.'

'I'm sure he will. He's in the same position as you were. Life or death? No choice, or had you forgotten?'

'Yer a good person, Spirit Tim. I'll do it!'

'There's something else. My sister and I would like to see Gerand and Carys before they're taken to Rome ...'

'How'd yer know they'll be goin' there?'

'Trust me. I know a lot. Including that you'll be promoted to standard bearer and eventually become a centurion!'

Marcus's smile almost stretched the full width of the stable.

'I'll be in touch!' Tim left to find Gwirocon and was relieved to see the druid king being led along the street towards a heavily guarded cell.

Tim stayed close to Gwirocon's side as he entered. Caradoc was pleased to see his old friend and trusted ally. The defeated king was bound with more chains than Marley's ghost in *A Christmas Carol*.

'Welcome, my friend!' Caradoc tried to stand but was held back by the chains. 'I'm sorry I cannot offer you my usual standard of hospitality.' He smiled, but the strain of an uncertain future overshadowed the forced sparkle in his eyes.

'Caradoc, I don't have much time.'

'What, no file to help me escape?'

'This is no laughing matter! I've come to offer some advice which may keep you and your family alive!'

'I hope it's sound advice, Gwirocon. The future doesn't have a long term feel about it.'

'I know you don't believe in signs from the spirits, but you must do exactly as I say.'

'Like following the horses to the ambush?'

'Precisely. Now, you're going to see ... well, something you won't believe. It's only a silly little thing, but it's to prove I'm in touch with the spirits of the future. They've told me what to say. Ready?'

Caradoc nodded. Had the druid been at the ale? His doubts dispelled when the chains lying across the floor rose of their own accord and wrapped themselves around his feet.

'I'm listening!'

'You, your family and the captives will soon be taken to Rome and paraded through the streets. You will be amazed to see the city; its buildings are as high as hills and made of stone. Thousands of people live there, not hundreds as in our villages. They regard you as a hero; this will be to your advantage.'

'A hero, eh?'

'Do not show any fear! Astonishment at the size of the city, yes, but not fear. You are a king, not a coward, meeting your fate with a proud and brave heart! You will be taken to the emperor.'

'Claudius?'

'Who else, assuming he hasn't been assassinated? Your captured kinfolk will plead for mercy and look pathetic and weak. When Claudius allows you to speak, do so with reason and dignity. The Romans will like that.'

'What do your spirits want me to say? Will they help me rehearse?'

'Caradoc, this is serious! Say that, if you had come to the city as a friend, you would have been treated with respect and honour. Say that you cannot imagine why the might of Rome should want to overrun a poor country with filthy hovels and a low standard of living compared to the buildings and prosperity of their wonderful city. Tell them you had palaces, lands, servants; is it no surprise you did not want to give them up to satisfy their own greed!'

'Is all that supposed to save my life?'

'Then say your execution will, in time, be forgotten. But if Claudius lets you live, his clemency and justice will shine out for generations to come.'

'Nice one! Will it work?'

'I strongly believe so. You will never, however, be allowed to return to Britain. Oh! I almost forgot. When you have finished your speech, bow to both Claudius and his wife Agrippina; she'll be sitting a short distance away. It's vital that you bow to her as well as the emperor!'

'Power behind the throne?'

'More than you can ever imagine! Never give her cause to complain!'

'So the Romans win after all.'

'Not entirely. Madrun will renew attacks in Ordovicia; hit and run ambushes, not pitched battles.'

'Huh! At least he's learned something!'

'And Venutius will lead the Brigantians in a revolt. Scapula thinks the war is over; it isn't, and he will die a broken man!'

'That's a great comfort. Thanks, Gwirocon, my friend.'

The chains unwound themselves.

'And thanks also to your spirits!' he added with a smile.

The following days passed far too quickly. Branwena was reunited with Caradoc in his cell while the children remained in their own; it was the Roman governor's way of ensuring the captive king made no attempt to escape.

Scapula treated them well and looked forward to a Triumph held in his honour in Rome, a privilege granted very rarely. He knew he would have to return to Britain to finish his period of duty, but believed it should be plain sailing from now on. Little did he know.

Marcus proved to be a valuable friend and offered to stand guard outside Gerand's and Carys's cell, even to the point of bribing his comrades so he could do this boring chore. No one noticed him surreptitiously open the door several times to let unseen visitors in and out.

If anyone with a lit candle had looked inside, they'd have wondered what on earth was going on. Tim and Carys cuddled up to each other in one corner of the cell while Caroline and Gerand did the same in another.

It crossed Caroline's mind that, if all four of them had been visible, it would have looked just like the party they'd thrown while their parents were away at a wedding; writhing, quietly smooching couples littering every square centimetre all over the house. If only their parents could see them now!

These wonderful heart-warming, breath-taking moments couldn't last forever: they knew separation would come sooner than they'd like. They were right.

The last view they had was of Marcus leading the Fourteenth Legion eastwards along Sarn Wydellin. Caradoc and his family were treated as royalty, which they were, and carried, still chained together, in a horse drawn wagon. The other prisoners, shackled by hand and foot, shuffled miserably between the lines of soldiers. It was a formidably long way to Rome and many wouldn't survive the journey.

Gwirocon's horses trotted beside the long train, to Scapula's amusement. One came very close to Marcus.

'Told you you'd be standard bearer!' called a voice discreetly from nowhere.

Marcus smiled, keeping his eye fixed on the road ahead.

'And me brother's joined the auxiliary! Thanks, Tim. Yer've been a great mate!'

The horses stopped on either side of Gwirocon, who stood watching from the end of the lane leading to his farmstead.

He waved back to Gerand and Carys as they passed, although their eyes were fixed on the spaces above the horses' saddles.

The weather began to get decidedly cooler and wetter. The time for the Cornovians to prepare for their usual winter occupation in The Wrekin hill fort was fast approaching.

Gwirocon, Caroline and Tim rode up the hill to see how much work needed to be done to repair the huts and clear the remnants of rotten grain from the storage pits. It was Gwirocon's duty as king to make sure his folk in the neighbourhood finished all repair work before the annual migration began.

After making mental notes, they sat down on a rock near the Needle's Eye.

Gwirocon looked at their vague outlines and smiled.

'Who'd have thought it?' he mused. 'Wraiths from the future saving me, my people and Caradoc!'

'Is there anything else we can do to help?' asked Caroline. 'We could be here for ever!'

'No, I somehow don't think so,' said Gwirocon. 'You came here for a purpose, I'm sure. And I think you've achieved it. I've learned so much from you. I feel like you're the family I never had. I'll miss you when you go.'

His voice trembled. Tears welled up in his eyes.

Tim noticed. A lump rose in his throat. He wanted to say something, but couldn't. It was all too emotional. They'd been through a lot together and the respect he felt for Gwirocon couldn't be put into words.

He stood, resting his hand on the druid king's shoulder. He squeezed it gently, not knowing what else he could do.

Tears streamed uncontrollably down Caroline's cheeks like droplets on a shower room wall. She leapt up and threw her arms around Gwirocon's neck. Her pendant brushed against the original one resting on the druid king's chest.

An almighty CRACK! knocked Gwirocon backwards, hurling him unceremoniously to the ground several metres away.

The last thing he saw was Caroline and Tim engulfed in an enormous sheet of ice-white, shimmering flame.

The Horseshoe Inn.

CHAPTER 20

Archaeology Rules, OK?

The hill walker simply didn't notice them. Two bodies suddenly appeared on the ground just as he was striding along the grass-covered slope towards the Needle's Eye.

'I'm terribly sorry,' he said most apologetically. 'I didn't see you. Left my glasses in the car.' He helped them up, very concerned that they were shaking so much.

'It's OK. We're fine,' Caroline managed to mutter. Her legs felt like jelly.

The walker gave them a quick glance to make sure, nodded and continued on his way.

Tim gazed around the top of the hill. The Iron Age huts and fort ramparts had disappeared. Clouds of steam belched reassuringly from Buildwas Power Station like they had before their adventure began. Tim glanced at his watch; it was working again!

'We're back! Caroline, we're back!' he exclaimed, far more relieved than he'd expected. The journey through nothingness had been really weird.

The relief was more than his sister could bear; floods of tears sprang from her eyes and trickled down her cheeks into the corners of her mouth. She clung to Tim, sobbing loudly.

The walker turned and looked at them briefly before scurrying out of sight down a gully.

'C'mon, dry up,' said Tim, gently. 'It's all over now. Let's go and find mom and dad.'

Their parents were still lying on the car blanket, just as the twins had left them years (or was it minutes?) before.

Mr Dale drowsily opened his eyes.

'That was quick! Been through the Eye already?'

'Oh, dad!' said Caroline, kneeling down to give him a massive hug.

'Steady on! What have I done to deserve this?'

Mrs Da'le gave Tim a brief but all-encompassing mother's scrutiny. She was aghast.

'What on earth! Tim! Just look at your clothes, they're worn out!' She sniffed the air around him. 'You stink something dreadful! And what have you done to your hair? Are you wearing a wig?'

Caroline clung to her father, not daring to move except to look at Tim through the corner of her eye. Of course! They hadn't had a decent wash and had worn the same clothes for at least two years! And Tim's hair was halfway down his back! Actually, it quite suited him.

Tim shuffled uneasily.

'Is that my rope? What the hell have you done to it? It's worn out!' Mr Dale shoved Caroline away and stood up. He was rather cross. 'You're just the same as him! Filthy!'

Caroline saw Tim's scarlet, guilt-ridden face and burst into tears again.

'We're going home! Now!' Their mother rammed everything into the picnic bag and stormed off towards Heaven Gate.

'You heard your mother! Get moving! You've got some serious explaining to do!'

No one said another word until they arrived home. While the children took showers, Mrs Dale shoved their grime-ridden threadbare clothes into the bin and emptied out their backpacks.

Her mood hadn't improved by the time they came downstairs. She was livid.

Mr Dale stood with his arms folded and looked deadly serious. He nodded towards two daggers lying on the table.

'You know what I think about knives,' he said. 'Where did you get these?'

Tim and Caroline struggled, without success, to stop themselves grinning. The daggers proved it had all happened!

'It's not a laughing matter!'

'Where did you get that pendant from?' demanded Mrs Dale. 'I've never seen it before and it looks expensive.'

Caroline looked down at her chest. She gasped.

'Tim! It looks brand new! Not a mark on it!'

'Dad ... mum. I think you should sit down. You won't believe what's happened to us.'

He was right. By the time he and Caroline finished recounting their adventures, their parents, who hadn't uttered a word, exchanged one of those 'I don't know where they get it from' looks and quietly suggested the twins might like to channel their vivid imaginations into doing their school assignments.

Oddly enough, this didn't upset Caroline or Tim at all. In fact, they couldn't wait to get started and went meekly (just to please mum and dad) to the study straight away.

Mrs Dale sat quietly, watching while her husband examined the daggers in some detail.

'Well?' she asked. 'What do you think they've really been up to?'

'All I can say for sure is that these daggers seem to be in too good a condition to be genuine, but I'll get them checked out. What puzzles me is how their hair grew so long in such a short time.'

'And how they got so smelly. It's impossible! Everything they've said is impossible!'

'But what harm have they done?' said Mr Dale. 'Ruined some old clothes and a rope. Let's see what they write for their home-work; we may discover the truth. And we'd better take them to the hairdresser tomorrow; they can't go around looking like that!'

'Why not? It suited you when you were younger!'

'Before it started falling out ... Kids, eh? Who'd have 'em?'

There was a strange atmosphere in the house for several days. After their hair had been clipped to normal length, Tim dropped his film off at Tesco's and waited in the Coffee Shop until it had been processed. The hour service seemed to take forever.

He tore open the envelope, aching to prove to his parents that their adventure had been real. His heart sank. Almost every photo had the same sticker smack in the middle. It read, 'This photograph has been incorrectly exposed or the film may be out of date. Consult your camera manual for advice.'

'Let me see,' said Caroline, snatching them. She couldn't believe it! Most of the pictures were fuzzy or completely blank.

'That's you in the sacred grove,' said Tim, pointing at a photo of Caroline, who could be seen facing the camera. There was no sign of Gwirocon standing behind her, the stone altar or the trees. 'And that's Marcus,' he added, glancing at another. 'And there's Gwirocon's roundhouse on The Wrekin!'

'Are you sure they weren't taken at the Wroxeter display? They do say the camera never lies,' observed Mr Dale drily.

'There weren't any roundhouses there! What we told you is true!' insisted Caroline. 'You've read my diary: why don't you believe us?'

'Let's go home,' said Mrs Dale, shaking her head. 'Finish your essays and we'll read them. We'd like to believe you, but, well, these things just don't happen in real life. Do they?'

A week passed. Mr Dale had only just finished reading Tim's account of Caradoc's struggle against the Romans when the post arrived. Caroline had written about King Gwirocon and the Cornovian way of life.

He slit the envelope and took out a sheet of paper. It was headed 'Thomas Downs, Forensic Consultant'.

'That's interesting. Tom says the daggers are extremely good replicas. Exact in every detail. Carbon dating implies they're only a few years old, not long enough to date accurately.'

'Where do you think they got them from? And Caroline's silver pendant?'

'No idea. Haven't a clue.'

They heard Tim and Caroline coming down the stairs. Mr Dale quickly stuffed the letter under a folder on the table.

'Well,' said Caroline. 'What did you think of our assignments?'

'They're excellent. Easily the best you've ever done by far. Trouble is, the detail you've included can't be proved.'

Tim was stunned. His parents knew they never lied, yet they still didn't believe them! Caroline's eyes filled with tears. She struggled unsuccessfully to hold them back. It really wasn't fair! How could they think they'd made it all up?

'You've kept your part of the bargain by doing your homework,' said Mrs Dale. 'Although goodness knows what Mr Hart will make of it. We'll take you to The Horseshoe Inn for lunch tomorrow.'

Her suggestion cheered them up slightly, but nothing could ease the hurt they felt.

How could their parents be so cruel?!

The short journey from Wellington-under-The-Wrekin was only five miles along the old A5 former main road heading towards Shrewsbury, Unfortunately, there was more traffic than usual and it took some time before Mrs Dale could overtake a very slow-moving yellow JCB digger.

The Horseshoe Inn was one of those old fashioned country pubs that had been refurbished and now catered for families. Mr Dale bought drinks from the bar while his wife ordered food. It didn't take long to arrive. The earth shook as the digger trundled past and up a narrow lane behind the pub.

They hadn't quite finished their meal when the pendant around Caroline's neck began to twitch. Mrs Dale was first to notice. She sat, transfixed. She nudged her husband.

'Er, Caroline,' he said. 'What are you doing to your pendant?'

'Nothing. Why?' She looked down at it.

The pendant was swinging, first one way, then the other. It stopped and suddenly shot into a horizontal position, as if being pulled by an unseen hand. 'It's pulling me!' she exclaimed.

The pendant tugged harder and harder. Caroline stood up and, seeing the look of complete astonishment on Tim's and her parents' faces, let it take her outside. It tugged, almost dragged, her along the potholed lane behind the pub, past a stable block on the left and left again at a bend in the road.

They stopped for a moment at the entrance to a field in which were several blue portakabins. The Wrekin summit was just visible in the distance. The digger chugged deafeningly as it scraped topsoil from an area marked out with pegs and string. A sign read:

SEVERN WATER, SERVING THE COMMUNITY WELL
Project to connect artesian borehole to Telford mains supply
KEEP OUT

The pendant yanked Caroline towards the digger. The driver noticed, switched off the engine and strode towards them.

'Can't you lot read?' he shouted, pointing to the sign. 'Hey! You can't go there!' he added angrily as Caroline walked, or rather, stumbled past. 'Here, what's goin' on?'

'Come with us,' answered Mr Dale. 'Something strange is happening!'

'You're tellin' me!'

The pendant fell back on Caroline's chest as soon as she reached the marked out area. Instead of pulling her forwards, the pendant was spinning wildly above the ground.

'Here,' said Mr Dale, whipping a note from his wallet and stuffing it into the bemused driver's hand. 'Dig where she's standing. Gently, mind. Bit at a time!'

'Oh, I don't know, guv.'

'You're supposed to be serving the community and you're digging there anyway! C'mon, man, get on with it!'

The digger scraped away the soil; the pendant kept on spinning. The JCB scraped a little deeper until Tim heard the metal bucket drag across something hard.

'Stop! Stop!' he yelled, waving his hands frantically. The man cut the engine.

Caroline's pendant stopped moving.

'Have you got a spade and broom?' said Tim.

'On the back of the cab.'

The man handed him a spade caked with hardened mortar. Union rules forbade him using it; he was a driver, highly skilled. Spades were for labourers.

Tim gently scraped the soil away until hundreds of small, flat stones were exposed.

'Tesserae! That's a mosaic!' gasped Mr Dale.

Even the driver was intrigued by the discovery. It took almost an hour of grossly unprofessional work scraping and brushing soil away until a large part of the mosaic was exposed. There was a pattern there, but the little stones were too dirty to make out what it was.

'We need water,' said Mr Dale, 'to highlight the pattern.'

'That's what Severn Water does best!' grinned the driver. 'I can fix a hose to the artesian well and squirt it over.'

He was as good as his word. While he directed the hose, Mrs Dale brushed water gently over the mosaic.

'It the same pattern as on my pendant, Gwirocon's talisman!' shrieked Caroline. 'Look, this is the hill in the centre, there's a moon and star and ...' She turned round. 'The sun should be somewhere over there, under the digger! Can you move it out of the way a few metres?

The digger moved backwards. Suddenly, the ground gave way on one side. The engine roared as the driver forced the caterpillar track out of the hole.

Mrs Dale went to have a look.

'There seems to be a step here!'

They all rushed over to have a look. Sure enough, the ground had given way under the weight of the JCB and dirt had fallen into a large hole.

While Tim cleared more of the dirt away with the spade while Caroline helped with her bare hands, Mr Dale ran back to his car and came back with a torch. He shone it into the hole.

'More steps. There seems to be a cellar underneath the mosaic!'

'I'm going in!' said Tim, grabbing the torch.

'Only if I go as well!' insisted his father.

'Are you sure it's safe?' asked Mrs Dale.

'No. But don't try to stop us!'

They slid carefully into the hole, following the steps until their feet reached the bottom. Tim shone the torch around a small room with Roman amphorae lying between columns of bricks used to support the room above. Some amphorae had broken and spilt their contents on the ground. One, smaller and narrower than the rest, had a round piece of wood sticking out of the rim.

'That's the end of a scroll, unless I'm very much mistaken. Give me a hand.'

Tim held the fractured amphora upright while his father gently teased the scroll out. Mr Dale unfurled it with great care. The scroll was made of papyrus and slightly brittle at the edges.

'What's it say?' asked Tim eagerly.

He shone the torch onto it and saw it was covered in brown handwritten text.

'Not enough light. We'll take it out with us after we've had a good ferret about here.' He rolled up the scroll and put it carefully on the floor near the steps.

They examined more amphorae. Two, with letters scratched roughly into the surface, particularly caught their eye. One said 'CARATACUS', the other 'BOUDICCA'.

'Let's get back to the others,' said Mr Dale, thrilled beyond words. He led the way back to the open air.

'Well?' asked Caroline. 'Did you find anything?'

'It's amazing!' said Mr Dale, slowly unfurling the scroll until he could see the first few lines of writing. 'There's more like this down there!'

Everyone crowded around him.

'Can you read it?' asked Tim nervously.

'Hm. Let's see ...' Mr Dale squinted to make sense of the faded lettering. '... GWIROCONI PRAESCRIPTIO.'

'Gwirocon's Introduction,' said Tim without thinking. 'What else?'

'Where did you learn Latin?' asked his father incredulously.

'Do you believe us now?' demanded Caroline. What more proof did they need? First the mosaic with the pendant pattern, and now this, written evidence that Gwirocon existed. 'Where do you think we learned it?'

Mrs Dale's eyes almost popped out of their sockets.

'Carry on, dad!' urged Caroline.

While the others, including the JCB driver, listened with utter amazement, Mr Dale laboriously read more from the scroll. Tim and Caroline translated his words in unison.

The scroll said:

GWIROCONI PRÆSCRIPTIO

NUNTIUS MIHI NUPER ADFERTUR DE CLADE TERRIBILI PER QUAM OPPIDA ROMANA POMPEII ET ERCULANO VASTATA SUNT. QUAE CLADES EQUIDEM TOT MILIBUS SINE ULLO MONITU DEORUM OBRUTIS, INDUXIT ANIMUM COGITARE UT TUM, CUM MORIEMUR, MEMORIA OMNIUM QUAE EXPERTI SUMUS NOBISCUM MORITURA SIT.

CONSUETUDO TAMEN DRUIDUM, QUOS CONSECTANDOS ROMANI CURAVERUNT, RES MEMORIA COMPREHENDERE, NOS ADIUVAVIT AD NOSTROS USUS ET MORES ALIQUA EX PARTE CONSERVANDOS, SED CUM LEGIONES ROMANAE NOSTRA LITORA INVASERINT, TAM MULTA EX CONSUETUDINE NOSTRAE VITAE IN BRITANNIA MUTATA SUNT UT, NISI EVENTUS RECENTES HISTORIAE NOSTRAE NUNC RECORDANTUR, TIMEO NE VERITAS RERUM IN PERPETUUM PEREAT.

IAM SUM SEPTUAGINTA ANNOS NATUS; ETSI ETIAM NUNC SIC SUM MEMORIA CLARA PRAEDITUS, TAMQUAM CUM CLAUDIUS IMPERATOR FACTUS EST, VIRES TAMEN DEFICERE COEPERUNT. HINC NECESSE EST MIHI SCRIPTIS MANDARE EA QUAE EXPERTUS SUM, LATINE NIMIRUM QUONIAM BRITANNI VIDENTUR LINGUAM SUAM NEGLEGERE, ANTEQUAM E VITA DECEDAM.

ITAQUE HIC SEDEO ABDITUS IN VILLA MEA SUBURBANA SITA IN VICINIA OPPIDI CRESCENTIS QUOD NOMEN MEUM HABET: UIROCONIUM. PER FENESTRAM PROSPICIO IN SUMMUM MONTEM: HIC ETIAM E MEO NOMINE VOCATUS—MONS GWIROCONI—UBI MAIORE EX PARTE ANNOS QUINQUE ET TRIGINTA HABITAVI; PER QUOD TEMPUS EI QUI NOS DEVICERUNT ME SOCIUM INAESTIMABILEM HABERE CONSUERUNT; QUOD FIDUS MINISTER ET SATELLES FUERIM ME SUMMO HONORE HONESTAVERUNT: NOVUM OPPIDUM IN CIVITATE CORNOVIORUM SITUM EX NOMINE MEO APPELLAVERUNT.

SI MODO COGNOVISSENT QUID RE VERA APPETEREM...

Gwirocon's scroll.

Gwirocon's Introduction

I have just received news of the terrible catastrophe which has destroyed the Roman cities of Pompeii and Herculaneum. So many thousands overwhelmed without any warning from the gods has caused me to reflect on the fact that, when we die, the memory of all we have experienced is going to die with us.

The practice of the Druids, whom the Romans have studiously persecuted, of committing events to memory, has helped to some extent to preserve our culture and our traditions, but there have been so many changes to our British way of life since the Roman legions invaded our shores that, unless details of our recent history are recorded now, I fear the truth of events will be lost forever.

I am now almost 70 years old and, while my memory may still be as clear as it was when Claudius became emperor, my body is failing me rapidly. Hence the need to commit my experiences to papyrus (using the Latin language, for it seems our British tongue is in much decline), before my own earthly existence expires.

And so I sit here in the privacy of my own villa situated on the outskirts of the growing township which bears my name: Viroconium. Through the window I can see the summit of the mount which is also named after me — Gwirocon's Hill — my home for most of the last 35 years, during which time our conquerors have come to regard me as an invaluable ally. It is because of my loyal support and service that they have honoured me with the highest accolade they can bestow: a new city named after me in my own Cornovian territory.

If only they'd known what I was actually trying to achieve …

No one noticed Mrs Dale faint; she slumped to the ground sometime during the translation. The driver obligingly shot water in her face to revive her: unfortunately, his enthusiasm got the better of him and she got a good soaking.

'I must call the Shropshire archeological people straight away,' said Mr Dale. 'This has to be the most significant archaeological find for centuries! Just think! These scrolls are unique! And they'll give the British version of events! I'll be able to translate them ...'

'With our help,' pointed out Caroline.

'... and produce a series of books. I can see it now: *Wroxeter Chronicles*! First Gwirocon's story, then Caradoc's and Boudicca's! And whatever else is in the cellar!'

It was a unique moment.

Mr Dale, the JCB driver, Caroline, Tim, and even their mother, who was so enthralled she didn't realise she was still dripping water over the ground, experienced the tremendous thrill of being involved in an incredible historical discovery.

The school holidays came to an abrupt end. Caroline and Tim handed their assignments to Mr Hart but had to wait until the following Monday afternoon to see what marks they'd been given.

Mr Dale popped into the school at lunchtime and gave Tim the day's first edition of the *Shropshire Daily*, shortly before the history lesson was due to begin.

Brave entered the classroom. His beard had a new stain; gravy from his school dinner had dribbled down it and looked like something never mentioned in polite circles.

He tapped his desk with an old wooden ruler.

'Ladies and gentlemen, your attention, please!'

The din subsided immediately, a fact which took him by surprise. But then, it was the beginning of term. Things would get back to normal as the weeks progressed.

'I've marked your assignments. On the whole, not bad. Top marks to Susan.'

The class groaned and hurled the usual array of daggers in her direction.

'But the most ... er, *interesting* ones were done by Tim and Caroline.'

The Dale twins grinned from ear to ear.

Their joy was short lived.

'However, they are more like fairytales than history essays! I don't think I've ever read such poppycock! Virtually nothing you've written could possibly have happened! It's pure fantasy! The only way this could be true is if you witnessed the events first hand, and that's hardly likely, is it?! Well, what do you have to say for yourselves?'

There was a look of malicious glee in his eyes. He didn't like the fact that their father was a successful historian and author.

Tim reached into his bag and produced the *Shropshire Daily*. He proudly held up the front page, high enough for everyone to see.

The headline read:

DRUID KING GWIROCON RULED, OK?
AMAZING DISCOVERY BY LOCAL HISTORIAN!

Brave snatched the paper and scanned the report.

The whole class watched him, wondering why his hands were shaking so much.

'Perhaps you'd like to have a word with our father before you mark our assignments again,' said Caroline. 'I'm sure he'd love to let you know all about his recent discovery!'

Brave turned away, completely and utterly dejected. How was he supposed to keep up to date with all the latest archaeological finds? He hated it when mere kids knew more than he did.

Caroline gave Tim a high five.

But Brave Hart had been right.

People make history.

Even if they have to travel back two thousand years to do it!

THE END

Allan Frost is a well-known popular historian specialising in the history of the Wellington area of Shropshire and has written several titles on the history of the town and its neighbourhood.

A full list of currently available books can be obtained by writing to Wrekin Books,
1 Buttermere Drive, Priorslee, Telford, Shropshire, TF2 9RE, England, or by making enquiries at any good bookseller.